CAUSTIC OCTOBER

ALSO BY KEN PRATT

The Royal Potter's Shop

When the Wolf Comes Knocking

Matt Bannister Series

The Jessup County Chronicles

CAUSTIC OCTOBER

THE JESSUP COUNTY CHRONICLES
BOOK 2

KEN PRATT

Caustic October
Paperback Edition
Copyright © 2025 by Ken Pratt

CKN Christian Publishing
An Imprint of Wolfpack Publishing
1707 E. Diana Street
Tampa, FL 33609

www.cknchristianpublishing.com

Paperback ISBN 979-8-89567-040-8
Ebook ISBN 979-8-89567-039-2
LCCN 2024952416

FOREWORD

The Jessup County Chronicles is a continuation of the Matt Bannister Series. Do you need to read the Matt Bannister Series to understand what's taking place in The Gypsum Creek Massacre? No. I will say if you did read the Matt Bannister Series, it would add to the depth of the story and those to follow because you'll understand the character's histories and relationships better. However, any essential details that are relevant to the story will be covered in this series.

It was 2004 when I first took a pencil in my hand and wrote the first words to what would become my first book. Seven years later, Willow Falls was written. A literary agent I had reached out to responded that *Willow Falls would never be published because it was too secular for the Christian market and too Christian for the secular market. It went straight down the middle and crossed the lines of both genres and there was no genre like that.*

I think she was wrong. I remember walking along the sidewalk in Sisters, Oregon, when I got a notification to open a link from my publisher. To my surprise, Willow Falls was the #1 Best Seller on Amazon, and it stayed there for a while. That book she thought would never resonate with people was just the beginning. The Matt Bannister Series went on to have eighteen books, and sixteen of them were the #1 Best Sellers on Amazon. The other two reached as high as #3 and #2 but didn't reach that #1 spot.

There is a wide following for the Matt Bannister Series, and I have met many great people and made many new friends who have supported me in more ways than they know. I recall many reviews that inspired me when I felt uninspired, direct messages with incredible encouragement when I was discouraged. In so many ways, my life has been touched by the people who have read my books and reached out to me in very positive ways. The fanbase for the Matt Bannister Series is made up of incredible people, and so, with that, I dedicate this first book of the new series to my friends, the wonderful fans of the Matt Bannister Series.

Thank you. Matt is Back!

AUTHOR'S NOTE

I was asked once, "Whatever happened to the young couple who were attacked in the cellar in the book *Hollister?*"

Caustic October answer's that question.

This is Laura Whitehead and Jake Thomas's story.

CAUSTIC OCTOBER

PROLOGUE

ALEX WENTWORTH LOOKED WITH GLOWING PRIDE at the front page of Saturday's *Jessup County Chronicles* Newspaper. An old photo from 1884 that he retrieved from the *Portland Oregonian* showed a good-quality photograph of the collapsed railroad trestle and the burned remains of a train laying a hundred feet below the tracks at the bottom of a deep gully. The photograph was taken from aboard a boat on the Columbia River. The headline read "The Gypsum Creek Massacre: Legendary Lawman Matt Bannister Grants Interview." His name, Alexander Wentworth, was in smaller print below the heading, indicating he was the journalist who interviewed the legendary US Marshal. It was a privilege that no other journalist had succeeded in doing, including a journalist from back east for *Harper's Weekly*.

Alex grabbed the copy of the paper and neatly placed it in a briefcase before carrying it to his car to drive across the city of Branson and up Bannister Hill to the large home of Matt and Christine Bannister, overlooking the valley.

He was invited inside and was pleased to find the elderly couple waiting for him in the sitting room. Christine was seated in her wheelchair with a pillow on the seat next to the davenport, where Matt was sitting. He held her hand.

Alex entered with a proud grin. "Mr. and Mrs. Bannister, I want you to know that we have never sold more papers than we did yesterday!" He sat down across from them and opened the briefcase to reveal the article.

"Congratulations, Alex. That is exciting," Christine said fondly.

Matt's lips rose just a bit. "I read the article. You did a good job with it. Lucky for you, you didn't mislead or outright lie about me."

Alex grinned. "I didn't want my picture added to your collection of dead men on your office wall."

Matt chuckled. "I'm glad to hear that."

Christine added with an encouraging tone, "Alex, you wrote a wonderful article. Matt and I have been discussing what story to tell you next. We thought of one in particular that might be of interest—"

Alex held up a finger to interject a thought. "I'm sorry for interrupting. Last week, you told me that my grandfather was your deputy marshal and was killed at the Sperry home by Charlie Walker. I did some research about the Sperry family and discovered that there are still several descendants of the Sperry family living in Natoma. I drove over there and spoke with a man named Lonnie Sperry. He is a son of Jack Sperry, who you may have known."

Matt nodded. "Jack was Morton's youngest brother, between Vince and Daisy."

"Yes. I had a long talk with Lonnie. He told me all about

his father, aunts, and uncles. I take it they were a wild bunch?"

Matt nodded. "They were a troublesome bunch sometimes."

"Lonnie let me borrow a little book titled *The Hollister Sheep Shooter's War*. He proudly claimed there were a couple of Sperrys in the book. It's basically thirty-five pages of a badly written memoir by a fellow named Barry McCracken. The author claims he was a part of the Hollister Sheep Shooters and involved in the land war between the cattlemen and a sheep rancher. Interestingly, the only Sperry mentioned in the book was your deputy, Morton. Mr. McCracken mentioned you several times, of course, so I tend to believe the events he referred to are factual. It's a story about a group called the Hollister Sheep Shooters and a war they had with a large sheep rancher by the name of Robert Fairchild, who hired a group of gunmen. Is that right?"

Matt nodded. "Yes. That took place in the town of Hollister. I knew Barry McCracken and everyone he mentioned in the book."

"So, everything he wrote is true?"

"Well, for the most part. Barry exaggerated his importance in the feud and made himself a bigger player in it than he really was, but that's a lying writer for you. What else would you expect? I have his book in my library. Robert Fairchild decided to move to the middle of the cattle capital of Jessup County and brought thousands of sheep with him. When it wasn't well received, Robert hired the Blackburn Marshals to protect him and his wife, as well as his shepherds and sheep flocks from the Hollister Sheep Shooters. It did get bad. My deputies and I got involved, and despite our efforts, things turned tragic just when the feud was supposedly settled and over."

Alex leaned forward with interest. "McCracken's book mentioned a supposed agreement that technically ended the feud, but the book also ended rather abruptly, unexpectedly, in fact. There wasn't a summary or even an explanation of why the sheep shooters attacked the Fairchild Estate. McCracken merely described what happened and his role in it. It isn't a well-written book at all.

"Interestingly, though, there was a small line that caught my attention. It was near the end of the book and written as the justification for what happened on that fatal night. Maybe you could enlighten me because I'm missing something. The line was:

'The rage that night was born when two Blackburn Marshals outraged the town. Robert Fairchild, the burden of every cattleman, paid the price.'

"Do you know what he was referring to when he says they outraged the town? I couldn't find anything about that in my research."

Matt nodded. "I do. What Jesse Helms and Cass Travers did to little Laura Whitehead and Jake Thomas was the final straw that broke the proverbial camel's back and sealed the caskets of Robert Fairchild and the notorious Blackburn Marshals."

"What did they do to Laura and Jake?"

Matt frowned. "Laura was fourteen, and her parents forbade her from being courted by Jake, who was eighteen. They were in love, so she sneaked out after her parents were asleep and met Jake in an abandoned cellar behind the church. It was the only place they could talk and spend an hour or two together. Jesse and Cass quit the Blackburn Marshals that night and followed Jake to the cellar, where they found Laura with him. They had a message for Jake's father, and that was to slice that young man's mouth open clear up to his ear across one cheek. They forced themselves upon Laura that night. They attacked her sexually and then beat that little girl something fierce. Morton and I tracked them, and I put a bullet through Cass Travers's head. I should have killed Jesse then and there, but we arrested him. He was released while we were away in Portland. I wish I would have killed that man then."

"Why?"

"Because he came back." Matt stood slowly, walked to the glass cabinet across the room and opened it. He pulled out a small, white, ceramic replica of a grand piano with black and white piano keys. He turned it over and spun a key that played "Canon" by Pachelbel. The piano had a broken leg that had been glued back on. He handed it to Alex.

"What's this?" Alex asked.

"A music box that once belonged to the young and beautiful widow, Holly Fairchild. She told me her husband Robert had brought it home from France as a gift. It was custom-made and quite expensive." Matt sat down and looked at Alex. "Barry McCracken never wrote about what happened next in Hollister because it had nothing to do with sheep. It had everything to do with Laura Whitehead. I had to go back to Hollister. It isn't the story Christine and I had planned to tell you, but if you want to hear it, I'll tell you what happened."

Alex hesitated. "I was thinking you could tell me what happened during the Sheep Shooter's War."

Matt shook his head. "No need. McCracken's book about the Hollister Sheep Shooter's War summed it up pretty well. Mind you, his role was much smaller than he made it out to be. It's what happened *afterward* that's never been told and should be."

Alex shrugged his shoulders. "Well, I'll take whatever story I can get. I am meeting Lonnie Sperry tomorrow to return the book. I'll have to tell him I only found one Sperry in the book."

Matt offered a half laugh. "The other Sperry relative mentioned in the book that you may not have put together yet is Jesse Helms."

"The Sperry-Helms Gang!" Alex exclaimed with a smack to his head with his palm. "Of course. I should've figured that out on my own."

"As I said, Jesse came back. And he plays a larger role in this story than I'd like."

Alex lifted the music box. "I'm guessing this has something to do with it?"

Matt pointed at the ceramic piano in Alex's hand. "That piano music box is the only thing I'm aware of that has survived from the original Fairchild Estate in Hollister. The Fairchild Estate was burned to the ground the night those two kids were attacked. The Hollister sheriff, Pat Emmerson, didn't actually take it from the house, we found out later, but he did give it to Laura Whitehead the day after the house was burned." He pointed at the music box with a slow-jabbing finger. "If not for that music box and the day it got broken, I may not have a story to tell you today. Trust me when I say it will be worth your time."

"I told my editor I planned to write about the Hollister Sheep Shooter's War this week."

Matt shrugged. "Well, you can write that article based on the information in Barry's book. Then, you can write this story the week after. Fair enough?"

"Sure."

Matt took a drink from a glass of water. "It's important to know that the Sperry-Helms Gang disbanded after Morton changed his life around and started working with me. Cass Travers, Jesse Helms, and Elliot Zook were hired on as Blackburn Marshals to protect the Fairchild Estate during the Sheep Shooter's War, as Barry McCracken called it. One morning, they found Elliot Zook and a couple of other dead Blackburn Marshals hanging from the Fairchild Estate headgate. It's not the Sperry or Helms way to let something go, so Jesse wanted Gunther Thomas's blood. He and Cass ended up quitting and sought vengeance on their own. Unfortunately, Gunther's eighteen-year-old son Jake, and Laura, paid the price. Let me tell you about it."

PART ONE

CHAPTER ONE

Laura walked down the eight concrete steps to the door and pushed it open. Inside, the lantern's light cast Jake's shadow on the wall as he waited for her with the loving gaze that always softened his eyes when he saw her.

Laura closed the door behind her before leaping into his arms to press her lips against his in a firm kiss. She broke the kiss and said, "I have been waiting for this all day! I saw you ride by the store earlier today and my heart melted like butter on a griddle. You, Jake Thomas, make my heart melt. I love you so much." She kissed him again.

He chuckled contently with a large grin. "I'm glad to hear that because I can hardly stand the hours away from you. I swear, as soon as your father says you're of marrying age, I'm asking him if I can have your hand in marriage. I know he'll refuse, so we're eloping! I don't need his permission to love you."

"Apparently, you don't need to ask my permission either because I did not hear a marriage proposal in there," she teased.

He kissed her gently. "I assumed you would agree. That is unless you drop me like a rotten apple and take up with Aaron Longley."

"I would never do that to you."

The door burst open with a bang that made the pair of lovers jolt in fright. Jesse Helms asked, *"Well, what are you two kids doing all alone in here?"*

Cass Travers closed the door behind them. *"My oh my,"* he said, taking a look at Laura.

Laura clung tighter to Jake as he moved in front of her protectively. *"What are you doing here? You're not supposed to be here,"* Jake said nervously. Jake didn't wear a gun belt nor did he have a weapon of any kind.

Jesse put his finger to his lips. *"Shhh. I came to talk to you because I have a message for your father."*

Jake's hands shook visibly as he could not hide the fear that overwhelmed him. Laura was frightened as well and it showed in their nervous expressions. *"W...w...what do you want me to tell him?"*

Jesse exhaled as he tightened his lips and nodded slowly. *"You can tell him..."*

"What?" Jake asked with concern.

Jesse hit Jake in the stomach with a hard right fist that knocked the wind out of him and doubled Jake over. Jesse grabbed the back of Jake's hair and rammed his face into a rising knee. He kneed his face again and let the boy fall to the blanket Jake had spread out on the concrete floor. Jesse dropped down on the young man's chest, pulled his knife from the sheath on his belt, and set the sharp blade against Jake's throat.

Laura screamed and then tried to run, but she was grabbed by the throat and slammed against the shelves by Cass. His revolver was quickly pressed against her head. *"Hush!"* Cass snarled. *"I don't want to hurt a pretty jewel like you."* He jerked her body forward and slipped around behind her, keeping an arm over her breast to hold her tight. *"You just be quiet and watch or you'll never* leave this cellar alive." He warned with the barrel of his gun gently caressing her cheek.

Jake was on his back with a knife blade pressed against his throat. Despite his defenseless position, his eyes and concern were on the fierce stranger holding Laura. "Please, don't hurt her. I'll do anything you want. Just please, don't hurt her," he pleaded.

Jesse tapped the side of the blade against Jake's cheek to get his attention. "Your father killed Elliot?" Jesse asked plainly.

Tears ran down Jake's face as he stated truthfully, "I don't know who Elliot is! I don't know." With fearful desperation he begged, "Please, let her go."

"Elliot was my friend that your father shot in the back of the head before he was hung up by his feet!" Jesse snarled.

"It wasn't me! I swear I had nothing to do with it," Jake said as he broke into frightened sobs.

Jesse narrowed his brow. "You already told me who did it. I'm only here to send a message to your father. Do you know what my message is?"

"No," Jake wept with his eyes watching Cass. "Please stop it. Let her go."

Jesse looked back to see Cass had holstered his revolver and was allowing his hands to roam over her body. Jesse moved the knife blade from Jake's throat to the inside of Jake's mouth and pressed the blade against his left cheek. "Here is my message to your father. Listen carefully; tell your father Jesse Helms will be seeing him soon. This is for shoving that badge into Elliot's mouth." Jesse ripped the knife sideways, slicing through Jake's cheek from the corner of the lips to nearly the joint of the jaw.

Jake cried out and turned to his stomach to not choke on the blood that was pouring out.

Laura screamed, but Cass quickly covered her mouth. He drew his mouth close to her ear and chuckled wickedly. "Now it's our turn."

Laura awoke with a loud scream as she sat up in bed sobbing in terror. Almost immediately, her mother, Helen, quickly entered her dimly lit room and wrapped her daughter in her arms as she sat on the bed.

Her father, Mitch, followed and stood in the doorway, watching his only child cling to her mother, sobbing in terror. He knew why the nightmares were starting again. It had been almost four months since that night in the cellar and nearly four months of trying to reassure Laura that the men who hurt her would never return. Laura had just recently, in the last few weeks, begun sleeping through the night. It had been a welcomed relief and a sign that she was recovering from the trauma of what had happened. Her dreams were not peaceful, but no longer nightmares that brought a panicked scream and sobbing in the middle of the night—until now.

Four days prior, the town doctor confirmed that Laura was carrying the child of one of the two men that raped her; and the nightmares had returned. Laura was forced to live with the physical injuries she had received along with the psychological and emotional damage that changed the sweet and lively girl into a frightened, skittish, and depressed young lady who seldom left the house.

Everyone in the community knew what had happened to her and Jake Thomas. Everyone knew Laura had long been sneaking out of the house to meet Jake in the church cellar after all the responsible folks in town went to bed. There were no secrets in Hollister when it came to Laura; everyone knew Jake had kept a blanket and lantern in the cellar for their midnight meetings. One didn't have to use their imagination for too long to conclude that Jake had seduced her. Laura's reputation had been tarnished beyond repair despite what had happened to her that night. People talked, and people talked a lot in small towns. Gossip spread faster than a match could start a fire, and now everyone knew Laura was carrying an unwanted baby. Mitch hadn't mentioned it to Helen, but one of the ladies from church, named Claire Archibald, had suggested that maybe the child didn't belong to one of the rapists but to Jake. Claire emphasized that there were three, if not four, possibilities of who the father could be. It shouldn't be forgotten that Aaron Longley was courting her as well.

"I...don't...want...to...have...their...baby," Laura choked out in between her sobs. "Mama...I...don't... want...to...have...a baby!" she wailed into her mother's shoulder.

Mitch's bottom lip twitched as his eyes filled with empathetic tears to see his baby girl wailing for reasons that no female should ever have to know. His chest tightened with the powerful emotions that forced their way into his throat. He tried to fight the choking sensation, but no words came out of his mouth. Anger seethed within him, and he slammed his clenched fist into the door, slamming it against the wall with a loud bang.

"You don't have to be mad at her! She had a nightmare," Helen Whitehead snapped at her husband.

"I'm not mad at her!" he shouted. He was about to continue but stopped himself short of saying more. The thought had always plagued him. *What if Laura had given her innocence away to Jake in that cellar like a little harlot?* Now, after talking to Claire Archibald, he wondered if Jake was the father of her baby. If so, it would be Laura's fault and her consequence to pay. He had raised her to be a proper Christian girl, but somewhere, she was led astray by the wolf in sheep's clothing, Jake Thomas. Mitch knew it. He had caught them on the grain bags in the hardware store's back room laying in each other's arms, kissing deeply and intently like a married couple did on their honeymoon night. It was most concerning at the time, but now he was humiliated after everyone in town learned she had been sneaking out to meet Jake. No one needed a blanket on a hot July night. There was only one reason for the blanket and now he had to wonder, did the thing growing in her belly belong to one of the two rapists, or Jake Thomas? Laura had lied, snuck out of the house, and hid the truth from them, which left Mitch feeling torn between fury and empathy. His eyes burned with anger as they glared at Helen. He would say something, but it was better left unsaid. He turned and walked away.

Helen sighed as she looked at the dimly lit lantern left burning in her only child's room. Laura had been afraid to sleep in a dark room since the night she was attacked. After a few moments, Laura rested in her mother's embrace and sniffled as she calmed down after the terrifying nightmare.

Laura's soft voice said, "Father doesn't even look at me anymore. He hates me, doesn't he, Mother?"

"No, baby, he does not hate you. He's angry about what happened to you. But your father loves you very much." Her heart broke as she heard her beautiful blonde-haired daughter say such words. Laura was the only child she had been able to bring into the world, and now her baby was living a nightmare that no woman should ever have to experience.

"He doesn't act like it anymore." Laura whimpered softly. "He acts like he's ashamed of me."

"No, baby. That's not true. Get those thoughts out of your head, sweetheart. He loves you so much. Now, you lay down and try to sleep," Helen said comfortingly. She lay beside her daughter, gently stroking her hair until Laura relaxed enough to fall back to sleep.

———

MITCH WAS TOO angry to sleep. He despised Jake Thomas and considered the young man equal to the devil himself. Despite his most strenuous efforts to keep them apart, it had become town-wide news that his precious beloved daughter had been sneaking out of the house late at night tomeet Jake in the church's cellar while also being courted by Aaron Longley. The content of the rumors and town gossip spread faster than a prairie fire and humiliated Mitch to the deepest part of his soul. Everyone in town knew his daughter wasn't as pure as he expected her to be.

However, it wasn't Jake that Laura was having nightmares about. It wasn't Jake who had beaten her, knocked her tooth out or hurt her that night. It was Cass Travers and Jesse Helms. The United States Marshal Matt Bannister and his deputy, Morton Sperry, had tracked down the two criminals and killed Cass Travers but arrested Jesse. Mitch and the rest of the town expected to watch Jesse Helms hang for what he did to Laura, but within a week, Jesse was acquitted and released from the marshal's jail with no charges pending, riding away a free man. There would never be any justice for what happened to his daughter, and it infuriated Mitch.

He sat down at his desk and pulled out a piece of paper. He grabbed his pen and began to write. He wrote a letter to Matt Bannister and released all his fury onto the page, blaming Matt for failing to do his job. Jesse Helms was a free man while Laura was a prisoner of her own home, too scared to venture outside and now living the worst nightmare a rape victim could imagine. She was carrying her rapist's child.

Laura was scared enough, knowing that she could run into Jesse Helms again somewhere, anywhere, at any time she walked out their door. However, being told that she was pregnant brought a whole new basket of fears that were tormenting his daughter. An unwanted pregnancy was terrifying enough for a fifteen-year-old girl, but other worries crept in, like what if the unwelcomed child ended up being the spitting image of its father? What if the baby grew up to be just as criminal as its father? Evil begets evil, and there was no doubt in Mitch's mind that the child being knit together in his daughter's womb was nothing but pure evil. Every thought Mitch had, every bitter word he could spit out, was written with ink onto the page. When the ink was dry, he folded the letter, put it inside an envelope, and wrote Matt's name on it.

If Jesse Helms was dead, at least Laura could rest easier. The knowledge that Jesse was out there somewhere, a free man and able to roam anywhere he pleased, left a sickening feeling in Mitch's stomach. Enough was enough! Matt Bannister was to blame for arresting Jesse instead of killing him. He was responsible for Jesse walking out of jail as a free man. Undoubtedly, Jesse's cousin, Morton Sperry, had a lot to do with that. Mitch was going to hold Matt accountable. *Someone* had to.

It was nearly three in the morning when Helen quietly stepped into Mitch's office. "She's finally asleep." Her bottom lip quivered as she asked emotionally, "What are we going to do? That poor girl has been through enough." Helen was of average height and heavyset with ample proportions. Her curly brown hair was cut at neck length after a long fight with lice that she could not seem to get rid of until she cut her long, curled hair off. She had a round face and brown eyes that made her appear more masculine with shorter hair.

Mitch raised his six-foot frame from his desk. He was a tall and thin man with long arms and a thin neck that appeared slightly longer than average. His oblong-shaped face held his blue eyes and hooked nose where his spectacles set. He had a Dutch beard about three inches long that followed his jawline under his chin; he shaved the rest of his face daily. Mitch was slightly relieved to have his rage transferred to paper. He embraced his wife. "We don't have a choice, Helen. She's got to have the baby," he said with cold and bitter voice. "And then, we're going to get rid of it. I won't allow one of those rapist's spawn to live in this house, nor will I let my daughter raise it."

"I'm worried about her. What if she hurts herself trying to get rid of it, Mitch?"

"Do you want to abort it?" Mitch asked gruffly.

Helen's face wrinkled with mixed emotions. "I do, but I know we can't. We can't condemn the bordello for aborting that woman's baby and then ask them to help us do the same thing."

The ceiling blurred through the warm moisture that formed as Mitch rolled his eyes. "That whore died from that abortion. I won't risk that happening to Laura. That whore was carrying Jake Thomas's baby anyway," he said bitterly.

Helen embraced her husband, resting her head on his shoulder. "I'm afraid Laura will do anything to get rid of it, including killing herself."

Mitch gasped at the thought. "We could take her to Branson," Mitch suggested as the idea came to him. "Claire Archibald mentioned the idea to me. I don't think it's a bad idea. They have good doctors there who will keep Laura safe while doing it. I'm sure if we explained that two men attacked her, the doctor would understand and do it. And best of all, no one here will know. We could just say she lost it naturally."

Helen stepped back, breaking the embrace. "Mitch, we don't believe in that. The church doesn't believe in aborting babies. We'll be ostracized if anyone finds out."

Mitch spoke heatedly, raising his voice slightly, "She wasn't fornicating with some boy in a lily field, Helen. She was raped! I'll be damned before I let her have that baby. It's going to be just as evil as they are."

Helen hesitated. "She'd sleep better. Maybe she could put this all behind her if we take her there. We just can't let anyone know what we're doing. Okay?"

Mitch could feel his anguish ceasing. Whether the child belonged to Jake or one of the rapists, he could be rid of it. "Of course. We'll go next week after the freight wagons come. They should be here in the next few days. I wrote Matt Bannister a letter. I hope he reads it before we get there. I have a ton of bones to pick with him. I want to hear him explain why he let Jesse Helms go in front of Laura."

CHAPTER TWO

Jake Thomas patted the neck of his horse and tipped the brim of his hat downward, just a tug to keep the rising sun from glaring into his eyes. It was a cold October morning despite the cloudless blue sky. He had ridden up to the top of a butte that overlooked the grassy valley that rolled like ocean swells toward the beautiful Blue Mountain range. He had gotten his first view of the valley from the top of the butte when he was six years old when his family picnicked there. It was the most beautiful view he had ever seen and still, to this day, the very spot he wanted to build a home to raise his family. Jake had spent years dreaming about his future home and even drew pictures of the house he dreamed of overlooking the valley. He hadn't bought a ring yet, but he knew who his future bride would be. Laura Whitehead. He often dreamed of building her a fine house where they could raise their family and live their lives together on the Long T Ranch, just as his parents did. It promised to be a dream come true and, in his vision, a lifetime of paradise.

From the top of the butte, Jake could see the rooftops of Hollister in the distance. The Whitehead Hardware Store was a two-story building on the town's main street and was the only building with a tin roof. The sun's glare reflected off the tin like a mirror, making it the easiest building to identify. Unlike in the past, when Jake would smile when he saw the bright reflection of the roof, now it brought a sinking sensation that dropped an invisible knot down his throat into the bottomless pit of his soul. Jake knew under that roof, Laura would be waking up. There was a time, not long ago, when he would sit upon his horse and gaze at the hardware store's roof and pray that Laura would become his wife. He swore he'd give anything to be able to spend the rest of his life being married to her.

Unfortunately, her parents wouldn't give him their blessing to court her, and instead, they encouraged Laura to be courted by Jake's good friend, Aaron Longley. Laura was too young to marry anyone at the moment, but in another year or two, she would be of marrying age. Jake wanted to be the man she married with or without her parent's blessing.

He hadn't been able to see or speak to Laura since that night in the cellar when they were attacked. Her parents guarded her like a fortress of gold and blamed Jake for putting her where two ruthless men could assault her. It was Jake's fault that she was there, and he couldn't shake the guilt that haunted him day and night. He was there for every moment of it and was forced to watch the girl he loved being ravished by the two men who showed no mercy for her cries. Jake was heavily burdened on his own, but to hear Laura's father blame him was like a dull sword piercing his heart. The truth couldn't be denied; it was his fault that the two men were there. He was the one they wanted to hurt, and they followed him to the cellar. Laura became an innocent victim when she met him there.

Jake traced the scar on his left cheek with his finger. The scar was long and ugly, and it deformed his face with a thick, reddened line that tightened the left side of his face from the corner of his lip to the joint of his jaw. He hid the hideous scar under his bandanna because every time he looked in a mirror, it was a bold reminder of that night. He didn't want to see the scar and no one else did either. Jake had stopped leaving the Long T Ranch to avoid being stared at, accused, and gossiped about, as everyone in town knew what had happened to Laura was his fault. The blue bandanna covering the lower half of his face drew attention and the few times he had gone to town, undoubtedly someone would try to make light of the situation and put their hands up like he was a robber. His sense of humor had died, and now he avoided town like it was a leper colony. His life had become a solitary existence of riding with the cattle and working out on the range.

There was no reason to pray that she would become his wife anymore. From what he had heard, Laura had become a shadow of who she once was. Jake understood that Laura blamed him for what happened to her. He had been told by his old best friend, Aaron Longley, that she never wanted to speak to him again.

The sound of a man gagging over some phlegm caught Jake's attention. He turned his horse to look behind him. A cowhand named Jimmy Dawkins leaned over his saddle, vomiting nothing except air. His face turned red as his stomach contracted to force what was left out of his stomach.

"Good heavens!" Jimmy exclaimed, spitting the bitter taste of bile out of his mouth. He sniffled and wiped his mouth and nose with his sleeve. His watery eyes focused on Jake. "This lung infection I got. I'm telling you, I cough this green crap up and it gets caught right about here," he padded his upper chest. "I'm dry heaving my guts up this morning. The boys and I stayed too long at the saloon last night. It's a waste of money to puke up good whiskey, but crap." He sighed, appearing sick and queasy. "It was fun last night, just not so much this morning."

Jake was not amused. "We have work to do."

"I'm here!" Jimmy snapped, not appreciating Jake's tone. "Damn, Jake, I thought you'd be in a better mood knowing you're going to be a daddy."

Jake narrowed his eyes irritably. "What are you talking about? I'm not going to be a daddy."

Jimmy looked at Jake, realizing he had spoken out of turn. "I suppose I should have let that girl you're pining over tell you. I forgot her name, but I heard she's pregnant. It looks like her parents will have to let you marry her now," he said with a celebratory tone. Jimmy was a new ranch hand on the Long T Ranch and wasn't in the area when Jake and Laura were attacked.

Jake's breath rushed out of his lungs with a cold gasp. "What?" he questioned in a near whisper. His eyes suddenly grew warm with moisture.

"That girl you liked, the hardware store owner's daughter. She is pregnant. Everyone was talking about it in the saloon last night. You sealed the deal, Jake. I've heard of women getting pregnant to trap the man they love in marriage, but you reversed the game and sealed the deal!"

Jake's eyes continued to thicken with water as the shock of the news penetrated his soul.

Jimmy took notice of Jake's anguished expression. "I

heard about all those nights you'd sneak her out of the house. You sly devil, you. You *did* seal the deal, right?"

Jake's head shook slightly. "No." His brow twitched emotionally. "Never."

"You mean it's not yours? You mean to tell me there's no possible way it's yours?"

"No." Jake swallowed with a twitching bottom lip. "Who said she was with child?"

"The whole town's talking about it. Jake, I thought for sure it was yours." He chuckled awkwardly and then groaned. "Oh, crap. Jake, I'm sorry. That means the baby belongs to someone else. Doesn't it?"

Jake's mouth tightened as he nodded. "Go do something, Jimmy. Tell my pa that I'll be back later." He turned his horse and rode away.

"Hey Jake, where are you going? Your father and brothers are going to ask," Jimmy called after him, but there was no reply. Jake galloped his horse into the distance.

———

JAKE'S CHEST tightened with a growing pressure that felt like it might close the arteries going to his heart. He rode without any place in particular in mind, wishing he could get lost and hide from everyone in the world until his dying day. Four miles northwest of the Long T Ranch, he turned his gelding north along the Upper Flint River and followed it up a narrow valley into the tree coverage of the Wallowa Mountains. He followed the running river until he came to a bend where a wide open area invited him to rest his horse and dismount.

His chest rose and fell as he lifted his eyes toward the

blue sky while an angry scowl twisted his lips. He yelled venomously toward the sky, "Do you see me, God? Do *you* see me?" He yanked the bandanna down and pointed his hand at his cheek. "Is this not enough? What do you want from me? You know I love her! You knew it and you still allowed those animals to hurt her! I thought you were my Lord. I thought I could trust you. I thought you promised to watch out for your children! Laura never did anything wrong, Lord. How could you let this happen to her?" he screamed. Jake fell to his knees beside the river, landing on a small rock that sent a wave of pain up his leg. "Jesus, she is supposed to be my wife," he said and collapsed his hands and head to the ground. His eyes burned with tears as he continued, "Those two animals had no right to do what they did. You watched, but you didn't help us. Do you see me now, Jesus? I can't live like this. I don't want to live anymore." He pulled himself up to his knees, pulled his revolver from the holster, and pointed it at his head.

"Jesus, there's nothing for me to live for. Laura is all I ever wanted and she's been taken from me. I love her so much, Lord," he said, fighting the sobs that strangled his voice tighter than a noose around his neck. "How can you let her get pregnant from them? She is supposed to be my wife. She was supposed to have a child with *me*, not them!" He could no longer fight the tears and began to sob bitterly. He pulled the hammer back until it clicked, moved the barrel under his chin and closed his eyes. "Forgive me, Lord."

His soul felt like it was being torn and shredded like a piece of steak in a grinder with the handle being cranked by God himself. The life he had planned and dreamed of would never be. It was the end of his dream that would have been beautiful. The excitement and joy he once knew in life had become a wet leaf deteriorating on the ground before his very eyes. Feeling Laura's soft hand in his or smelling the scent of her hair as she leaned her head on his shoulder were now memories that he would never experience again. The loss of Laura in his life left a gash that split him open from head to toe, and nothing could ease the pain, guilt, and shame that filled him.

Three...two...one...pull the trigger. It sounded so simple to do. The intrusive thoughts raced through Jake's mind as he counted down silently. *Three...two...one...pull the trigger. Jake, you have nothing to live for. Laura is having another man's baby, and it's your fault. You should have saved her. You should have protected her.*

Jake's thoughts plagued him, urging him to pull the trigger and end his sorrow. His finger was on the trigger with the hammer pulled back. A quick jerk of his finger and his anguish would end. Tears blurred his vision as his lips pressed together. Jake closed his eyes as he began to apply more pressure on the trigger.

Breaking through the intrusive thoughts that encouraged him to pull the trigger and end his suffering, a memory of his mother's fragile voice echoed in his mind. *"Don't be a fool; why die before your time?"*

It was the day the US Marshal Matt Bannister had shot and killed their ranch hand, Monty Saunders. That evening, Jake's mother was troubled about what had taken place that day, so she sat in the family room reading her Bible. "Jake, listen to this. I'm just doing my Bible reading and Ecclesiastes 7:17 says, '*Do not be over-wicked and do not be a fool, why die before your time?*'" She closed her Bible to speak to Jake pointedly. "Monty's wickedness is what got him killed today long before his appointed time. Now I'm telling you, son, don't become a wicked man and don't be a fool. Don't die before *your* appointed time."

Jake lowered the gun, fell forward onto the gravel beside the river, and wept. "Jesus, you have no idea what it feels like to lose the girl you love. You have no idea what it's like to have watched what those men did to her!" He sobbed. "She's carrying one of those men's baby. It isn't right! She was supposed to marry me. She's the only girl in the world I'll ever love. Why didn't you stop them?" He clenched the pebbles of rock in his fists and wept. "Jesus, you could have stopped them."

CHAPTER THREE

It had been a long time since Christine Bannister had the privilege to make dinner for her husband. She had moved into Matt's two-bedroom brick house and spent her time making it homier and comfortable. The house hadn't known a lady's touch since Regina Bannister lived there with her family several years before. Gun oil and dirty towels were no longer left on the table at dinner time or trash left on the countertops. The dark and drab home was now kept clean, cheery, and bright. Christine had quit dancing at Bella's Dance Hall and traded her expensive gowns for simple dresses to maintain the house and cook in. She loved her new home, her new life and most of all, her husband.

Christine wore a simple tan dress with gray lily patterns in the material. Her long dark hair hung straight down over her shoulders to her mid-back. Her large brown eyes shone bright and narrowed with a smile to hear the front door open. She met Matt at the door with a giddiness she had not ever known before with her first husband, Richard

Knapp. The joy she felt with Richard fell short compared to the joy and value that Matt made her feel. "How was your day, handsome?" she asked as she approached Matt to greet him with a kiss.

He held her close and gazed into her eyes. "It just got a whole lot better. How are you, my beautiful lady?"

"I am feeling great. I made a roast with all the potatoes, carrots, and beets you can eat. And I think it turned out perfectly."

"I'm sure it did. It smells delicious."

"Thank you. So how was your day?" she asked again.

Matt took a deep breath. "I received a letter from Mitch Whitehead today. He spared no consideration to mixing his words about Jesse Helms being set free. He blamed me for that and not killing him when I had the chance. He thinks it's because Jesse is Morton's cousin that we set him free. They just discovered that his daughter is pregnant and either Jesse or Cass are the father," Matt said with a heavy heart.

"That's the young girl from Hollister?" Christine asked with an empathetic expression.

"Yes." Matt nodded. He washed his hands in a wash bowl.

"That's terrible. I can't imagine the anguish she must be going through."

"I can't arrest Jesse for what he did to her, no matter how much I want to. The district attorney dismissed the charges. That was because the Crowe Brothers were threatening his family's lives, and of course, I was in Portland. My hands are tied. I can take Mr. Whitehead's accusations and ridicule, but I don't like Jesse being set free any more than her father does."

"Is there anything you can do to make it right?"

Matt shook his head. "I arrested Jesse and thought he'd be put away for years. I knew there was the chance that the Crowe Brothers, the Helms, or Sperrys would try to intimidate the jury or the district attorney, but I wasn't here to stop it. The charges were dropped and Jesse was released. I wish I could do more, but I can't."

"I take it the letter was scalding?"

Matt offered a sad hint of a smile. "It was brutal. I can understand his anger though. I'm a lot of things, but to say I don't care about his daughter is not true. My heart goes out to her and her family. Anyway, did anything exciting happen around here?" he asked before sitting at the set table and taking her hand in his to thank the Lord for their well-prepared meal and life together.

Christine answered after praying. "Audrey came by to visit. She says Morton doesn't like working at the granite quarry. He's not used to laboring so hard. She thinks he'll be coming back to you soon enough."

Matt's eyes widened slightly with interest. "I hope so. Truet and Annie set their wedding date in May, and then he'll be moving onto the Big Z. Nate is coming along as a lawman but is still not experienced enough to face any real dangerous men with a gun. Nate's suitable for collecting taxes, delivering warrants, and such, but sending him into a potential dangerous situation, I'm not comfortable with that. With Morton and Truet, I am. I need to find an experienced lawman or two to hire."

"I agree. You need to hire five or six men so you can stay in your office and send them to do the dirty work. You're married to me now. I want to keep you safe in that office."

Matt chuckled as he took another bite of the roast. "I've never had a better-tasting piece of roast, Christine."

Her smile glowed. "Thank you."

"You're welcome."

"Are you going to respond to the letter from that young girl's father?"

Matt wrinkled his nose. "All I could tell him is that Jesse being free has nothing to do with me. I can empathize with his situation, but there is nothing else I can do."

"You should let him know that so he doesn't blame you."

"I will."

There was a knock on the door. Matt opened the door to see Morton Sperry holding his palms up, revealing the raw skin from torn-off blisters between his thumbs and index fingers. He was dressed in dusty clothes and had dust stuck to the dried sweat on his face. He appeared to be in a bad mood as he spoke earnestly. "I love your uncle Joel and uncle Luther too, but I want my job back until the election for the Branson sheriff's office comes. Slinging sledge-hammer all day isn't working for me. However, I need a raise because I can't afford to feed my family on what I was making before. How about five dollars more a month? That way, I can tell Audrey you offered me more money than at the granite quarry."

Matt laughed lightly. "You drive a hard bargain, but sure. I'm glad to have you back. Would you like to come in and have some dinner? Christine made a fantastic roast and we have plenty."

Morton shook his head and glanced down at his clothing and boots. "No. Christine will take the broom to me if I get dirt on her floor. I have to let Luther know I'm going back to the marshal's office and then tell Audrey. See you in the morning?"

"I'll have your badge ready. Have a good evening,

Morton." He closed the door and turned to look at Christine, still sitting at the table.

Christine shrugged a shoulder. "Audrey isn't going to be surprised. She told me how much he hated going to work."

TWO HOURS LATER, Matt sat on the edge of the davenport with his legs kicked up on a coffee table and his arm around Christine, who leaned against him with her legs stretched across the davenport, comfortably covered with a blanket. She was reading a book to Matt as they cuddled to the sound of the crackling fireplace. Matt listened attentively, enjoying the weight of her body pressed against him and the fragrance of her hair. He kissed the top of her head gently. The kiss did not interrupt her reading, but an unexpected knock on the door did.

Matt approached the door where his gun belt hung on a hook. "Who is it?' he asked, standing off to the side of the door.

"Lee," his brother Lee answered. "Open up, it's cold out here."

Matt opened the door and Lee came inside. "I think it's going to be another cold winter."

"It feels like. We don't have any coffee made or anything to warm you up," Matt said as Lee removed his long coat and hat.

"No. No. It's fine. I thought I'd stop by and visit for a bit. Christine, how are you?"

Christine sat upright. "I'm great, thank you. How are you and the family? Is everything okay?" she asked with concern. It was later than usual for anyone to stop by.

Lee sat on the smaller davenport facing them. "Yeah,

the family is fine. Regina sends her love. She's putting the girls to bed. Um..." Lee hesitated to get the point. "The Monarch Hotel Manager, Roger King and his wife have decided to move closer to their daughter over in the Willamette Valley. They told me that a month ago and are leaving in a couple of days." He paused and offered a slight grimace. "I know you and our dad aren't too close, but I've decided to hire him as the new Monarch Hotel Manager." He paused, waiting for Matt to respond, but Matt remained quiet. "You don't have anything to say about that?"

"No. What could I say? I don't own the hotel."

"I didn't know if it would bother you to have him living here. He's never been around, so it will be different to have him living in town. I figured since his wife is serving a ten-year prison sentence, and all of Dad's family is here, he might as well join us. Besides, he's got a lifetime of experience managing saloons and tenements, so he's a perfect fit. The hotel has to be easier. I just wanted you to know and ask if you're okay with that."

Christine said, "I think it's a wonderful idea."

Matt answered with a shrug of his shoulders. "Dad and I had a pretty good talk when I went to Portland to find Gabriel. I support the idea."

"Good!" Lee said with a relieved sigh. "Because I offered him the job two weeks ago, and Dad arrived today. He's staying at the hotel for now. We're having a family dinner tomorrow night at the Monarch Restaurant. I just wanted you to know and invite you and Christine to join us."

Matt scratched his head with a slow chuckle. "We'll be there."

CHAPTER FOUR

Mitch and Helen Whitehead had left Hollister early in the morning and traveled by wagon to Branson. It took all day to get there, but upon arriving, they hurried to the doctor's office before it closed for the day. When they entered the doctor's office, a teenage boy with greasy, uncombed blond hair was sitting in the small waiting room. He wore shabby clothing and boots with a hole in the leather revealing his big toe. His head rose with interest when he saw Laura. He smiled and offered her a nod. She looked away without interest.

"I'm Tad. My ma's in there seeing the doctor. She's been sick. What's your name?" the blond-haired young man asked. Being at the doctor's office made him nervous and talking to someone helped calm his nerves.

Laura turned her face downward, ignoring him. Mitch answered for her. "We're not in the mood to talk."

Tad nodded. "Fair enough. I was just being friendly, is all."

A man stepped out of a door and said, "Hello folks, I'm Doctor Ryland. Can I help you?"

Mitch said, "Yes. We want to talk to you in private if we can." He waved a hand toward Tad, who was sitting in the small room filled with eight chairs. "It's a delicate matter concerning my daughter."

"Okay," Dr. Ryland said, glancing at Laura. "What are your names?"

"I'm Mitch Whitehead. This is my wife Helen and our daughter Laura. She is the reason we came here, clear from Hollister."

"Let's go to the office where we can talk freely and you can tell me how I can help you." The doctor led the family into a side room.

Mitch nervously explained what had happened to Laura in the cellar and then said, "I know it's illegal, but we were hoping to get an abortion here instead of at the bordello back in Hollister. I care about my daughter and we want it done safely. We wanted to come to you because we don't know anything about how to go about it."

Dr. Ryland closed his eyes and rubbed them tiredly. "Mr. Whitehead, the only time I give an abortion is when it is absolutely necessary and to this date, I've only had to perform one to save the mother's life during surgery. It is illegal."

"I know that!" Mitch stammered, raising his voice. "That's why we traveled all this way, so that it could be done safely. My daughter doesn't want this baby, and we sure are not raising a rapist's child. Do you know who did this to her? It was the outlaws, the murderers, Cass Travers and Jesse Helms. My word, we don't want to know which one this thing is going to look like. My daughter has been through enough! Are you going to help us or not? If not, I'll take her to a bordello and pay them to do it."

Dr. Ryland's eyes narrowed irritably. "Keep your voice down. That young lady right there is your daughter, and you'll be risking her life if you take her to a bordello. I've been called to bordellos here in Branson more times than I want to count to save a young woman's life after an attempted abortion went wrong. I haven't been able to save all of the young ladies either. So before you threaten to take her to some madam, you better understand what you are risking. Sure, there are herbs, roots and medicines that can be taken to induce a miscarriage, but those things can go wrong. And they do. I've seen it and lost young lives like hers because of it."

"Then what are we supposed to do?" Mitch shouted, irate. "I want that thing out of her!"

Dr. Ryland rose from behind his desk and pointed at the door. "Mr. Whitehead, you need to go outside and cool off while I speak with your daughter and her mother. You're not helping her with your loud voice. You're certainly not intimidating me any either, so leave! I want to speak with your wife and daughter without you in here. Now go!"

"We came here for help! Don't you understand? She doesn't want those bastards' child in her!" Mitch yelled with angry tears forming in his eyes.

"I understand that. But I haven't heard your daughter or wife say one word and I'm not going to listen to you yell. Leave and wait out there until I call you back in. I want to talk to them without you in here."

"Fine!" Mitch exclaimed and stepped out into the waiting room. He cursed and sat down heavily in a chair.

Tad watched the angry father and questioned gently, "Your daughter is pregnant?"

Mitch shot an angry glance at Tad and waved him away with a hardened scoff.

"I'm sorry. I couldn't help overhearing."

"It's none of your business, is it?" Mitch snapped.

Tad shook his head. "No, sir. I hear Jesse Helms is a no-good rat, sir."

"He's a damn rapist, is what he is. If I ever see him, I'll blow his head off!"

"I don't blame you. Did you say you were from Hollister, sir?" Tad asked.

Mitch nodded without saying a word.

Another door opened, and Tad's mother, Jannie Sperry, stepped out of the back room. She was crying. "Ma?" Tad stood. He was shocked to see his tough and hearty mother broken into tears. "What did the doctor say?" he asked as his mother wrapped her arms around him and wept on his shoulder.

"Doctor, what's wrong? Is something wrong with my ma?" Tad questioned as Dr. Ambrose followed her out.

Dr. Ambrose spoke softly. "I'm sorry, son. She has Tuberculosis."

Tad's perplexed expression begged for an answer.

"Consumption, son. Your mother has a year left, maybe two. I'm sorry, but it's advanced. I don't know how she's gone this long without being diagnosed."

―――――

DR. RYLAND PUT his elbows on his desk and folded his hands. He spoke to Laura gently. "Young lady, I know you are scared and undoubtedly traumatized by what happened to you. I know you don't want to have a child at your age, and certainly, you don't want to have this one. But according to the law, you have to carry it to term and give birth. The illegality of the law aside, if you let some madam or well-meaning person with no formal training give you something to abort that baby through a miscarriage, you will be risking your life at the worst possible case. The second worst is damaging your uterus and never being able to have children again when you get married someday. Third, I have known several women who are haunted by regret and guilt from wondering who and what their child might have been.

"If I may be frank, how this baby was conceived is evil, but on that day, you were ovulating and your body conceived. Now, a child is growing inside of you. Just because some bastards forced themselves on you does not mean the child is guilty of the crime or that he or she will become evil. You don't want to be pregnant, but the fact is, despite the horror of what happened, you are. That makes you this baby's mother. The father is long gone and will never be a part of this child's life, so you are all this baby has right now. You don't have to raise your child; many families would adopt the baby. But as I mentioned, according to the law, you have to carry it to term and give birth. I am sorry this happened to you. I really am. Adoption is an option. But there are also those victims of rape who carry their child for nine months planning to put the baby up for adoption, but when they hold their child and look into the baby's eyes for the first time, they don't feel the same way anymore and choose to raise their child. It really just depends on the person."

Helen spoke, "Doctor, my husband wants that baby out of her."

"Trust me, I can understand your husband's hostility. Laura is with child while she is still a child herself. I do understand. But by law, I can't help you. Morally, I can't offer you any advice on what to take to induce a miscarriage either. I'm a doctor; I came into this profession to save lives, not end them. And that child developing inside of her is a living human being." He turned his palms upward. "I won't help you end that baby's life."

Helen closed her eyes and dropped her head in shame. "I know."

Laura's face rose to look at Dr. Ryland. "So I have to have it?"

Dr. Ryland nodded empathetically. "As hard as it may be, yes. Laura, nine months is a very temporary time of your life. You actually have five months or so to carry it and that is a very short time to endure the hardship of an unwanted pregnancy. By carrying the baby to full term, you won't put yourself at risk of an abortion going wrong and you'll know with a clear conscience that you gave your child a good home where he or she will be loved, whether with you or another family. Remember, the man who did this to you deserves to be hung, but the baby is as innocent as you are. I suggest that you accept the fact you are pregnant and you are this child's mother. The sooner you can, the easier it will be to love your baby. You'll be happier doing that than anything else in the long run. Five more months of your life is all your baby is asking for. Then you can put your little girl or boy up for adoption if you choose not to raise your child."

Helen lowered her voice, not wanting to be overheard. "Her father won't allow her to raise the baby even if she wanted to."

"Well, if I was in his shoes, I would probably feel the same way. But, the important thing is not aborting the baby. That can go wrong in many ways and affect you for the rest of your life. It's safer for you to have the baby and let a good home adopt it for your own piece of mind and future health."

———

THE COWBELL RANG as the marshal's office door was pushed open. Mitch Whitehead stepped inside the office, dragging Laura roughly inside by the arm. He jerked her forward as she fought from being dragged inside.

"Get in here!" he shouted angrily.

"I don't want to!" Laura protested, trying to pull her arm free of his grip. "You're hurting me!"

"I don't care what you want, Laura. You will do as I say," Mitch shouted. His eyes burned into her.

Nate Robinson stood from his desk. "You better let go of her arm before I break yours!"

Mitch pointed a finger at Nate and shouted, "You better mind your business, boy. Where's the marshal?"

Matt came out of his private office with a growing sense of pride for his deputy's response. Matt was in his midthirties, tall with broad shoulders and appeared to be quite muscular under his tan button-up shirt with the sleeves rolled up above his wrists. He was a handsome man with a neatly trimmed dark beard and mustache that covered the lower half of his square-shaped face. His long dark hair was pulled into a tight ponytail that fell below his shoulders. "I'm right here. Do you mind telling me what this is about?"

"It figures you wouldn't recognize me or my daughter. I'm Mitch Whitehead and this is my daughter Laura. The last time you saw her, her face was all beaten up, bloody and swollen. And you let the man who did that to her go!

Why don't you explain to my daughter why you set the man who hurt her free? Why is he riding around the county carefree while my daughter has to pay the consequences of his actions? Huh? Go on, Marshal Bannister, explain to her how your deputy is Jesse Helm's cousin. I know you did your deputy a favor and let that bastard go. I despise you! Go on, tell her!" he yelled.

Matt shifted his eyes to look at the young lady, a mere child, who he knew was carrying a child she never wanted. She hid her face under her free hand while staring downward. She was a pretty girl and had healed from the last time he'd seen her. "I think your daughter is scared enough without you humiliating her the way you are."

"Humiliating her?" Mitch scoffed. "She's carrying a child! Is that not more humiliating to her? I want to know why you let him go free!"

"I didn't. If it were up to me, Jesse Helms would be six feet underground. The district attorney, Jackson Weathers, didn't press charges. I was in Portland taking care of a personal matter when I got the news that Jesse was released. Take it up with Jackson for that answer, not me."

"You had nothing to do with him being set free?"

"I did not."

"You didn't kill him when you had the chance either, did you?"

"I don't make it a habit to kill men that surrender, no. The chance will come around again, I'm sure. But even if I had, your daughter would still be pregnant. It wouldn't have changed anything."

Mitch hollered, "He wouldn't be riding around free, would he?"

"How about you let me take care of him when the time comes, and you help your daughter come to terms with what happened to her?" Matt retorted. "Trust me, I was just as sickened to my stomach to learn he was set free as you were. I killed Cass Travers, but Jesse surrendered and I won't kill a man that surrenders, but I *will* hang him. I hoped that would be the case, but that isn't up to me to decide. That's the district attorney and the court of law who decide that. I got your letter, Mr. Whitehead, and I intended to respond to it. You are blaming the wrong man. Your daughter needs you to be her father and help guide her through the tragedy she is experiencing, not dragging her around in a state of rage that isn't going to do you one bit of good. I am sorry for what your family is going through; I really am. But there is nothing I can do about it legally. I'm sorry to say. The only bit of consolation I can give you is that Jesse will break the law again, and when he does, I will travel to the North Pole and back to track him down. I'd love to hang him, but because of that young lady right there, I'll gladly shoot him, too."

Mitch nodded once unapologetically. "Jackson Weathers, you say?"

"Yes. That's the man you want to talk to."

"Laura, let's go," he said. He left the marshal's office without another word.

CHAPTER FIVE

MITCH WHITEHEAD BEGRUDGINGLY HAD TAKEN his family to the Monarch Hotel to check in for the night. They had a lovely room on the second floor with two bedrooms that cost more than Mitch wanted to spend. There were cheaper hotels and boarding houses in Branson, but Helen insisted they stay at the Monarch. They seldom ever took a family trip to Branson, but when they did, they always stayed at much cheaper hotels that often had dirty sheets. The last time they stayed at Mitch's favorite cheap hotel, Helen came home with lice. Helen insisted they could afford to stay one night in the Monarch Hotel without draining their life savings. Mitch didn't like spending money on anything he could get cheaper.

Mitch sat in a comfortable padded chair in the hotel room, glaring at the floor. "Eight dollars for one night, Helen! We're not made of money and we could have stayed at the Shady Ben's Hotel for a quarter as much at the most."

"Well, dear, you look mighty comfortable in that chair.

The Shady Ben's doesn't offer a chair like that, now does it? I'll not have my daughter staying on Rose Street, Mitch. We can afford to stay here just fine, so stop mourning the loss of a few dollars and enjoy your family."

Mitch's burning eyes darted toward his wife. He pointed toward the bedroom where Laura was lying down. He hissed quietly, intentionally trying to keep his voice down, "Her child is not my family! God only knows whose kid that is!"

Helen's kind eyes turned harsh as she snapped, "That's enough, Mitch! Our daughter does not have a child inside her by choice. She is not a harlot, and I despise you speaking about her as if she was. This is not her fault!"

"Oh no?" he questioned. "How do we know that Jake Thomas's seed wasn't planted before those men got to her? Our daughter lost her values and gave herself away to who knows how many teenage boys and men!"

Helen struggled to keep her enraged voice low. "Because the doctor told us she was a virgin! What is wrong with you, Mitch? You know that! You were there when Dr. Anderson said so. Whatever has gotten into you needs to stop before you say something to your daughter that she won't forgive you for."

Mitch waved a hand begrudgingly and stood upright. "Yeah, well, Dr. Anderson also said she wouldn't get pregnant, didn't he? He was wrong about everything. I'm going for a walk. This has been a wasted trip. The doctors here are no more helpful than Dr. Anderson back in Hollister. We'd have better luck talking to the whores for help than a doctor. I never thought the world would be like that, but it is. I just wanted to get rid of that beast as safely as I could, but it's pointless! I'm going out for a while."

"Don't let me find you in the tavern downstairs, Mitch," Helen warned.

"It's called the Monarch Lounge, Helen. Women are not allowed inside, thankfully. So you won't find me inside even if you tried," Mitch said with a bitter tone. He paused to exhale with a heavy sigh. "I'm not going there, Helen. I promise. I'm just going for a walk to get some fresh air. I'll be back shortly."

———

"MOTHER," Laura said, stepping out of her hotel bedroom when she heard her father leave. "Does father think I'm a harlot?" her eyes were glistening with tears from the ache in her heart that felt much more like a nail driven into her chest.

Helen lifted her arm like a mother bird's wing to invite her daughter to sit close beside her. "No, baby." Her arm wrapped around Laura as she sat heavily on the davenport and leaned against her mother, beginning to weep quietly. Knowing Laura had overheard her father's words broke Helen's heart. "It's okay, baby girl. Shh. It's going to be okay."

"Why did God allow this to happen to me? They hurt me, Mama," Laura said with a fragile voice.

Tears burned Helen's eyes. "I don't know, sweetheart. That's a question that we can ask forever and they'll never be a satisfactory answer. What I am thankful for is I still have my little girl. Those men could have killed you and Jake, and we would never have known who did it. I am thankful for that. I thank God every day that you're still alive," Helen said with her chin resting on top of her daughter's head.

"Father blames me for what happened. I can see it in his eyes and hear it in his voice. He treats me differently now."

"How does he treat you differently?"

"Like, I'm infected with leprosy or something. He looks at me like I am disgusting. He used to hug me, but now he won't come near me." A tear slipped from Laura's eyes.

"This isn't easy for him. We have spent your whole life trying to watch over you and keep you safe, and we couldn't. That hurts him. What happened to you broke him. Your father has always been a strong man, but seeing you hurt broke him, Laura. He doesn't know how to handle this situation. Finding out you are with a child has devastated him. He doesn't know how to act or what he's supposed to do. He doesn't mean to hurt you, but he doesn't know how to help you. So he's doing what he knows how to do; he's trying to protect you. He may be going about it the wrong way, but that's what he's doing."

"By thinking I'm a harlot? It's not Jake's baby. I wish it was, but it's not."

"I know, Honey," Helen said gently, holding her daughter.

"I have to have this baby, don't I?" Laura questioned hopelessly.

Helen closed her eyes as a tear slipped down her cheek. "I'm afraid so," she whispered.

"I'm scared of having a baby." Her body began to shake as she wept on her mother's shoulder.

"I know you are, Laura. I promise you I will be there for you every day and every night through it all. I'll be there when it is born, and we'll find a good home to give the baby to. We will get through this, Laura, I promise you."

"Mother, is it wrong for me to pray that I have a miscarriage?"

Helen's brow lowered. "I don't know," she answered gently. The human part of her hoped Laura's body would reject the unwanted child, but the thought also brought a sense of guilt because she knew that the child growing inside of Laura was as precious to God as she or Laura was. "Do you feel like it's wrong?"

Laura shook her head slowly. "No. I was just wondering if it was wrong because I have been."

Helen leaned her cheek on the top of Laura's head affectionately. "I think that's normal for anyone in your position, sweetheart. I don't think anyone ever has wanted to have a man's baby that forced himself on her. My guess is every woman who's ever lived and gone through what you are going through has prayed for the same thing. I'm sure God answered some of those prayers and some he didn't. I think we should pray and ask the Lord for his will to be done. And that your father will..." She paused. "That he will start being himself again. He doesn't think you are disgusting or have leprosy. He just doesn't know how to help you or how to handle this situation. But don't doubt that he loves you because I know that he certainly does."

———

MITCH WALKED several blocks over to Rose Street and found himself walking past several saloons before he entered Madame Collet's Bordello. It was decorated with bright colors, primarily red drapes, and large paintings of nude women. The scent of lavender greeted his senses, and the sound of a lady's laughter could be heard from the other side of a door. More telling, the sound of creaking bed springs could be heard upstairs above him. It only took a moment to understand where he was, and for the price of a couple of expendable dollars, he could experience what the ladies were there for. For a brief second, the temptation aroused him.

A petite little lady who wore an elegant evening gown and had curly red hair approached him with a warm smile. "Hello, welcome. I haven't seen you come in here before, so this must be your first time. I am Collette. Would the fine gentleman like a drink?" She was in her late forties and holding a tall champagne glass in her delicate fingers.

Mitch could feel his aggravation diminishing with her welcoming presence. "Why not? Yes, I would. Two, if you don't mind, I could use them," Mitch said.

"My pleasure. And what might I call you, sir?" she asked as she stepped behind a small bar to pour him a shot glass of watered-down bourbon but paused. "Sir, you look like a man who has had a hard day. How about I pour you the good stuff?" She picked up a bottle from behind the bar. "This is tequila, brought up from Mexico. If you're having a tough day, a couple of shots of this will make it better."

"Sounds great," Mitch answered slowly.

"Do you have a particular type of lady in mind for some company? Or a specific name of a lady? Some of our new customers were recommended to Susan or Carrie, maybe?" she asked, handing him a tall shot glass to drink. "Carrie gets a lot of repeat customers and new ones too."

"No." Mitch's stomach tightened with anxiety. "My name is Mitch. I was curious to ask…"

Collette grinned with a slight snicker. "We don't have our prices posted like a meat market. We have top-notch ladies here. The girls are bathed and checked daily to guarantee they are clean and disease-free. The girls are beautiful and priced individually. We have ladies priced from two to five dollars for half an hour. It depends on the lady of your choice. Our available ladies are in the selection room at the moment. Are you ready to make a selection?"

"No." He swallowed his drink in one large gulp. He held the shot glass out as his eyes watered from the tequila. "Can I get another? That is good."

Collette smiled kindly. "Of course. Is this your first time visiting a place like this?"

"It is," he admitted.

"Let me guess: you're a loyal husband who has never cheated on his wife, but you're from out of town and had a bad day? Don't worry. Your wife will never know; your reputation is safe with us." She refilled his shot glass. "Am I close? It happens every day here, Mitch. Relax and let your manly needs be satisfied."

Mitch shook his head. "No, that's not why I'm here." He swallowed the second tall shot glass quickly. "Can I get another?"

Collette's brow raised. "Yes, but I'll warn you that tequila carries more of a kick than most of the watered-down whiskey you'll buy around here. It's a bit more expensive, too."

"That's fine. I don't drink normally, but I don't feel a thing. It's not much of a kick if you ask me."

She smiled with a slight shrug and poured him another tall shot. "So, Mitch, if you're not here for a lady's company, then why are you? You're not from the city here to collect taxes, are you?"

"No. Miss, I'm searching for someone to give my daughter..." He hesitated. "An abortion. Or at least tell me how to get rid of the monster inside her. The doctors are no help at all."

"How old is your daughter?"

"She just turned fifteen."

Collette asked questionably, "Who is the child's father to make it a monster?"

A touch of the fury stored up inside of Mitch became evident as he answered, "A pair of rapists! I don't know which one is the father and I don't care. I just want it gone! Now, what do you use to abort things you don't want? You must have women that get pregnant here. We have a whorehouse in Hollister too, but the last whore that got pregnant ended up dying while miscarrying. I don't want to risk harming my daughter. Those bastards hurt her enough. I can't stand to see her carrying a child like it's a favor to her. I'd kill them both if I could."

Collette could see the desperation and pain in his eyes. She nodded understandingly. "Unfortunately, I have lost a few ladies myself over the years for that very reason. I could give you four or five options that you could use, but no matter what antidote or method you use, they all carry a risk of death or injury. The woman's body chooses if it wants to miscarry a problem or not. When we use herbs, potions, or medicines to force it to do what the body doesn't want to do, it can backfire on us. I've lost some good friends for that very tragic reason. I don't give my girls anything anymore for that. I discovered a lady in Chinatown who uses her own special potion, which works like a dream. It's still quite uncomfortable for the lady and she will cramp like the dickens and suffer for a few hours. I won't lie to you, your daughter will hate life for a few hours, but not one person has died yet from her potion. I think she is a Chinese witch because she can heal almost anything. I warn you; her potion is not cheap. She charges about ten dollars for a small vial, but it is effective. By morning, the problem will be fixed. If you can afford that, and the tequila you've had and maybe a little extra for the information, I can give you her name and tell you where to find her."

"If it's safe and effective, I'll pay anything. I have the money to pay. I just want the problem gone," Mitch said, shaking the empty shot glass. He was considering another shot of tequila.

"Very well," Collette said. "Her name is Ling Sheng. She was married to Wu Pen Tseng but is now married to Ah-See, who is the new President of the Chinese Benevolence Society," she said with a knowing grin. "That woman is smart. As I said, I think she is a witch, I really do. Anyway, Ling Sheng has a special potion she makes up for a very high price that promises to make your daughter miscarry, and as I said, no one in town has died or had any complications yet. All of the bordellos and painted ladies go to her now for that problem and other cures. As I said, your daughter will hate life for a few hours but will enjoy the next nine months of her life normally. It is much safer than anything anyone else will give you. You'll find her in the big red building in the center of Chinatown. You can't miss it. Tell her husband, Ah-See, that I sent you."

Mitch pulled out his billfold to pay for the shots and information. "One more thing. How much for the bottle of tequila? I like that stuff."

———

THE IMPRESSION of Ling Sheng that Mitch had pictured was of an old Chinese woman without any teeth and with more wrinkles on her face than hair on a fluffy cat's back. His impression could not have been more wrong. Ling Sheng was undeniably a beautiful young lady in her late twenties. Her face was one of the prettiest Mitch had ever seen, and her black hair was long and glistened in the lantern's light. Ling Sheng busied herself, mixing a potion with careful measurements. She was dressed in a long pink kimono with darker pink lilies decorating the pattern. Mitch could not help but sneak glances over to the small room with an opened door where she worked mixing her herbs, spices, and magical potions to create the answer to his prayers. Ling Sheng was too beautiful not to stare at. Her husband, Ah-See, did not miss Mitch's roaming eyes as they leered hungrily on his bride.

"My wife is a beautiful lady, isn't she?" Ah-See asked, sitting in a wicker chair four feet in front of Mitch. They were in Ah-See and Ling's home on the second floor of the Chinese Benevolence Society building. Mitch had refused a cup of tea but held a bottle of Mexican liquor from which he was drinking.

"Yes," Mitch answered, putting his attention back on the small Chinese man in front of him. "Yes, she is. She makes my wife look like a dead, bloated cow."

Ah-See smiled slightly. "Perhaps every man's wife is a flower of its own kind. I'm sure your wife is beautiful in many ways, or you would not have married her. Yes?" Mitch ignored him and turned his head back to peer at Ling Shing. Ah-See changed the subject back to the one that Mitch seemed more passionate about. "Marshal Bannister is a good man. If it weren't for him, I would not be where I am today or married to Ling. I am sure you're mistaken. Marshal Bannister would not let any man who harmed a child go free to do so again. I know him well enough to know that."

Mitch's focus went back to Ah-See. "We have different views on that," he said with a touch of bitterness. "The man is as corrupt as a politician."

"Only one view is right. I believe it is mine since I know Matt better than you," Ah-See said.

"Perhaps," Mitch said to end the conversation that started with an angry rant about the marshal but didn't go the way he had hoped. "She doesn't speak English, does she?" Mitch asked, waving toward Ling.

"No. Ling is learning to speak it slowly. I am teaching her."

"So what do you do here? Are you a priest or something? There's like a Chinese church or something downstairs and you two live in a palace compared to the other shacks in Chinatown." He took a drink of the tequila. The alcohol was taking effect as his words were beginning to slur.

"A priest, no. I am the President of the Chinese Benevolence Society."

Mitch shrugged his shoulders. "I'm not from here. I have no idea what that is. It just looks like a shrine or something heathenistic to me."

Ah-See grinned. "In essence, I run Chinatown. Like the mayor of your town. Are you sure you don't want some tea?"

"No. I have my bottle, thank you. So basically, you're a politician? No wonder you live in a palace."

Ling came back into the room with a small glass vial with a cork stopper. She spoke in Chinese. Ah-See translated, "Ling says it is made strong to make the miscarriage faster. Your daughter must drink the potion with a glass of water, followed by two more glasses of water immediately. And then two more glasses of water every hour for six hours to wash it from her system. That is very important to do. In seven hours, the miscarriage will happen."

"Great. I was told my daughter would be uncomfortable for a while. Is that right?"

"No," Ah-See corrected him. "She will suffer excruciating pain for five to six hours, but it will pass."

Mitch nodded. His eyes gazed at Ling Sheng. "You have a beautiful wife. I didn't know Chinese women could be so dang pretty."

Ah-See faked a smile, annoyed with the intoxicated man. "Chinese women are the prettiest of flowers in all the world. My Ling is the most beautiful of them all." He spoke in Chinese to translate for Ling.

"Ah," she said with a wide smile. "Thank...you," she said, careful to pronounce the words correctly. She bowed politely with a lovely grin.

Mitch squinted his eyes to see the glass vial of brownish liquid with floating brown particles more clearly. "What is in here?"

"That is a secret," Ah-See replied.

CHAPTER SIX

MITCH HAD COLLECTED A PITCHER OF WATER from the young man working at the hotel's front desk and was reassured that someone would be attending the desk all night if he needed more water. Mitch carried the ceramic pitcher and his half-drunk bottle of tequila upstairs and entered his hotel room.

Helen was lying across the davenport with her eyes closed. They opened slowly and she lowered her brow curiously as he set a pitcher and a bottle of tequila on the table. He offered a lopsided grin as he looked at Helen and pulled a small vial of brown liquid out of his shirt pocket to make sure it hadn't leaked from the corked top. "I got the gold. Gold, I say."

"What are you doing? Are you drunk? I told you, you better not go to the tavern, Mitch."

"I didn't go to the tavern. I went to the whorehouse and bought the tequila. You should have some. Tequila!" he shouted and laughed. "It's even fun to say…tequila!"

"Whorehouse? Mitch, did you lay with a woman?"

Helen questioned with an aching in her heart, fearing her husband had cheated on her.

"Helen...no. I bought tequila. Tequila!" he exclaimed, followed with a laugh.

"Shh. It's getting late. You need to be quiet. I'm disappointed in you, Mitchell Whitehead, you're drunk."

"I got the gold elixir that...that is safer than anything else. Seven hours and she'll pop that evil seed out like vomit and then we can go home." He smiled. "Ling Sheng made it. Anything Ling Sheng makes is golden. It has to be golden. She's the most beautiful woman I've ever seen. If we have another baby girl, I want to name her Ling Sheng Whitehead. Ling Sheng...it sounds as beautiful as she is, doesn't it? Ling Sheng."

Helen sat up with an offended grimace. "Who are you talking about? A prostitute? If a prostitute has you that excited, then maybe you need to stay here while Laura and I go home."

"I wish Ling Sheng was a whore. She made the elixir, potion, medicine, whatever it is. It's guaranteed to work and work safely."

"What kind of medicine is it?"

"I don't know. Ling Sheng made it. The whores swear by it. Laura will have to drink a lot of water though."

"Is this to get rid of the baby?"

"Of course," Mitch said with a touch of surprise that Helen would have to ask. "If she drinks this now, it will be over by morning and then we can go home."

"Mitch, it's late. Laura's already gone to bed. We should do it tomorrow when we get home."

"Bullcrap! We're doing it *now*. I want that thing out of her. The sooner, the better. Seven hours is all it takes, Ling Sheng said."

"Who is Ling Sheng? Where did you meet her?"

Mitch scowled. "Chinatown! I already told you that. Did you think Ling Sheng was American? No. I never knew Chinese women were so beautiful. Helen, you should grow your hair long and let it hang free. Dye it black and buy one of those kimonos before we leave town." He paused to look at his wife's body. She was quite a bit thicker than Ling Sheng. He wrinkled his nose with distaste. "Maybe not. Cut back on the cakes and pies a bit and yeah, that might be okay."

"What are you talking about?" Helen questioned abruptly. "Are you suggesting I dress up like your lady friend?"

"No! I wouldn't. But if you lost fifty pounds, you might look good in a kimono."

Helen's brow furrowed while her eyes grew moist. Her mouth dropped open as she slowly shook her head, gazing at her husband. She was dumbfounded that he would compare her to another woman. "How dare you?" the words came out just above a whisper.

Mitch smacked his lips a few times. "My mouth's dry; I need a drink." He grabbed the bottle of liquor and took a long drink. "Collette said Ling Shing was a witch, but Ling Shing's too beautiful to be a witch. I was thinking maybe she can whip up a potion to help you lose fifty or sixty pounds. I mean, how does a little, ugly Chinese man find a wife like Ling Shing, and I get you?"

Helen stood. Her eyes burning with heated tears. Her throat was tight, and her stomach was feeling sick as she choked down a painful sob. "Good night. For all I care, you can sleep on the floor like a dog or go back to wherever you came from." She sniffled. The gas lantern's light reflected off from the layers of moisture clouding her eyes. "You are a real ass."

"We have to wake up Laura. I have the golden elixir."

"Good night! Go to sleep and dream about Ling Sheng or whatever her name is. But leave Laura alone. She's sleeping unless you woke her." Helen went into her bedroom and closed the door abruptly.

"Ling Sheng wouldn't slam the door!" Mitch shouted toward the bedroom. He filled a glass of water from the pitcher and entered Laura's room. He turned the gas lantern on the wall from dim to bright and kicked on the edge of her bed to jar her awake. "Laura, wake up. I need you to sit up."

"What are you doing?" Laura asked, squinting her eyes in the light. She had been in a deep sleep. She sat and scooted against the headboard to gaze at her father with a combination of curiosity and alarm. "What's the matter?"

"Drink this, and then I need you to drink two glasses of water," Mitch said, removing the cork cap and holding the vial of brown liquid out for her to drink.

"Huh? What's this?"

"Just drink it."

Laura took the vial and held it up to the light to see floating particles in the dirty brown liquid that smelled like a saloon's outhouse once she put it up to her nose. "No! That stinks. I'm not drinking that." She handed it back to her father.

"Drink it!" he said impatiently.

"No. You drink it. I'd vomit before it touched my lips. It smells like feces, literally."

"Laura," Mitch said, controlling his voice, "plug your nose and swallow it."

"No!" she exclaimed with a shake of her head. "It smells disgusting."

"Laura, do it now before I force it down your throat!" Mitch ordered with a raised voice. His eyes were wide and glaring.

Laura could feel the intimidation rise into her throat. Her voice shook as she sputtered, "I...I don't even know what it is. Why do you want me to drink it?"

"It's the fix to your problem."

"What problem? The baby?" Laura asked with a horrified expression.

"Yes. Now drink it so we can get this over with."

"No..." she said lightly, shaking her head rebelliously.

Mitch's eyes hardened. He spoke in a deeper and more threatening tone, "Just drink it and get it over with, Laura!"

"No. I don't want to drink it. It stinks."

Mitch grabbed her jaw with his left hand and squeezed to open her mouth. In his right hand, he held the opened vial, waiting to pour the contents down her throat. Laura screamed as she fought to turn her head while she pulled at her father's hand to break free of his grip. "Mother!" she cried out.

"Hold still! Damn it!" he seethed.

Helen burst into the room. "Mitch, what are you doing?" she shouted.

Mitch ordered, "Hold her arms down!"

Helen was firm. "No! You can wait until we get home." A cold chill ran down her spine when Mitch turned his glare to her. His eyes were reddened and fierce. She had never seen him look so cold, dangerous, and deadly in all the years of their marriage. His eyes were mad and wild, and if she didn't know better, she would say he looked demonic. She took a step back.

Mitch sneered as he cursed.. His voice was cold and seething with malice. "Hold her arms down, Helen or I'll shove this vial down your throat and see what it does to you! Get over here!" he yelled. He quickly grabbed Helen's wrist with a mighty grasp and jerked her forward mercilessly.

"You're hurting me!" she cried out.

"I will hurt you if you don't do what I tell you!" He pushed her down over the bed's side on top of Laura's body. "Hold her arms down with your fat ass!"

Shocked by the madness of his expression and the venom in his voice, Helen was too afraid to disobey the strange madness that had overcome him. She closed her eyes and wept quietly while her daughter struggled to break free.

To feel her mother grab her arm and lay across her body to stop her squirming felt as violating as the men who attacked her. In a panic, Laura screamed through her sobs, crying out for help.

Mitch cursed and squeezed Laura's jaw again to force her mouth open. He put the vial to her bottom lip and began to pour the liquid into her mouth. Laura tried to shake her head free of his grasp, slicing her cheek on a tooth in the process. She spat the foul-tasting liquid out, letting it run down her chin as she gagged. It tasted as foul as it smelled.

Cursing with more foul words than either Helen or Laura had ever heard escape his lips, Mitch stood and put the cork back into the vial and carefully laid the vial on a dresser. He unbuckled his belt and ripped it free from the pant loops, folded it over and ordered Helen to get up. He yanked the blankets from Laura and swung the belt as hard as he could, with a loud crack of the leather striking the night dress covering her stomach. He swung it again as Laura cried out in pain.

"Are you going to drink it?" her father shouted.

Laura sobbed without answering.

He swung the belt again, harder, aimed at the bloomers on her legs. Her scream echoed through the building as she sat up to protect her legs. The next strike of the belt hit her back with a loud crack that was sure to leave a welt. He struck her again and again, enraged.

"Are you going to drink it now?" he shouted.

"Yes!" she cried out through uncontrollable sobs.

"Good." He set the belt on the dresser, uncorked the potion and handed it to his sobbing daughter, whose body was shaking in anguish. "Drink it!"

Laura held the vial in her trembling hands and tried to calm her wailing enough to catch a breath.

"Drink it!" her father ordered.

Laura in a flare of anger, threw the vial against the wall with a loud defiant, "No!" The vial shattered, allowing the brown liquid to run down the wall.

Enraged, Mitch grabbed his belt and stepped toward the bed. Laura, fearing her father's fury, scooted toward the wall, holding a protective arm up and whimpered, "Daddy..."

Mitch swung the belt with all the fury that burned within him, striking Laura with a downward slash across her cheek and arm. "That cost ten dollars! If you don't want to drink it, then I'll beat that thing out of you!" he yelled and swung the belt like a madman. Laura screamed with the continuing blows that her body endured without any mercy or care of where the leather belt landed, leaving a welt everywhere it hit her.

The sound of someone banging on the hotel room's door did not register with Mitch as he mindlessly swung the belt, aiming at Laura's abdomen but hitting her arms, side, back, and legs as Laura squirmed with every burning sting of the belt. She leaned forward to protect her legs and the belt hit the side of her face, leaving an immediate red mark over her cheek and eye. Screaming, she turned away from him and tried to bury herself into the mattress, exposing her back to another brutal sting of the belt.

Mitch stopped, panting. He ordered his wife, "Hold her arms down. I'm going to beat that thing out of her!"

The wailing of her daughter unsettled Helen's nerves. She shook her head just enough to be noticed as she meekly said, "She's had enough, Mitch. Please stop," she asked gently, hoping her calm voice would ease his drunken wrath. "Someone's at the door."

Mitch turned his shoulders toward his wife and swung the belt with a powerful overhand swing that hit the top of Helen's shoulder. She wailed with a scream and nearly dropped to her knees with the force of the blow. She began sobbing and hurried to leave the room and open the hotel door, but Mitch hit Helen across the back with a loud snap of the leather and then quickly grabbed her hair and dragged her across the floor toward the bed. "I told you to hold her arms down!" He pushed her onto the bed.

Sobbing with deep guttural cries, Helen begged, "Please stop! Mitch, stop." Helen received a crack of the belt across her back for disobeying his order.

Hearing her mother's deep, gut-wrenching cries, Laura took advantage of her father's attention being elsewhere and scampered off the bed to run to the door, but Mitch quickly caught her and roughly slammed her back onto the bed. He forced her arms down and ordered Helen to hold them down. Sobbing, Helen surrendered to his demand and obeyed.

"Mommy...make him stop!" Laura screamed.

"I can't, baby...I'm so sorry," Helen wept bitterly. She closed her eyes shamefully.

The banging on the door grew more urgent. "Open this door!" a voice demanded.

Mitch gripped the belt tightly and swung the belt over his head down upon Laura's stomach. Her scream was loud and painful as she kicked her legs uncontrollably. He glared at Laura mercilessly. "You asked for this!" He swung the belt with another loud crack that brought another deafening scream.

The front door lock opened, and Matt Bannister entered the bedroom with his Colt.45 drawn. His hardened eyes scanned the room to see a woman pinning a young girl down while her father beat her with a belt. Matt grit his teeth and leveled the revolver at Mitch's head, fighting the temptation to pull the trigger. His deep voice shouted with deadly venom, "Hit her again, and I'll blow your head off!" Matt's brown eyes were cold as ice and shifted between the stunned father and bawling daughter with red, raised welts covering her face and neck. Undoubtedly, there were many more under her nightdress and bloomers.

Mitch's attention shifted to Matt. Like a rabid dog, oblivious of danger, Mitch stepped forward, raising his belt at the intruder with devilish intent.

Matt stepped back to miss the arching speed of the belt and then stepped forward and whipped his revolver through the air cracking the butt of the grip down on Mitch's head. The man stumbled back against the wall and came at Matt again. Matt slammed the cylinder against the side of Mitch's head with a forceful blow. Mitch collapsed to the floor, beginning to bleed but intent on getting back to his feet. Matt slammed the revolver against his head again, sending Mitch slumping to the floor unconscious.

"You have no idea how badly I wanted to pull the trigger!" Matt turned his angry gaze at Helen. "Get away from her!" Helen began apologizing as she tried to comfort her wailing daughter, who was still squirming in pain.

"Christine!" Matt yelled, watching Laura withering in pain. He roughly jerked Helen away from Laura pulling her to the floor. "I said get away from her! Christine!"

"Yes?" Christine said, coming into the room. "Oh, my," she gasped, seeing Laura on the bed with her arms locked over her bent knees, rocking back and forth in agony. She went to Laura quickly and took hold of Laura's arm. "Come with me, sweetheart. It's going to be okay." She helped Laura to stand.

"Take her to my room," Floyd Bannister said to Christine. He had followed Matt into the bedroom.

"Laura..." Helen cried as she remained on her knees, bellowing out, "I'm sorry!"

Christine looked back at Helen with disgust burning in her eyes as they left the bedroom.

"Stay put!" Matt ordered Helen when she tried to stand and follow.

"She's my daughter," Helen's tear-stricken and anguished expression pleaded with Matt as she pointed at her husband's unconscious body. "It was him!"

Matt had no pity. "I'm taking her to the doctor and if she's injured in any way, I'm throwing both of you in jail and I'm leaving you there while I find her a new home. You both make me sick!"

Helen shook her head as she rested her arm and head on the mattress. "It wasn't me!" she sobbed. "Bring my daughter back. Please, bring her back. I didn't do anything."

"You're right, you didn't! You should have stopped him. What I witnessed is unforgivable, Mrs. Whitehead. I know who you are. We met in Hollister the day after your daughter was attacked. I'm Matt Bannister. Christine is my wife. Your daughter's safety is all I care about. She's clearly not safe here, and I won't leave her with you."

Helen cried out, "He made me do it! I couldn't stop him." She collapsed to the floor, wailing.

Matt watched her without an ounce of mercy. He shook his head with disgust and left the hotel room, walking past his father.

Floyd Bannister was in his midsixties, with short silver hair combed straight back. He kept a groomed silver goatee and was dressed in a gray suit. He stood in the room, watching his son quietly. As the new manager of the Monarch Hotel, he made his first executive decision. "I want you and your husband out of here by ten in the morning. You will not be welcomed back."

CHAPTER SEVEN

MATT AND CHRISTINE MET HIS BROTHERS, LEE and Albert, and their families at the Monarch Restaurant to have dinner with their father, Floyd. When dinner had come to an end, Lee and Albert took their families home to put their younger children to bed for the night. Matt and Christine stayed to visit Floyd in the comfort of his hotel room. It was getting late and nearing the time for Matt and Christine to go home when they heard blood-curdling screams coming from the Whitehead's room.

Matt had met the Whitehead family in Hollister the day after Cass Travers and Jesse Helms had attacked Laura and Jake. What those two men had done to Laura made her unrecognizable compared to the pretty young lady who sat in Matt and Christine's family room now. Matt dared not allow her to stay in the presence of her parents after witnessing what they were doing to her. Laura was not shy about telling them what her father wanted her to do and how she tossed the vial against the wall. Her body was covered with reddened, raised welts that were slowly going down, including the one across her face.

Laura wiped the tears from her eyes. "My father has never beat me like that before. Honest, he hasn't," she said with a troubled voice. "I don't understand why he hates me so much now."

Matt had gone to bed, and Christine cuddled in a blanket on one end of the davenport while Laura sat on the other end, wrapped in a blanket as well. "Sweetheart, you could smell the liquor on your father's breath. He was drunk. That's no excuse, but it does make people do things they would never do if they were sober. I can't imagine he doesn't love you though."

"He thinks it is my fault that those men did what they did to me. He thinks the baby is Jake's, but we never did anything but kiss and talk."

"Who is Jake?" Christine asked.

Laura's face drew longer. "The boy I love. We were going to elope next year and get married. My parents hate him and won't let him see me. That's why we'd meet in the cellar. It was the only way," she said with a sad shrug. "I don't go anywhere since those men...." She looked at Christine with a frightened gaze. "I'm afraid of it happening again, so I don't go anywhere without my mother. My father doesn't want to be seen with me, I don't think."

"I'm sorry that happened to you, sweetheart, but it wasn't your fault. Those men made a decision, and they'll pay for it, whether in this world or the next. The Bible says vengeance is the Lord's, and he'll see to it. But for you, it's going to take time to heal and feel comfortable being out in the world again."

"This is not a world I want to live in anymore," Laura said softly.

Christine asked empathetically, "Do you ever think about ending it all and committing suicide?"

Laura's eyes filled with thick layers of tears like a bucket filled to the brim. She nodded while her chin twitched with emotion. "I don't want to have this baby," she said with a strained voice. "I don't want it in me, and I keep praying the Lord will let me miscarry it. I'm afraid of what could happen if I take something to try to get it out." She paused to sniffle and wipe her nose. "Our reverend said what happened to me was God's will, and this baby is God's will too. But if it was evil for them to do what they did to me, then how could it be God's will? God doesn't will evil, does he?"

"No," Christine replied softly. "God doesn't will evil. But evil exists in this world, and we're not always protected from it. God allows evil because we live in a fallen world, but that does not mean it is *his* will. The manner in which that child was put inside of you is criminal, wicked, and evil, and definitely *not* God's will. However, the timing was right, and you conceived. As women, our first baby is supposed to be an experience between a husband and wife, but they robbed you of that. And now you have a baby growing inside of you..."

"I don't want it inside of me!" Laura exclaimed. "I didn't drink that stuff tonight, but that doesn't mean I want this baby. My father says if it was conceived by evil, then it will be born evil. I will never forget what those men looked like, and I don't want to see their faces again! I'm afraid of having the baby because I don't want to see them."

"Laura, look at me," Christine said gently. "Do you know who my father is?"

"No."

"Take a guess. Who do you think my father might be?"

Laura shrugged. "The mayor of Branson, Mr. Slater? My father showed us his mansion up on the hill. Is he your father?"

Christine chuckled lightly. "No. I don't know who my father is. He was one of several young men that raped my mother. I am just like that child inside of you. My mother didn't ask to be raped either, nor did she want to get pregnant, but that's how I was conceived. I'm the product of my mother being raped, just like that child inside of you is. I'm sure my mother would have liked to have gotten rid of me too at first, but she loved me instead. Now, here I am. How I was conceived was wrong in every way, but that doesn't define my value or who I am. I was just as innocent and human as any married couple's baby across town. My life is just as valuable as anyone else's. My father, whoever he is, committed a monstrous act against an innocent girl not much older than you are. The fact is, it isn't how we're brought into the world that makes us a monster, but how much we are loved or not loved by our parents plays a much bigger role than how we were conceived."

"Your mother was like me?"

Christine nodded. "She was a year or two older is the only difference."

"Do you think she prayed for a miscarriage too?"

"I'm sure she did. But luckily for me, the Lord did not answer that prayer. My grandparents were thankful for me, and I know Matt is glad the Lord didn't answer that prayer too. There's not another woman in the world who would put up with him like I do, trust me," she said with a smile.

"Keep in mind, Laura, that we can only see what's happening right now. God sees the future and knows who and what that little one inside of you is going to be. Who knows, that little one could be the next great theologian or a scientist. Maybe even the woman who changes the world somehow. We never know what God has planned, but he sees what's ahead and far beyond what we see. All I can say is trust him. This little one could become the biggest joy and pride of your life."

"Your mother must be proud of you."

"My mother ended up committing suicide when I was three months old. She grew up in a small town and knew who the boys were. They teased her, spread gossip, and ruined her reputation. They were vicious, and the gossip spread, making my mother's life hell. My mother couldn't take it anymore."

"How do you know she loved you then?"

Christine smiled sadly. "My mother wrote me a letter the night she died. She didn't commit suicide because of me. She loved me very much. One of her tears smeared the ink on the paper as she wrote. It was the people in her town who thought she was more unwholesome than a harlot for giving herself to several boys at once. No one believed those fine, upstanding boys had forced themselves upon her. She couldn't take it anymore and gave up. I grew up in the same town as the fatherless child. But Laura, that doesn't define me; who I am and my integrity are what defines me. It could be the same with your child too. God does not will evil, but he can bring goodness and joy out of it. We have an amazing God that way."

"I never would have guessed your father was a rapist," Laura said, gazing at Christine.

Christine nodded. "Yes, he was." She pat Laura's foot.

"My mother experienced what you're going through, but she had me. I'm grateful to her for that. I can not put myself in her shoes or know what she was facing when she went to town; I just know it was bad. What I do know is she committed suicide and gave up the chance of ever knowing me. I like to think she would have been proud of who I grew up to be. My grandparents raised me, and they were certainly proud of me. My father, whoever he is, got my mother pregnant, but he did not make me who I am. So, before your father wants you to drink another vial that just smells better, you have to ask yourself if my life, which was conceived by rape, has the same value as yours or not."

"You don't have any children, do you?" Laura asked thoughtfully.

"Matt and I just got married a couple of months ago. Give us some time," Christine said with a chuckle. "No," Christine said as her smile faded. "I was shot about a year ago and the bullet damaged my ovaries. I don't know if I can get pregnant. I'd like to, but Doctor Ryland said I may not ever. Matt and I decided to leave that up to the Lord and enjoy our lives either way."

"Would you like to adopt my baby?" Laura asked.

Christine grinned. "I don't know. That's a tough question to answer without asking Matt too. How about you carry that baby and give birth and then if you don't want to keep him or her, you can ask me then."

"I don't know if my father will let me."

"Laura, I know the next five months won't be easy. If you allow me to, I'll help you get through this as much as I can. You're always welcome here and I'm only one letter or telegram away. My husband and I will come to get you if that's what it takes to keep you safe, alive, and well. That's a promise. But you have to promise me that you won't do what my mother did when those suicidal thoughts come to you. Cast those thoughts away like a dead rat and know for a fact that feelings are just feelings. It doesn't mean what you're feeling is true or a fact. The truth is your future is brighter than you know. Maybe you'll marry Jake, maybe not, but someday, you will be married, and you'll be thankful that you never gave in to those dark feelings and ended your life. Okay?"

Laura smiled slowly at her new friend. "Okay. I promise you, I won't."

CHAPTER EIGHT

MITCH WHITEHEAD WOKE UP WITH A HEADACHE brewing behind his temples. He was lying on the floor in Laura's room, still dressed and wearing his boots. He touched the side of his head and winced at the touch of a bump on the upper left side of his head. A crumbling of dry blood revealed a cut at the center of the bump. He sat up and widened his eyes to stretch his eyelids in the hopes of waking up and forcing the nauseousness away. His stomach was upset and he nearly vomited as he swallowed. His belt lay on the floor and vaguely, he recalled hitting Laura with it. The broken vial lay on the floor where a dried brown substance had run down the wall, leaving a faint foul odor.

He picked up his belt and stood to loop it around his pants before leaving the room. Helen was sitting on the davenport drinking a cup of coffee. "Where's Laura? Still sleeping?" he asked, rubbing his temple.

Helen's eyes fired a glaring ray of fury at her husband. "Do you not remember anything?" Her tone held the advanced warning of a pending storm of wrath.

"Hmm, not too much. I remember asking her to drink that elixir the Chinese woman made." He sat heavily in a padded chair. "Will you get me a glass of water? My head is starting to pound. I don't feel well."

Helen had no compassion for him. "Have Ling Sheng get it for you."

"Huh?" he questioned with a perplexed glance at his wife.

"Maybe you'd find me more attractive if I squinted my eyes." She squinted her eyes at him with a hostile grimace brewing in her expression. "Maybe you could pretend this robe is a kimono and lift it over my face and pretend I'm Ling Sheng! I'll keep my eyes squinted."

Mitch closed his eyes with a pounding of a growing headache. "If I said something offensive, I apologize. Helen, I don't feel well, and I don't know where all this anger is coming from. Did Laura drink that medicine?"

"No! She threw it against the wall because it smelled like feces and it looked like it too. I'm not convinced that's not what it was and you spent ten dollars on it, you said. Did you say something offensive? Yes, I would say so. But that's not what I'm angry about. You beat my daughter in a drunken rage! I could not stop you and when I tried, you beat me," her voice trembled with emotion. "No, you can talk about some Chinese woman all you want as far as I'm concerned. You can go to every whorehouse you can find and catch leprosy, as far as I'm concerned. You will never touch me again!" Her voice hardened as a dangerous sneer twisted her lips. "And you will *never* lay your hands on my daughter again! You tortured her, Mitch. It was not a beating; you beat her until there was nothing but welts on her. God might forgive you, but I doubt she ever will. She asked if you hated her when you left, and now I'm afraid she is convinced that you do. And I'm not so sure that you don't because no father should do that to their child! You are an unforgivable fool, Mitch."

Mitch's brow lowered. He could vaguely remember whipping his daughter for refusing to drink the vial he had bought. "I was drunk."

Helen scoffed. "I hope it was worth it. Do you know how humiliating it was for our neighbors to hear my daughter screaming for help and you shouting? Or for them to watch Matt Bannister take our daughter out of here?"

"To jail?" Mitch questioned with concern.

"No," she said with her eyes burning into him. "He took her away to protect her from *us!*" she shouted. "I'm her mother and you made me hold her down so you could beat that baby out of her. As her father, you are supposed to love her no matter what. How could you be so hate-filled that you could beat her like that? I will never look at you the same way again, Mitchell Whitehead. Go find yourself a Chinese woman if that is what you want, but don't you ever strike my daughter or me again!"

Mitch leaned forward and buried his face in his hands. "I'm sorry."

Helen spoke heatedly. "Saying you're sorry cannot make up for what you did!"

"What do you want from me?" Mitch shouted. His eyes glared with profound venom. "I said I'm sorry! What more do you want from me? I can't change what I did. I don't even remember what happened, but I can't change it now, can I, Helen?" He sighed heavily and rubbed his temples while closing his eyes. He continued reasonably, "Nothing you said hurt me more than hearing Laura thinks I hate her. I love my daughter more than anything. This headache is killing me. She should have drank that medicine last night."

"How dare you spend our money on some vial of crap that could have killed our daughter. We don't know what that was, Mitch. Go lick it off the wall if you trust that Chinese woman so much. It might even cure your headache. Did you forget her name? It's Ling Sheng. I should lose what did you say, fifty, sixty pounds?"

Mitch buried his aching head in his hands and groaned. He spoke softly. "I was angry. I had a drink, which led to others, and now I'm miserable. Nothing would have happened last night if I had not tried that tequila."

"There's still some in the bottle you bought if you'd like some more. It might be more fitting than water."

"No. Never again."

"I've heard that before."

Mitch shot an angry glance at Helen. "I'm done talking. I said I'm sorry, and that's it. I'm going to change my clothes and going downstairs to get something to eat. Are you coming or not?"

"No. You've humiliated me enough for this trip."

"Starve then." He stood to step toward the door.

Helen said, "I would have breakfast with you, but I want to look more like Ling Sheng. Maybe we can ask the doctor to stitch my eyes closed so they're slanted."

Mitch shook his head. "You work on that." He was in no mood to listen to her sarcasm.

"By the way, you made such a big scene last night that we have to leave by ten. And we can never come back, thank you. I hope they refuse to serve you breakfast."

"The other hotels are cheaper anyway," he said as he walked out the door.

Helen did not bother to tell him that his face was covered with dried blood from his head wounds.

———

MITCH WAS STILL BREWING over the fact that Helen had not told him his face was covered with dried blood when he went down to the restaurant. The hotel room's door opened, and Laura entered more like a skittish mouse than the witty and spirited girl they had raised. Matt and Christine followed her in.

"Laura!" Helen said, standing from her seat. "I'm so sorry about last night, baby. I'm so sorry. Forgive me." Her arms wrapped around her daughter as she squeezed her eyes shut tightly. "I'm sorry," she whispered, followed by a sniffle as her eyes watered heavily.

Mitch stood awkwardly from his chair. He nodded to Matt once and slowly stepped near his wife and daughter. What he had done the night before was fully realized when he saw the slight hint of a welt on her cheek. He quietly gasped as the air was sucked out of his lungs from the weight of the guilt that suddenly filled him. "Laura...." His throat went dry.

"Mother," Laura said, ignoring her father, "this is Christine, Matt's wife."

"Hello, Mr. and Mrs. Whitehead," Christine said without her usual friendly countenance.

"Hi," Helen said with a questionable lowering of her brow. "Marshal Bannister," she greeted Matt without any substance in her voice. He merely offered a cold nod in return.

"Mother, can we sit down and talk?"

"Of course," Helen said uneasily. She worried her

daughter would refuse to go home with them. "What is this all about, Laura?"

Matt could not hold his anger back any longer and spoke heatedly. "When I came in here last night, what I witnessed was some of the worst abuse I have seen, and I've seen a lot. Mr. Whitehead, you're lucky I didn't blow your head off last night. That's all I have to say to you. You're lucky. I know your family has a lot going on right now, but there is no excuse for what I witnessed. Not ever!"

Mitch closed his eyes shamefully. "I know. What I did is inexcusable." He looked at Laura, who had not said a word to him. "Laura, I am sorry. I don't know what got into me."

"It didn't get into you, Father; it got into me. I'm the one that's pregnant, remember? That's why we're here in Branson, to get rid of it. That's why we came here, and why you despise me." Her bottom lip quivered as she finished.

Mitch shook his head as he tried to catch a breath that was suddenly stolen from him. "I don't despise you. I love you too much to see you go through this." His voice quivered as his eyes watered. "It's hard enough to live with what happened to you without watching you carrying one of those bastards' seed. I wanted to help you."

Laura wiped the tears from her eyes. "Father,"—she swallowed heavily—"Mother, I am keeping the baby. At least until it's born, I won't drink anything to miscarry it."

"What?" Mitch gasped. "Laura, no decent man wants to marry a mother with a rapist's child. Think of your future. You're fifteen and pregnant. Can you imagine how ridiculed you're going to be walking around with a baby in your belly? People are going to start thinking you want that thing. What's that going to do to our family, Laura? What's that going to do to you? We need to get rid of it before it's too late."

Matt spoke firmly. "It is against the law to intentionally induce an abortion. If you force her to do so, I will arrest you."

Mitch spoke heatedly. "Do you think I'm afraid of being arrested? Do you think the DA is going to hold this against me after he let Jesse…"

"Stop it!" Helen shouted. "I'm tired of hearing you talk about Jesse Helms! Can we please just move on and forget about him? I'm tired of the fighting, Mitch. If Laura wants to carry this child until it's born because she thinks it's the right thing to do, then she is going to do it. And we, meaning you and I, are going to support her. I will not allow you to ruin this family because of what happened to Laura. It was *not* her fault! And I am tired of saying *that*. I just want to go home and get back to living our lives as normally as we can. Please!"

Mitch took a deep breath and gazed at his daughter with a blank expression.

Christine offered softly, "Mr. Whitehead, I know you must be heartbroken from what happened to Laura and horrified to learn she is pregnant from it. Laura can tell you what happened to my mother, but in short, she was raped at Laura's age by several young men. I was conceived that day from a violent rape. My father, whoever he may be, was a heartless animal who drove my mother to kill herself. His actions do not make me any less human or more evil than you or Laura. I think I turned out okay, and Laura's baby will, too."

Mitch gazed at his beautiful daughter for a moment and then gave a resigned sigh. "I don't like it, but what other choice do we have? We'll get through it if you want to be the hub of community gossip."

"That's the best you could do?" Helen asked with a scowl. "We can handle the gossip, but a house divided cannot stand. You need to decide if you can let go of your anger and be supportive of Laura or not. If not, Laura and I will go home without you. And if you ever treat Laura or me like you did last night again, I will divorce you. Do you understand me?"

Mitch closed his eyes. "What happened last night will never happen again. I'll never drink again. I swear it. Yes, I will try to change. I'm not going to jump and down and clap my hands to celebrate her being with child because I don't think it's exciting at all. But I love my daughter enough that, yes, I will try to let the past go and move forward."

PART TWO

CHAPTER NINE

Jake Thomas drove the buggy into Hollister with a stirring in his stomach that wouldn't settle. Fearing the possibility of running into Laura at the church bazaar caused his hands to shake as he held the reins of the single horse that pulled the carriage.

His aging and disabled mother sat beside him on the padded seat, wrapped in her warmest fur coat. "Maude's jam is always worth the price. So is Lona's relish. I always buy twelve jars a piece and it gets us through the year," she explained once again, knowing Jake didn't want to take her to town.

"Ma, you know, I don't feel comfortable going to town anymore," Jake said.

Sasha Thomas put a deformed, arthritic hand on his thigh. "Jake, the scar on your cheek isn't going away no matter how long you hide it. It is time that you show your face without looking downward. That scarf doesn't hide anything."

"It's a bandanna, Mother, not a scarf."

Sasha smiled at his quick response. "You are a wonderful young man with a bright future and you can not hide away forever. It's time, Jacob, to start living your life like a man. You have nothing to be ashamed of. So take that scarf off and stand proud just the way you are."

"Proud of what, Mother? My scar?" Jake asked. He wasn't allowed to wear the bandanna over his face in his mother's presence, but it was tied around his neck. He yearned to pull it over his scarred face as they got closer to Hollister.

"No. You should be proud of being a Thomas. You are your father's and my son. You are Jake Thomas and I think that's plenty to be proud of. That scar isn't going to change who you are; it's just a scar. You're still alive and breathing, so you might as well act like it and pick up your mat and start walking into the future, Jake."

"Mother, you don't have a scar that's deformed your face."

She chuckled good-naturedly. "Well, you're right. Instead of a scar, I have a body full of rheumatism that has deformed every part of me." Sasha's rheumatism had severely affected every joint in her body, twisting her fingers into knots and curving her upper back until her head was permanently downward. Her feet, ankles, knees, and hips had become so inflamed that she was confined to a wheelchair. Sasha was no longer able to be self-sufficient and depended on her daughter Darra to care for her.

"I apologize, Mother."

Sasha smiled. "Son, we all have thorns that make our lives difficult at times, but life is still life and it is good. Your beauty has not been diminished. You'll see, people will stare only until they don't notice it anymore. Learn to accept it and don't let it bother you. They stare at me, too, but I'm respected, and you are, as well."

The church bazaar was being held in the community center where several tables were set up filled with jars of home canned goods ranging from jam to bear meat. There were crafts and knitted hats to quilts that promised to keep a warm bed during the approaching cold winter. Sasha always purchased certain items for her family that she could no longer make herself: a new blanket, a pair of knitted gloves to keep her hands warm, socks, and a scarf. Sasha didn't get to leave the house too often to do any shopping, but she had never missed a church bazaar.

Jake strolled along slowly, pushing his mother's wheelchair along the tables so she could socialize with her friends and do some shopping along the way. It was more of a social event for the town's women to visit and commend each other on how great their products were, whether it was canned apple butter or a bar of soap. Sasha bought a little bit of everything to help fund the community school and the seller's family.

"Jake!" A woman named Claire Archibald exclaimed. She was surprised to see him with his mother. He had not been in church for at least a year. "It is good to see you." She lowered her brow as she studied his scar. "They really did cut you open, didn't they?"

A flicker of aggravation passed through his brown eyes. Jake was of average height and had a lean build. His dark hair was cut short, and he kept a clean-shaven, oblong, handsome face, which now had a long red scar from the corner of his lip to near his ear. The sutures that Doctor Anderson used to close the wound slightly deformed the left side of Jake's face. "Yes, they did. It left a scar, too."

"I see that. I'm sure you've heard about Laura's condition, right? That poor girl." She lowered her voice to a mere whisper. "I happen to know Mitch and Helen took her to Branson to do away with that problem. No one here wants a rapist's child growing up in our community anyway. Certainly, it would follow in its father's footsteps. As they say, the apple doesn't fall far from the tree. Am I right? It's like letting your child play with a rattlesnake if you ask me. Thankfully, they took her to Branson to wipe that problem away. Maybe now we can get back to normal living around here. Right, Sasha?"

"Yes." Sasha wasn't particularly fond of Claire. "Except, I do not agree with what you said about her baby. That child is no different than any other. Now, if you'll excuse me, I must get to Maude's jam before it is gone."

"Yes. Maude's is good, but my daughter Nora's jam is excellent. You should buy some. Oh, don't forget to stop at my table. We butchered our big sow and made pickled pork. Fifty cents for a jar. I think it's a fair deal." She grimaced as her eyes went to the entrance door. "Oh, no. Just when we thought we might get back to normal living around here. That rich blonde woman is back. And look, she has a new gang of gunfighters with her. I hear she was a lady of the evening back east when the late Robert Fairchild married her. She married well for being a two-bit harlot. He's dead now, and she's richer than most of us have ever dreamed of being. There's no doubt those men with her are fawning all over her. You should too, Jake." Claire put a hand on his shoulder with emphasis. She continued as he twisted his shoulder away from her, "You might as well seek that woman's gold like them fellows are instead of wasting time pining over a piece of used-up tin like Laura."

"Laura's not used up," Jake said, aggravated.

Claire raised her brow questionably. "Hmm. That's not what I heard."

Sasha said with her fragile voice, "I think the phrase you used for Laura is uncalled for. What happened to her is tragic."

"I never said it wasn't," Claire said with an innocent shrug. She waved a hand toward the tall, blonde-haired young widow Holly Fairchild, who had entered the community hall with three men dressed in suits. One wore a gun belt. "The Whiteheads couldn't even make it to the church bazaar today. We support their business, but they don't support us. Well, good day, my friends. I must get back to my table and raise my prices now that the royal highness is here."

Sasha had her son lean closer and said quietly, "Claire always wanted to be friends, but I couldn't trust her. If she talks about others the way she does, then you can count on her talking that way about us, too. That's not the kind of woman I ever wanted to be friends with. Men can be the same way, so choose your friends carefully, son."

————

HOLLY FAIRCHILD HAD FALLEN in love and married the much older millionaire, Robert Fairchild. Robert owned three newspapers along the East Coast and a political magazine that had made him a very wealthy and influential man. Robert may have been in his sixties, but he was far too ambitious to retire and sit in his rocking chair. Robert saw a business opportunity in wool and found the open country of the far north side of Jessup County to be the perfect environment for sheep to graze. Robert knew it was the cattle capital of Jessup County when he bought property along Gibbons Lake. He had his estate built before bringing in thousands of sheep and several experienced sheep herders from South America. He had expected some trouble, but he had misjudged the character of his new neighbors and a secretive group calling themselves the Hollister Sheep Shooters who began killing his sheep. It escalated rapidly when a sheepherder was murdered, and another shepherd's chest was branded with a branding iron that burned a sheep into his flesh.

Robert Fairchild did not become a successful businessman by running from trouble or hiding from confrontation. He hired a group of professional gunmen known as the Blackburn Marshals to protect his investments and home. One might expect a significant gun battle was pending, but what was being called the Hollister Sheep Shooter's War was merely tit for tat with threats and minor annoyances until Robert poisoned the Long T Ranch's cattle pond. It was a declaration of an all-out battle that loomed ahead. Holly, being a reasonable and sound-minded lady, went against Robert's wishes and rode alone out to the Long T Ranch to make financial restitution to Gunther Thomas for his lost cattle and pond.

Enraged by Robert's actions, Gunther could only see an opportunity to strike back when Holly rode onto his ranch. He ordered his cowboys to molest the young and attractive bride of the old man, and they would have if not for US Marshal Matt Bannister arriving in time to stop it.

Sasha Thomas was greatly distressed to hear of her husband Gunther's actions and insisted that each man who partook in that order was to be fired immediately. She held Gunther accountable, and he humbly came to apologize to Robert and Holly Fairchild. However, Robert was not so quick to forgive and sent a few of the Blackburn Marshals to poison the Thomas family's water well. An anonymous note by a good-hearted Blackburn Marshal is the only thing that saved the Thomas family's lives. The letter stated Robert had no knowledge of the poison attempt and that one of the Blackburn Marshals that the Thomas's killed was the one who planned it on his own accord.

The close call had sobered both parties and Robert and Gunther, along with the Jessup Cattleman Association, came to an agreement that ended the hostilities. However, when two Blackburn Marshals attacked Jake Thomas and Laura Whitehead in the church cellar, hostilities reached a new climax that enraged the townspeople of Hollister. That night, the Hollister Sheep Shooters were joined by ordinary townspeople and attacked the Fairchild Estate, murdering everyone except the maidservants. The Blackburn Marshals were wiped out, and Robert Fairchild was taken from his house and forced to watch his estate burn to the ground before being hung from the headgate of his property. Only later was it discovered that the two Blackburn Marshals that attacked the two teens had quit their employment with the Blackburn Marshals and the attack on the youths had nothing to do with Robert Fairchild or anyone else who was killed that night.

Holly was in Branson when it happened. Since then, she had gone back east to take care of the funeral and settle Robert's estate. Robert had never had any heirs, so Holly had become the sole owner of a vast empire and sold a good portion of it. She had more money than she'd ever need, but there was one thing she was determined to do for her late husband. She was intent on rebuilding the Fairchild Estate just like it was on the lake outside Hollister and completing what would be Robert's final dream, to build the most modern and largest woolen mill outside of Hollister called the R. F. Fairchild Woolen Mill.

Holly had not been back to Hollister since Robert's death but had hired the same company to clean up and rebuild the estate house and horse barn just as it was according to their blueprints. The only thing that would not be rebuilt was the bunkhouse the Blackburn Marshals lived in. Over the past four months, the estate house was completed and no trace of the fire remained. She stopped by the Fairchild Estate for a moment and was pleasantly surprised to see it looking exactly as it used to and furnished, although not like it was before. The visit to her home was kept short as she wanted to confront the local sheriff about the investigation into her husband's death.

To her expectation, the sheriff had failed to identify anyone involved. Seeing a sign for the church bazaar, she and her new security guards approached the community hall and went inside to see what could be found. Her reception was cold and unfriendly, but she paid no mind as she strolled from table to table. It was merely entertaining her to see how cold and rude a person could be until Holly looked at the things for sale on their table.

"Mrs. Fairchild, welcome back to Hollister," Claire Archibald said from behind a table with jars of slightly green liquid with cuts of white meat and a few carrot slices. "Have you ever tried pickled pork?"

"No, I can't say I have ever heard of it. Is it cooked?" Holly questioned with a slight expression of distaste.

"It's cured but still needs to be cooked. The pickling process adds to the flavor. It's a bit tangier than ham. It's delicious. I'm only charging a dollar fifty per jar."

"I'll try a few jars. I guess since I'll be living here, I might as well start eating like a local."

"I saw that the old Fairchild Estate is rebuilt. I thought you might sell that land after what happened there. Bad memories and all that death out there..." Claire trailed off.

"Luckily, my memories are good. And I'll be making plenty more," Holly said with a coy smile. Holly was in her late twenties, tall and shapely, with a darker shade of curly, long blonde hair that fell over her shoulders. She had an oval-shaped face with large, round blue eyes that appeared to bulge just enough to add to her beauty.

There was a touch of malice in Claire's eyes as she said, "That canal they are building on the lake is going to drain the lake, some people fear. You don't plan to drain the lake to make more sheep pens, do you? Everyone has been questioning that, but there's not been much of an answer from the workers camped out there."

"No," Holly answered as she picked up a jar to gaze at the meat inquisitively. "The employees are under stringent orders not to say a word to anyone about what they are doing or they'll be fired. Good jobs that pay well and supply everything they need are hard to find." She set the jar down. "To answer your question, it is a canal for the waterwheel that will power the woolen mill. No, it will not drain the lake."

"Yes. We've all noticed the building of that woolen mill. It's awfully big for a place where all of the sheep are dead and there are no people to work in it. It seems a waste of money?"

"To my knowledge, sheep are not extinct. I'm sure we can bring in more. We still have a written agreement with the cattle association that I plan on sticking to."

"The agreement was burned, wasn't it?" Claire asked. She was under the assumption that the contract with Robert Fairchild had been burned in the fire. She knew the Hollister Cattle Association had already burned their copy.

Holly shook her head. "No. It is fine. It was in the safe. In the spring, my flocks will arrive, and by summer's end, the woolen mill should be complete and fully operational. As far as a workforce goes, maybe you haven't noticed all the men camped outside of town working to build it all. There will be plenty of Chinese and American men wanting jobs when the work is done."

"Well, Gunther and the rest of the cattle association won't stand for that. Do you want to start the fighting all over again?" Claire asked with a certain sharpness to her voice.

Holly shook her head. "There shouldn't be any fighting. We have our agreement and we'll stick to it. I'm not looking for any trouble, and my business won't interfere with anyone else's."

"Aren't you afraid the sheep shooters will start up again?"

Holly chuckled. "No. If they do, keep in mind you only have so many men in town. If needed, I can bring in an entire army of men and then another army, if needed. I won't let what happened last time happen again. But I don't expect to have any quarrels with anyone except for the sheriff finding out who hung my husband. I think Matt Bannister will be back to investigate that though. So, I'll take five jars of your pork."

"That's seven dollars and fifty cents."

Sasha Thomas spoke from her wheelchair as Jake pushed her to the table. "You raised your price for her, Claire? It was fifty cents a jar for everyone else," Sasha explained to Holly.

Claire's eyes deepened with aggravation as they shifted from Sasha to Holly.

Holly grinned with a careless shrug. "The laws of supply and demand are adjustable in a free market. It's fine. I'm sure the taste will be worth the price."

"I'm Sasha Thomas, Gunther's wife."

Holly smiled warmly. "I know. It's a pleasure to meet you again. I met you and your beautiful daughter in church once before all the sheep trouble started," Holly said, giving her attention to Sasha while one of her guards paid Claire. "I'm Holly Fairchild."

"I know who you are," Sasha said. "I want to apologize for what happened when you came out to our place last time. I made sure Gunther fired all those men. I will not have those kinds of men working for us or around our daughter. I trust my husband apologized to you?"

"He did. I thank you." Her smile faded when her eyes moved to Jake behind the wheelchair. "You were with that girl in the cellar the night they blamed my husband, am I right?"

Jake nodded. His teeth clenched. He despised not having the bandanna over his face now that Holly Fairchild was gazing at him.

"I heard what they did to you and her. How is she doing?"

Claire Archibald offered, "She's pregnant."

Holly's brow lowered empathetically. She asked Jake, "When you see her, will you tell her that I have thought of her often and my heart goes out to her? I want to meet her sometime. Perhaps you and her could bring your families out to my place for supper one of these evenings?"

Jake's throat was dry, and his voice cracked as he said, "I haven't seen her since."

"You haven't?"

"No, ma'am. Her folks won't let me near her."

"What is her name?"

"Laura. Laura Whitehead."

Holly watched Jake's eyes as she asked, "Can I ask you a question? Do you love her?"

Jake tried to swallow and nearly choked. He could feel the warm moisture fill his eyes as Holly's pretty face blurred.

Claire answered for him. "It doesn't matter. Her parents won't let him near her. Besides, she's already courting Aaron Longley. She's moved on. That girl is like a whirl-wind moving from one boy to another. That baby could be Jake's, Aaron's, or anyone with a dollar for all we know," she finished with a fake chuckle.

Infuriated, Jake stepped toward the table. "You know darn well that is not true! You are a lying sack of..."

"Jake!" Sasha snapped, interrupting him. Her deformed hand reached for his. "This is not the place to raise your voice. Am I being clear?"

Jake glared at Claire and shook his head. "You know you're lying about her and me. I hope everyone here knows you're a liar."

"I was merely trying to make light of a horrific tragedy. Of course, I know she is a wholesome young lady. A joke, in other words." She laughed.

Holly turned her attention to Sasha. "It was a pleasure to meet you and your son. I can tell you are a no-nonsense and honest lady, and I respect that. I would love to get to know you better. How about having lunch sometime soon? We'll cook up some of this pork and give it a shot. What do you think?"

Sasha smiled with a short nod of her crooked neck. "I would like that. Jake will drive me."

"That sounds perfect."

Claire offered, "Mrs. Fairchild, I also make a delicious berry pie. I could bring one for lunch?" She hinted at being invited.

"Another time, perhaps. I'll see you two soon. I'm going to wander around and see what else I can find."

"Maude's jam over there is the best in town," Sasha pointed with a crooked finger toward a table.

"I'll buy some. Thank you," Holly said with a friendly smile.

"She seems nice," Jake said.

"Remember what I said earlier? That's the kind of person I like to be friends with."

CHAPTER TEN

KENT KRUSE WAS A BLACKBURN MARSHAL employed by Robert Fairchild when the Hollister Sheep Shooters attacked the Fairchild Estate. Kent didn't know if it was a providential act of God or plain luck that he had decided to take Robert's rowboat out to the middle of the lake and fallen asleep that night. He was awoken by gunfire and watched from the lake as his friends were slaughtered. There was nothing he could do except remain unseen out on the lake until the buildings were piles of burning rubble and the aggressors left the area.

Kent was hired to protect the lives and assets of Robert and Holly Fairchild. Holly did not feel comfortable with the other Blackburn Marshals, so she often asked Kent to ride with her, as her husband did not want her riding off on her own. Kent and Holly created a friendship, and it didn't take long until he was drawn to her like a moth to a lantern. All he could think about was Holly, and he made every effort to keep her safe. He would have died for her in a heartbeat if she had been at the estate house the night it was burned down. Fortunately, she was in Branson, so he remained unnoticed on the lake.

When the sun came up over the smoldering flames, he knew Holly had become a widow and went to Branson to let her know her husband was dead and her beloved home was lost in Hollister. He was expecting to be welcomed as her friend and become the shoulder she could cry on, but to his horror, she accused him of cowardness for hiding on the lake and sent him away, stating she never wanted to see him again.

Holly went back to Boston and New York to settle Robert's affairs and had been gone for months. In the meantime, Kent discovered that Holly had hired the same construction company to rebuild the estate and then the woolen mill. Being unemployed, Kent took a job as a menial laborer with the company to stay close to Holly so that when she did come back to Hollister, he would be there for her.

The day he'd been longing for had finally arrived. He was laboring in the construction of the canal when he watched the black and gold carriage with bags stacked on top being driven by two men wearing wool coats over their suits drive down her long driveway. Kent got a distant but quick glance through the coach's window at the woman of his dreams; she was talking to another man. Kent felt the swell of jealousy rise within him like a balloon until it was ready to burst.

"Kruse, that pick won't swing itself!" the boss man yelled.

Kent wiped the sweat from his brow and nodded. The digging of the canal was a big job that started with engineers and a crew of Chinese laborers digging a hole six feet wide and five feet deep with banks at a 45-degree angle, creating a twelve-foot-wide canal from edge to edge. A two-hundred-foot section of railway was built alongside the canal. Freight wagons brought iron wheels and axles, heavy wooden beams, and steel beams to manufacture a railroad flat car. They then brought the steam shovel, which was assembled on the flatcar beside the canal, piece by piece. The steam shovel did the majority of digging to keep the construction moving forward, cutting through the hills and valleys to keep the track and canal on the correct grade from the lake to the woolen mill almost a mile away.

Once the canal was at the proper depth, grade, and leveled, and the banks were at the correct angle, another crew cemented cobblestones on the two banks and laid river rock along the floor of the canal. At the same time, a crew of Chinese would disassemble the section of ties and rails from behind the steam shovel to carry it to the newly leveled ground in front of the steam shovel so the work could continue. Mules were used to pull the steam shovel forward for the next section of digging.

Kent's father was a stone mason and he was hired to lay stones along the bottom and canal walls to keep the banks from eroding. The W. F. Fairchild Woolen Mill's canal was to be functional but also as appealing to the eye as the surrounding area. The cost of such a structure and the brick woolen mill that was presently being built had to be extraordinary, but as of yet, there had not been any mention of a final estimate or cost.

Kent swung the pick to break up a stubborn rock that refused to break loose from the side of the bank. The canal was going to be almost a mile long and as vital to the woolen mill as a man's heart was to his life. A dam would be built right above the woolen mill's water wheel that would be powered when the dam was opened, releasing a powerful, narrow flow of water to power the machinery inside the woolen mill. The goal was to have the canal completed and filled during the spring flood while there was excess water from the melting snow. The canal ended at the woolen mill and drained into the Lower Flint River, which flowed from the lake.

It was honest, hard work with long days exposed to the weather, but Kent's wait was finally over. Holly had come home.

———

THE LARGE HOUSE WAS FAMILIAR. Everything was exactly the same: the house's design, the materials, and the paint. Yet, it was missing the heart of the home she had known. Everything Holly had owned was burned in the fire —every painting, every knick-knack, every bit of personal touch that she or Robert had done to make the house into a home was gone. The furniture was new, with blankets, towels, and potholders, which she had requested but had not personally chosen. It was a strange feeling of reminiscence to be in the house and look out at the horse barn, knowing her prized horses and custom-made saddles were no longer there. Her favorite dress and broken-in riding boots were gone. Her walk-in closet was large and spacious but empty. The matching walk-in closet across the room was also empty and would remain empty now that Robert was gone. She should have requested that the closet be opened up into part of the large bedroom or added space to the back deck. The closet door would always be a reminder that Robert was no longer there.

She lay on the bed and closed her eyes as her body sunk into the goose-feather-filled mattress. Soft, molding, and relaxing, the bed felt the same as when she last lay beside Robert in the same room, but he had never been in this house. The house looked the same but lacked the warmth of her memories.

It had been a long day and she was tired. The sheriff, Pat Emmerson, claimed he had nothing to do with the destruction of the Fairchild Estate nor the death of her husband. He had no information about who was involved since it was the Hollister Sheep Shooters who had committed the crime. Unfortunately, they were a secretive group from which the sheriff had not been able to penetrate a single bit of information. Not one man's name had ever been uttered about that group.

Holly suspected as much. She despised Pat Emmerson and thought of him as the crooked and corrupted lawman that she knew him to be. Holly knew she couldn't do a lot about him, but what she could do was build the W. F. Fairchild Woolen Mill and let it become the largest employer in the town.

There was a soft knocking on her door. "Miss Holly, one of the construction fellas is here to talk to you. He says it's important," Ross Hall said through the door. Ross was one of her paid security guards.

"Okay," Holly said with a groan. She had hoped to rest for an hour or two. She had not hired a cook, gardener, or maid yet, but she was hoping to find the families that had worked for her before and rehire them. Ross had offered to cook the pickled pork and his mother's cornbread recipe for supper, and she was fine with that.

She descended the stairs and stepped out onto the front porch. To her surprise, she saw Kent Kruse standing at the edge of the porch wearing soiled clothing and muddy boots, smiling at her with a dirty face. "Kent?" she questioned in near disbelief.

"Holly, you are more beautiful than ever. Welcome home," he said, gazing at her affectionately.

Holly's head shook, perplexed. "What are you doing here?"

"Working. I'm working for Dutch's construction crew digging the canal, but I built the foundation of your house, too."

"Oh," is all she said.

"I know I'm not cleaned up, but I was hoping we could take a walk like the old days and talk?" he said with a hopeful wave toward the lake.

"I don't think so. I was just lying down."

"I imagine you are tired after all the traveling. Maybe tomorrow? It gets dark early nowadays, but a walk along the lake would be nice."

A tall and broad-chested man came out onto the porch. He had dark-brown hair that was greased straight back, about mid-neck length. His square face had brown eyes and a thick, dark-brown, full-faced beard. "Is everything okay, miss?" he asked. He wore a gun belt that was set too low on his thigh.

"Yes, Wolfgang, it is. This is Kent Kruse. My husband employed him as one of the Blackburn Marshals."

Wolfgang's brow raised curiously. "Oh. You don't look much like a gunman."

Kent's jealousy rose to the surface, and it could be seen on his face. Wolfgang was the man in the carriage with her. "I'm not one anymore. Who are you?" he asked, reaching his hand over the porch steps, refusing to step on the clean boards with his muddy boots.

"I'm Wolfgang Grubbs. I'm the head of Miss Holly's

security detail. I've heard of you." He shook Kent's hand firmly with his powerful grip.

"Good things, I hope."

"No," Holly said plainly. "I told him how you hid out on the lake while those murderers dragged Robert off and hung him."

Kent sighed heavily with a shake of his head. "That's not true, Holly. I fell asleep in the boat and was awoken by thirty-some men or more shooting my friends. There was nothing I could do. I didn't have my guns with me."

"You could have tried to save Robert." Her blue eyes burned into him.

Kent dropped his head with frustration and took a deep breath. "I would have been killed too. Robert would still be dead and it wouldn't have changed a thing if I had. Sorry to say."

Holly asked sharply, "If I had been here and they dragged me out of the house with Robert, would you still have hidden on the lake?"

"I wasn't hiding," Kent said firmly. "I would have died for you, Holly."

"Then you should have done the same for Robert. He was the one paying you, not me."

Kent scoffed with defeat. "I wasn't falling in love with Robert; I was falling in love with you, Holly. Okay? Now, you know, I'm in love with you."

Holly closed her eyes with a disapproving scoff. "I have nothing left to say. You work for Dutch, not me. Please, from now on, stay over there with the rest of Dutch's employees, or I will have you fired." Holly turned around and walked back into the house, leaving Kent standing outside with Wolfgang.

"You heard her," Wolfgang said.

Kent nodded as his heart felt like it was being ripped in two by a pair of ice-cold hands. "Yeah, I did. You're her new security, huh?"

Wolfgang nodded. "Two others and me."

Kent took a disappointed, deep breath. "Well, guard her well. She isn't liked too much around here." Kent turned around and took a few steps to return to the Dutch Lyons Builder Company's makeshift labor camp, which was a small city of tents and thrown-together board shacks to accommodate the laborers a mile and a mile away.

" Will do," Wolfgang answered.

Kent turned around and pointed a finger at the big man. "You better! Because if she gets hurt, I'll hold you accountable. The people here are not a joke. Watch over her! If you ever need help, come get me. I mean it. Pull your holster up and tighten that belt so you can grab that grip in a hurry if you need to. And eventually, you will."

————

DARKNESS CAME EARLY in October and it was Holly's first night staying in the new house. Ross Hall had fried up the pickled pork, and the general consensus was it wasn't worth the money after all. However, Ross's mother's cornbread recipe was a saving grace that helped them finish supper. Holly was determined to find her house staff and bring them back to the newly constructed Fairchild Estate before she was reduced to eating beans straight from the can.

Wolfgang Grubbs was a large, powerfully built man of German descent in his midforties who had a background as a New York City policeman before entering the security field and eventually becoming a detective for the Simpson

Detective Agency. He had the reputation of being as loyal as a dog, quiet, sincere, and deadly serious when he needed to be. Holly hired Wolfgang to acquire a security team to move out west with her as a permanent position.

Ross Hall was a longtime friend of Wolfgang's from the New York City Police Department, and he had proven his loyalty and mettle to Wolfgang long before. Ross had lost his wife four years ago and had no children or any other reason to stay on the East Coast. Ross was in his midforties, not too overly tall at five foot nine and a little pudgy around the belly, with thinning brown hair that he kept short and combed to the side when he wasn't wearing his standard derby hat. His face was oblong and clean-shaven, with blue eyes and ears that appeared a little too big for the size of his head. His smile was infectious, but his easygoing nature could turn cold and hard when needed. He was a man of integrity, and that was what Holly was looking for.

Alessandro Baccari was the youngest of the three men. He was an Italian with thick black hair that he kept short and a mustache and goatee that he kept trimmed and neat. His brown eyes were alert and watchful. He was thirty-seven years old, of medium height, and thickly built. Alessandro knew Wolfgang from the Simpson Detective Agency and had proven himself as a man of upstanding character and courage. Alessandro was hesitant to come west until he met Holly, and then he was all in. She was not just the wealthiest woman he had ever met; she was also beautiful and alluring.

The three men got along well, and their friendship grew with Holly, which made them more like her family than employees. "Gentlemen, to us. And what we are creating to put this town on the map," she said, lifting her glass of wine in a toast.

"Cheers," Ross said with the others.

"Thank you, gentlemen, for bringing me home. I hope you all aren't disappointed that Hollister isn't like New York City."

Wolfgang snickered. "Well, I didn't see any beggars urinating on the sidewalk while in town."

Alessandro added, "I didn't see a sidewalk. I don't think I saw an ounce of mortar, brick, or concrete at all."

Ross wiped his mouth with a cloth napkin. "I felt a bit overdressed in a suit. I didn't notice anyone else wearing a derby. I might need to change my appearance a bit."

"Fellas," Holly said sincerely, "now that we are here, what do you gentlemen think about the place? You're not going to get bored and leave me, are you?"

Wolfgang shook his head. "Nope. I'm here for the long haul."

Ross said, "I love it. It is the most beautiful and peaceful place I have ever seen. I have to be honest; on the train ride across the plains, I thought I was going to die without anything to look at. That's hell. But the mountains and lake...I love it."

"Alessandro?" Holly asked.

"I didn't see any pretty women at the church bazaar today, and I'm assuming there are bears around here, right?" He had been born and raised in New York City.

Ross gazed at Alessandro, perplexed. "Those are real mountains, Alessandro. There are bears, wolves, and mountain lions, too." Ross continued, "And not to scare you, but there are probably a bunch of wild Indians up there hiding. If you go out at night or wander too far off, you might lose your pretty scalp. That wouldn't be so bad; you'd just look more like me."

"I quit!" Alessandro exclaimed and then laughed. "No, I think it's pretty here. I'm glad I came."

Wolfgang spoke seriously. "Miss Holly, I don't mean to sour the conversation at dinner time, but I think it's something we all need to know about. That old friend of yours, named Kent, told me he'd hold me accountable if you got hurt. He looked very sincere when he said it. Now, he doesn't scare me, but the context of what he was alluding to is concerning. It doesn't sound like that old sheep war you told us about is over. Or at least he doesn't seem to think so. Do you think we have to worry about this place being burned down again?"

"No," Holly said pointedly. "I have an agreement with the cattle association and I'm going to keep it. The murderers of my husband are getting away with it and they ought to be happy with that. And like I said to that woman today, if trouble comes, I won't hesitate to hire a hundred to a thousand more men. We're not here to cause an issue with anyone. My husband was murdered because of the Blackburn Marshals and they no longer exist. There won't be any trouble."

Wolfgang spoke gently. "It's none of our business, but did you and Kent have something special going on? He did say he loved you."

Holly closed her eyes as she sighed. "No. Kent was just one of the Blackburn Marshals that Robert hired. Occasionally, he would ride along with me and once, I had him row me out onto the lake, but there was *nothing* special between us. The last time I saw him, I told him I never wanted to see him again. No. There was nothing between us. He apparently felt ways that I certainly did not and do not share. If you see Kent come to this house, ask him to leave.

He's not welcome here. And that's all I have to say about
him."

CHAPTER ELEVEN

"Aunt Mattie, it sure is good to see you. How are you doing?" Jesse Helms asked as he kissed his favorite aunt, Mattie Sperry, on the forehead. "My ma told me about Jannie having consumption. I'm sorry to hear that. How is she feeling?"

Mattie's anguish showed on her downtrodden expression. The world she had known was altered the day she invited a mail bride into her home. She had perhaps used a bit of trickery to propose marriage to a lady named Audrey Butler to marry her son Alan, who had just come home from prison. However, Alan's brother Morton took a liking to Audrey too. In a fight that went too far, Alan took a shot at Morton and accidentally killed their youngest sister, Daisy. Morton, infuriated about Daisy, killed Alan. In the matter of one day, Mattie's life changed with the loss of three of her beloved children as Morton left and never came back. Now, Morton was married to the jezebel Audrey and had the gall to go into Mattie's home and take Daisy's three children and her grandson Travis with him.

Mattie's son Jack had moved to Branson and worked at the silver mine. She heard that he was marrying a woman that Jack had never brought to Mattie's home, nor had she heard from Jack since Daisy and Alan's funerals. Her oldest son, Dwight, was killed many years before in the Snake War, and her husband soon after disappeared. Loss was nothing new in Mattie's life, but it was slowly destroying her home. And now the news came that Jannie was slowly dying of tuberculosis.

She had raised eight children in her pieced-together large home, and now the only two that lived at home were Vince, her twenty-seven-year-old single son, who worked at the Helm's Dairy, and her thirty-two-year-old daughter, Jannie. Three of Jannie's children lived with their grandmother too, but the house had become quiet, lonely, and felt barren of life. Mattie's son Henry and his wife Bernice had recently moved out after a bitter fight. They lived across town in a house of their own and no longer had anything to do with her. Vince, and her grandson Tad, were the only two that she could depend on to keep food on the table, and their wages were meager.

"Where have you been?" Mattie asked Jesse. He had disappeared after being released from the jail several months ago.

"A little bit of everywhere. How is Jannie?"

"Sick," Mattie said without the strength in her voice that she had always had. "She's down at the saloon, making herself worse. She says if she's dying, she might as well enjoy herself doing it. I can't stop her."

"Hmm. Well, she might have a point." He sat in a chair beside Mattie and took her hand in his affectionately. "I'm sorry to hear that, though."

Mattie nodded toward the window. There were four

men outside waiting on horseback. "Who are your friends?"

"My new gang. We just got back from Nevada. I spent some time in California, too." He reached into his shirt pocket and pulled out a leather-bound billfold. He pulled out a few dollar bills. "I took this off a man on a stagecoach we robbed. It's nice, huh?"

Mattie didn't seem as interested in it or the dollars he handed her as she had been in the past. Jesse continued, "I figured it was time to come home and see the folks, and you. I thought I'd ask if there was anything I could do for you while I'm around. Do you still want Morton and his wife killed? I'll have my men out there do it if you want. I got Colin Kennedy riding with me now. He's a heck of a gunman. Perhaps even as good as me."

"No," Mattie said without any life in her tone. "Leave Morton alone, Jesse. Our family is stained with bloodshed. I won't risk causing a drop more. I know Morton and his wife will raise those children with the kind of love that Daisy would've wanted. Daisy was different than us. Her heart was pure and kind—she didn't have our family's poison in her veins."

"Daisy was a sweetheart," Jesse agreed. "Aunt Mattie, I'd hate not to settle the score for what the marshal and Mort did to Cass, but if you don't want me to kill him, I won't."

"No. I want them to raise those children right." Her eyes watered. "I miss my family the way it was, Jesse. The cemetery is going to be full of my children before I get there, I'm afraid. It isn't supposed to be that way; I should have died before any of my children. And now that nit-wit Tad is aching for a gunfight. I doubt he has the grit to finish one while still standing. Dwight had bad luck, and I think

Tad does, too. He's wearing a gun belt now. I can't stop him."

Jesse chuckled lightly. "I should take Tad with me and teach him what I know so he has a fighting chance, at least. But then again, the men I collected won't put up with his mouth, whether he's my relation or not." He paused to look around the house. "Dang, Aunt Mattie, I wasn't going to ask Vince to join us, but under the circumstances, I imagine you could use the money."

"I need Vince here, Jesse. He's all I have left in the world. All the rest of my children are dead, dying, or have left me for good."

He released his aunt's hand and patted her forearm. "Well, Aunt Mattie, I'm sorry to hear that. But you're my favorite aunt, if that helps. Listen, my friends are waiting. I guess we'll go down to the saloon and visit with Vince and Jannie for a bit. I'll be back tonight."

Mattie reached over and grabbed his leg to keep him seated beside her. "Jesse, wait. Cass was sterile, wasn't he? Isn't that right?"

Jesse grinned. "Don't tell me Jannie's pregnant again. It's not Cass's brat. He always said he was grateful for that horse kicking him in the jewels when it came to Jannie. He thought she was ugly as sin, but being the only woman around, she looked good enough after he had enough to drink. He'd hide his face in his grave if he knew he got her pregnant."

"Was he sterile or not?" Mattie asked with her penetrating green eyes glaring at him impatiently.

"He said he was. Cass got kicked by a horse when he was sixteen or so. He said his jewels swelled up like grapefruits before eventually going back to normal. He still had them, apparently, but he said they didn't work. Why? If Jannie's pregnant again, you can't blame him."

Mattie's eyes softened as a hint of a warm smile tugged at her lips. "Jannie's not pregnant, which is pretty good proof that he was sterile. I swear if a man spills his seed ten feet around that girl, she'll get pregnant. Jesse, listen to me: The parents of that harlot were at the doctor's office when Tad took his mother there. They wanted to abort her baby. I'm assuming it's your child."

"Who?" Jesse grimaced. "Who are you talking about?"

Mattie's temper hardened her voice. "Who do you think? What other woman accused you and Cass of raping her? The one from Hollister. She's pregnant. It has to be your child if Cass was sterile, right? It was either you or Cass that got her pregnant. That's what her father told Tad anyway."

"How do you know?"

"Tad spoke with her father. Go talk to Tad and ask him. Jesse, the doctor didn't give her anything to touch that baby. It's the only child you're ever going to have, most likely. You need to bring that baby home, my home, so it's raised with family."

Jesse laughed. "Aunt Mattie, I probably have a few kids out there by now."

Mattie grabbed Jesse's wrist with a firm grasp. "I'm serious, Jesse. You asked what you could do for me. I want you to bring your child home for me to raise. I need new life around here. Bring me that woman and she can have that child right here."

Jesse was perplexed. "Aunt Mattie, I don't think she'd agree to come home with me."

Mattie's expression hardened like stone. "Do you think I'm asking? All of my children are gone. I have spent my lifetime raising children, and now I have nothing left. I need new life around here, or I'm going to die. I have nothing left to live for Jesse. I need a purpose to keep on living. Without a purpose, I'm just going to sit here, wither to nothing and die. Raising your baby will give me something to live for."

"Umm, Aunt Mattie," Jesse said carefully before pausing. He knew what she was asking was not just a dangerous thing to do, but crazy. He wondered if she had gone mad over the past few months. "How would you explain her being here or the baby to Henry and Bernice or *Morton?*" he emphasized.

"Don't you worry about that. That's for me to worry about," Mattie snapped.

"No. It's my neck on the line if I'm caught up there. That's one area I'm trying to stay clear of. There's a whole bunch of cowboys up there that would like to hang me on sight, Aunt Mattie. Cass and I were Blackburn Marshals and that whole thing turned south real quick. I don't think it's worth the risk for me to go back to Hollister."

Mattie pointed out the window. "You have four gang members right outside. Are those cowboys going to hang them on sight? You have a brain. Use it! Stay out of sight and let them do the work for you. You were going to have your friend kill my son for me, but you can't have your friends figure out a way to grab her? I'm disappointed in you, Jesse. I'm an old woman, and I can figure this out. Please tell me you can, too."

Jesse was offended. "Oh, I can. I'm not stupid, Aunt Mattie. But then what? How are you going to keep your family and the rest of the town from finding out who she is? Marshal Bannister would love to put a noose around my neck already. If he found out I kidnapped a girl, I doubt he'd take me to jail. He'd hang me from the nearest tree with a solid limb."

Mattie stared at Jesse thoughtfully for a moment. "I'll say I ordered Vince a mail bride that just so happens is with child. I promise you she won't say a word to anyone once I have broken her spirit and have her trained. I'll change her name, and she'll either fall in love with Vince or disappear once the child is old enough to eat solid food. You can leave all of that to me. That will give me a purpose to keep on living. My question is, are you smart enough to do that for me without getting caught, or are you not brave enough to try, Jesse?"

Jesse could feel the indignation beginning to swirl behind his eyes. His intelligence and courage were being brought into question, which he took personally. "I could do it and get away with it, Aunt Mattie. That's not a problem. The thing is, the men in my gang won't like risking their lives for free."

Mattie forced a tear and wiped it from her eyes. She sniffled. "Jannie is dying, Jesse. Dwight, Alan, and Daisy are dead; my husband's dead. Morton wants nothing to do with me, and neither does Henry or Jack. I have nothing else to live for. I'm fading away every day now. I need a child to raise as my own. That's what gives me a sense of life and would fill the emptiness in my heart and this home. I need something to do and I'm still fit enough to raise a child, but I'll wither away and die sitting here alone. If you love me, please bring them here for me. It's the only thing that's going to save my life."

Jesse wasn't convinced it was a good idea. "Just a moment ago, you said it was better for Morton to raise Daisy's children because of the poison in our veins..."

"That's just talk, Jesse!" Mattie snapped. "I don't want

Morton killed because he's my son and your cousin. He's family, just like that baby is our family. Do you want the only child you'll ever have aborted or given to some other family to raise? That woman doesn't want it! That baby is trash to her. But that baby is life to me, my life. I need it, and it needs me. I'm the only hope that baby has of survival, and my survival depends on that baby. So please, go bring that woman here, and I'll take care of the rest. I promise you, no one will ever find out who she is."

Jesse was quiet for a moment as he gazed at his four friends out the window. His eyes focused on the youngest of the four men, and an idea slowly formed in his mind. "That's a dangerous request, Aunt Mattie, but I think I may have an idea that might just work."

The corners of Mattie's lips tugged upward. "That child is your only real legacy. It doesn't belong anywhere except here."

———

IT WAS late afternoon when Jesse Helms and his new friends rode into Branson. It was with prideful resentment that he wanted to stop at the US Marshal's Office, look Matt Bannister in the eyes and smile at him as a free man. He knew it would get under the marshal's skin, and there was nothing the marshal could do about it.

Tim Hazelton looked at his new friend and leader of what was being called the Powder Creek Gang in the Elko Newspaper in Northern Nevada. None of their identities had been discovered yet, and they left the area before they could be caught. It was better to be anonymous than it was to put a man's name on the crime. It took a little while to convince Jesse Helms of that, as he wanted it to be known as the Jesse Helms Gang. Now that he wasn't wanted for the crimes that he would have been, he was more agreeable to being called whatever the local papers wished to call their gang. Tim looked at Jesse with a questionable expression. "You have to be kidding me. You're not afraid of inviting trouble, are you? That is Marshal Matt Bannister's office. You know who he is, right?"

Jesse snickered. "Yes, I do. Why don't you fellas go over to Rose Street and get us a room or two for tonight? We'll leave in the morning. I'll meet you there."

Jesse opened the office door as the cowbell rang and stopped at the three-foot-high barrier. He smiled at his cousin Morton Sperry, who stood from his desk slowly, surprised to see Jesse walk into the office. Jesse chuckled a bit too intentionally. "Morton, you look like you've seen a ghost. I just wanted to stop by and tell you that there won't be any retaliation from me or anyone else. Your ma says the past is the past."

The deputy, Phillip Forrester, who maintained the office duties, rose from his desk and slowly stepped to Matt's private office and tapped on the door. "You might want to come out here," he said lightly, skeptical of Jesse Helms or what he may have planned.

"Really?" Morton asked skeptically. His hand was near the butt of his revolver. "That doesn't sound like the mother I know."

Jesse reached up and removed his worn hat, revealing his short-cropped brown hair. Jesse was just below average height but stocky and muscular. He had a broad, square-shaped face and a thick brown goatee that was about three inches long. "Mort, you know me better than anyone else I know. We're good. Your Ma wants you and your Missus to raise those kids as best you can. Raise them to be as good as Daisy would want them to be. And I'm sure you will. You're a good man, Mort. You've always been one."

Morton nodded. "Thank you."

"Unfortunately," Jesse continued, "in other news, your sister is dying. She has consumption."

A cold chill ran up Morton's spine. "Jannie? What are you talking about?"

"That's the only sister you have left. The doctor told her she has about a year left to live."

Morton frowned as his heart broke. "I'll let Travis know when I go home."

Jesse looked at Matt, who had come out of his office and was leaning against the wall with his hand close to his revolver. "Marshal Bannister. I just wanted to let my cousin know that he has nothing to fear from our family. Now, I guess I'll walk out of here and stroll around town." The condescending smirk on his face was intentional. The enjoyment he felt knowing how much Matt despised him and would love to throw him in jail but could not for any valid reason made Jesse all the more pleased with himself.

Matt didn't reply.

"Where have you been?" Morton asked.

"Around. I've been in Natoma for a few days visiting the family. I'm leaving tomorrow. I thought I'd head south and visit our family down that way. I shouldn't be gone too long, though. Who knows, maybe I'll bring home a wife like you did. Well..." He gave with a slight chuckle. "Not quite like you. I won't steal my brother's fiancée. Someone else's fiancée, maybe, but not my brother's."

Morton nodded. "Say what you will, but I'm happily married."

"Glad to hear it. I really am. Well, I'll be off. I guess I'll walk around town and see what kind of fun I can have. Hope you don't mind, Marshal." He chuckled.

"Not at all. I'll see you around," Matt said calmly, but his resentment was made clear.

"I'll see you later, Morton. Maybe I'll invite you both to my wedding when the time comes." He laughed and walked out the door to the sound of the cowbell ringing.

"I don't like him," Matt said.

"The man gives me a bad feeling," Phillip stated.

Morton sank into his chair and gazed out the window. "He's up to something."

"What are you thinking?" Matt asked, still leaning against the door frame.

"I don't know, but it's not good."

"I'm sure we'll hear about it. In the meantime, let's call it a day. I'm going to take my wife out for dinner."

———

MATT STEPPED into his home and stopped in a gaze of wonder at his wife, Christine. She had spread a blanket out on the floor and was on her knees, hovering over Saul and Abby Wolf's baby daughter, Kathryn Jane. Christine was gently tickling Kathryn's ribs while making a silly face. The delightful sound of the five-month-old's laughter brought the sweet sound of Christine's laugh, which was one of Matt's favorite sounds to hear.

She gazed at him with a bright smile that beamed with such beauty and joy. "Hi, how was your day?" she asked before turning her attention back to Kathryn and tickling her again while making a goofy face. Kathryn's laughter rang out like a sweet wind chime on a quiet day. "A baby's laughter is the greatest sound in the world, isn't it?" Christine asked with a wide grin.

"It has to be the most joyful, that's for sure," Matt agreed, unable to stop smiling. "Where's Saul and Abby?"

"They went to see Doctor Ryland. Abby thinks she's pregnant again."

"Already?" Matt questioned. Kathryn was only five months old.

Christine wrinkled her nose. "Well, yeah, Matt. It happens. I think they'll end up with a whole passel of children. They asked if I would watch Kathryn, and of course I will." She leaned her face over Kathryn's and tickled her neck while speaking in a loving, higher-pitched voice, "I said of course I will. I love this little girl. Yes, I do."

Matt removed his boots and sat on the floor against the front of the davenport. He watched Christine play with Kathryn; the joy reflected on her face was unmistakable. His beautiful wife shined brighter than Matt had ever seen her shine before. Like a bucket with a hole at the bottom, he could feel the joy fading from him when he thought of the fact that Christine may not ever be able to have children. Dr. Ryland had removed one of her ovaries, and the other was damaged from a bullet that was fired into her in an attempt to stop Matt from following the murderer, Martin Ballenger, out of the dance hall.

Christine turned her attention to him. "You look sad. You can't be sad when there is a baby to play with, now can you?"

Matt shook his head. "No." It was the fear of him that caused Martin to shoot Christine. The only reason she couldn't conceive was because of the damage the bullet caused. The Lord had spared her life, but there were times when life seemed to be most unfair. An innocent young girl like Laura Whitehead didn't want to be pregnant and was. Christine wanted to be pregnant and couldn't conceive. Even if Christine did happen to conceive, Dr. Ryland had told them that the chances were against her carrying the baby to full term. Watching Christine's playful nature shine with little Kathryn made Matt wish he could give her a baby that they could play with together. He felt a wave of envy flow through him at the thought of Christine's first husband, Richard Knapp, who may not have lived long, but he got to have a child with Christine and, for over a year, play with that baby girl side by side with Christine.

"Is something wrong?" Christine asked, taking notice of his downtrodden expression. "Do you need to talk to me?"

Matt forced the thoughts away. "No. I'm just enjoying watching you."

"Someday, we'll have a baby of our own." She wrinkled her nose and leaned down to rub her nose against Kathryn's. The laughter and affection between the two was infectious. Christine lifted herself upright on her knees and put her attention on Matt. "The night that Laura stayed here. She asked me if we would be interested in adopting her baby when it is born. I told her I would have to talk to you before I could answer that. I want to, Matt." Her brown eyes filled with her gentle tears. "I miss being a mother. Dr. Ryland doesn't think I can conceive, but I won't give up hope. I could hope and pray forever, but if the Lord's answer is no, then the answer is no. What do you think about adopting Laura's baby? She doesn't want it, and I want a baby, Matt."

Matt frowned. "That baby's father is either someone I killed or a man that I probably will eventually. Either way, the father is not a good linage."

Christine's expression turned sour. "What were we

telling Laura while she was here? That baby doesn't know who its father is. It will be a baby, just as innocent and beautiful as Kathryn. You can't condemn it because of the sins of its father. If you don't want to adopt a baby, then tell me so, and we won't. But do not refuse Laura's because of who the father is. That is not fair to the baby, Matt."

"You're right. Jesse Helms came into the office today to boast about being free, and I'm a bit bitter about it, I think. I understand the baby is innocent, but if we adopted that child, I don't know how I'd feel about seeing Jesse's or Cass's face every time I look at our kid and knowing I killed its father."

"Did Tom see your face every time he looked at Gabriel?" she asked of Matt's son, who another man raised. "Don't answer that; the answer is no. He saw Gabriel, and that's all. I won't argue with you because there are orphanages full of children that need to be adopted into a family. We don't have to adopt Laura's baby if you can't do so in good conscience. I can understand that. But we may never have a baby of our own if Dr. Ryland is right, and he may be. I'm not pregnant yet."

"We've only been married for a couple of months," Matt replied.

"That's true. Will you think about adopting Laura's baby? We have several months before she gives birth to decide. But if I'm not pregnant by then, I may never be." She picked Kathryn up in her arms to hold her. "I would like a family."

Matt reached out his arms to take Kathrine. "I'll think about it. It's my turn to play with her though," he said with a smile.

CHAPTER TWELVE

LAURA WAS GLAD TO BE BACK IN THE SAFETY OF her bedroom above the hardware store. The Whitehead family didn't have a luxurious home like the ones she had seen in Branson on what the locals called King's Hill. There were mansions there and all were owned by business owners, such as the owner of the Slater Silver Mine. They were beautiful homes that Laura dreamed she could live in. Her father reminded her that they owned a home just as big as some of the mansions, but most of their house was filled with rows and rows of hardware supplies. Laura smiled as she thought of her father telling her that. It may not be a mansion, but it was nice to be home.

Her father had been so guilt-filled and convicted by his actions that it took all he could do emotionally to apologize to Laura and reassure her that he loved her the same as he always had. He admitted to being furious about what had happened to her and that fury increased to desperation when they learned that she was pregnant. As a man of standing in the church and the community, he had fallen into the trap of caring too much about his family's reputation in the eyes of those around them. He had been wrong, and all he could do was accept the fact that his daughter was pregnant. For the first time since that night in the cellar, Laura felt like she had her father's love and approval.

Laura lay on her bed and held a ceramic grand piano with a turnkey that she twisted to hear the beautiful music that it played. The music box had some French writing on the bottom, including the word *France*, which was the only word Laura could read. Pat Emmerson, the town sheriff, had given the music box to her the day after she had been attacked in the cellar. Laura was in a bad way, physically and emotionally, but when she turned the key for the music to play, the gentle beginning and soothing melody that followed brought a sense of comfort to her. It sounded like little bells chiming, but what a beautiful sound filled her room. Laura had no idea what the musical number was called, but she had fallen in love with it. It was soothing, and the more she listened to it, the more peaceful it was to hear.

She rubbed her hand over her stomach and could feel the beginnings of a bump. It wouldn't be noticeable to anyone who saw her in her regular clothes, but with her belly exposed, it was evident to her. She rose from her bed and stood in front of the mirror on her dresser. She gasped as the shock of the tight ball pressing against her stomach. The shock of her swollen belly sent a wave of fear through her. She called out her door, "Mother! Mother, come here, please."

"Yes?" Helen answered from the kitchen, where she was washing the morning dishes.

"Mother, come here."

The urgency in Laura's voice was alarming. Helen dried

her hands with a dish towel before walking briskly to Laura's room. "What is it, hon?"

"Look." Laura was rubbing the bump of her belly with frightened tears welling in her blue eyes. "I'm getting fat."

Helen smiled warmly. "I think you're just bloated. It happens with pregnancy. Your baby is not that big yet. Drink plenty of water and lie down for a while, and you'll be fine."

"I don't like this," Laura said with a trembling voice.

Helen frowned, sat on the edge of the bed, and patted the mattress beside her. "I know you don't. Your body is changing, and it will change a lot more in the weeks ahead. Pregnancy can be a miserable time with bloating, heartburn, cravings, nausea, constipation, and all kinds of things that are not fun. But sweetheart, like the doctor in Branson said, it is only temporary. A year from now, this pregnancy will only be a memory."

"By then, I'll be a mom." Laura's chin quivered with emotion.

"Technically so. But you don't have to raise the child. We can put it up for adoption and find him or her a good home. Unfortunately, you have to carry and deliver the baby. As I said, your body is going to change a lot, and it will be uncomfortable at best. Someday, you will have another child with your husband, and this will all seem like a bad dream. I know right now that it seems like that will never happen, but it will. I am glad you threw that vial against the wall because if anything had gone wrong, you may not be here, or you may never have been able to have children again."

Laura sat down beside her mother. "How come you never had any more children after me?"

Helen sighed. "My sister, your aunt Ruth, could barely

share a room with your uncle Grant and not get pregnant. She'd pop those kids out one after another like she was destined to populate the world. They have eight children, as you know. But me? The Lord blessed me with one beautiful daughter." She offered a warm smile. "And that is enough for me. I quit asking why and thanked God for you. We almost lost you when you were five. Did you know that?"

"No, I don't know," Laura said with interest.

"You had influenza. We were so scared we'd lose you. After that, I never asked why again. I was just thankful to have you. Laura, how you got into this position is one of the most horrible things I can imagine any girl could go through, but you are going to be a very beautiful pregnant young woman."

"Thanks, Mother."

"We will need to start making you some larger dresses because you're going to get bigger and bigger."

"I don't know what I'm supposed to do."

Helen smiled slowly. "Eat and eat a lot. That's what you are supposed to do. Speaking of, are you hungry?"

"No. Mother, is it possible that you could take me to see Jake?"

Helen wrinkled her nose hesitantly. "No. I don't think that's a good idea."

"Please?"

"No, I can't." She could see the crestfallen expression on her daughter's face. "You'll see him again, Laura. We live in a small town. We can't stop that, but if you do see him in town, don't be surprised if he ignores you. That's what we're trying to protect you from, sweetheart. Boys will walk away from you when you need them the most, just like your father did after that night you were assaulted.

No man loves you more than your father, and you experienced the way he acted. Jake will do worse and may even say things that aren't true to make himself feel better about what happened."

"Jake wouldn't do that."

Helen watched her daughter, hesitating to speak. She took a deep breath and said, "Do you remember that young prostitute who used to come in here that died trying to miscarry her baby?"

"Yes. She had a name. It was Angelica, but she went by Angel."

"Yes," Helen answered, wondering how her daughter knew so much about her. "Well, she said Jake was the baby's father..."

"No," Laura said. "That's not true."

"Aaron was Jake's best friend and Jake told him it was. My point is that Jake refused to take responsibility for his baby and its mother. He certainly isn't going to want you now that you're carrying another man's baby." Helen said with a wave of guilt as she watched her daughter's eyes fill with thick tears and slip down her cheeks. "I'm sorry to tell you that, but you need to know Jake isn't who you think he is."

"I don't believe you," Laura whimpered with a high-pitched voice.

Helen pat Laura's arm lovingly. "It's true, Laura. Aaron told your father that some time back, but we didn't want to make you feel any worse than you already did. But you need to know the truth. That's why we say you can do better. And you certainly can. Aaron is a nice and respectable young man."

———

AARON LONGLEY and his family owned the Longley Ranch, six miles outside of Hollister on Dixon Creek. It was a beautiful piece of land, but their ranch wasn't as big as some of the others, such as the Long T Ranch. There was a Hollister Cattle Association meeting later that evening, and Aaron rode into town earlier than usual to visit the Whitehead family.

Aaron was a tall and stout young man with a handsome, clean-cut, round-shaped face. His brown hair was cut short under his black flat-brim hat with a rattlesnake skin band. He wore a gun belt on his waist but had never had cause to use it except when the Hollister Sheep Shooters were killing sheep or that night when the Fairchild Estate burned to the ground.

"Oh, hello, Aaron. Please, come in," Helen said with a welcoming smile when she answered the knock on the door. "I'm guessing you're here to see Laura?"

He nodded with a slight smirk. "Yes, ma'am. Mr. White-head just told me that she was with child, but I already heard that. You know how news gets around."

Helen's heart sank. "Do I ever. I'm afraid the gossip is just beginning when it comes to Laura. Please have a seat, and I'll let her know you are here."

"Wonderful." Aaron sat in a wooden rocking chair and watched Helen walk down a hallway toward Laura's room. He had sat in the same chair several times while visiting Laura. He had been convinced that her heart belonged to him until he heard that she had been meeting Jake in the abandoned cellar all along.

"She'll be out here in a moment," Helen said as she returned to the family room.

Aaron could tell by the frustrated expression on Helen's

face that something wasn't right. "How is she doing with the whole baby thing?"

"She doesn't have much of a choice, does she, Aaron?" Helen answered sharply.

"No. I suppose not. Should I leave?" he asked.

"No. It will be good for Laura to visit with a friend."

Laura overheard her mother as she came into the family room. "Yes, it will, Mother. Hi Aaron. Do you want to go for a walk?"

"Sure," Aaron said.

Helen was quick to reply. "I don't think that's a good idea. Why don't you two remain here? I'll go downstairs and help your father in the store."

"Why can't we go for a walk?" Laura questioned.

"I don't think it's a good idea in your condition."

"My condition isn't going to change anytime soon. Do you plan to keep me in the house forever?"

Helen spoke sternly with a hardened expression. "No, I don't. But today, I do. Do not leave this house, Laura." Helen knew all too well that there was a Hollister Cattlemen's Association meeting that evening and the Thomas family would be there, possibly even Jake. Helen wasn't willing to risk Laura running into him on the street.

"Fine! I'll sit here and talk to Aaron then," Laura said with a roll of her eyes and arms crossed. She plopped heavily into her mother's rocking chair across from a small table where Aaron sat in her father's chair.

"Good. I'll be watching the stairs, just so you know," Helen warned and went down the stairs into the store.

Aaron offered an empathetic smile. "A walk would have been nice."

"I feel like a prisoner in my own home. I can't do anything anymore."

"You can talk to me," Aaron said with an uneasy shrug.

Laura smiled lightly. "Aaron, why do you keep coming here? You know I was meeting Jake when you were courting me. You know that, right?"

The question took him off guard. "I found out. Hell, the whole town found out. And that hurt me. I thought we were in love."

Laura shook her head. "I'm in love with Jake. That's why I'd sneak out to meet him. It was the only time I could see him."

"What about me? You kissed me too."

"You're a nice person, Aaron. I love you as a *friend*, but not anything more than that."

"Don't tell me you're still hooked on Jake," Aaron spat out like sour milk.

"Jake and I are going to be married."

"Laura," Aaron said gently. He leaned forward in the rocking chair and placed his elbows on his knees. "How many times has he come by to check on you?"

Laura's brow wrinkled. "None. But you know he can't. My parents won't let him."

Aaron scoffed bitterly. "If I were him, your parents would not be able to *stop* me from seeing you. That's what love does, Laura. If he loved you, he'd be here every day trying to see you. A man in love will bend over backward and crawl through a rattlesnake pit to reach the woman he loves. Like I have! You hurt me deeply, but love endures hardship, and it endures the pain. Love doesn't give up, and I'm not giving up on you that easily."

Laura offered an empathetic hint of a smile. "We're eloping when I turn sixteen."

"He has no intention of marrying you, Laura. He never did."

"Is it true that you told my father that it was Jake who got Angel pregnant?"

Aaron's brow lowered, taken off guard by the question. "Yes, I did."

"How do you know it was him? They were just friends."

Aaron chuckled. "Right," he said sarcastically. "Jake was my best friend. He told me everything. Angel told him it was his. I'm guessing she'd know," he said with an awkward shrug of his shoulders. The truth was Angel had told Aaron that he was the father, but Aaron had never confided that to anyone. Jake was too committed to Laura to become a customer of Angel's.

"Maybe you should leave," Laura said softly. Her eyes grew moist.

"All right, I'll go, but the difference between Jake and me is that after what happened to you, he never wanted to see you again, and I haven't stopped trying to see you."

After Aaron left, Laura went into her room, took hold of her piano music box, turned the key, and lay on her bed listening to the peaceful music that soothed her soul. She wept.

———

HOLLISTER, Oregon, was not a large town; it was the center hub of Jessup and Waller County's cattle towns, and the Hollister Cattlemen's Association was the heartbeat of the community. It was a large, heavy-timbered, two-story building painted dark-brown with a large set of bull horns over the door. Jake's father, Gunther Thomas, was the president of the association, but Jake had skipped every meeting since his cheek was sliced open. It was his first time back, and his welcome had been warm and inviting, except for his former best friend, Aaron Longley. Aaron refused to look at him, let alone applaud his return.

When the meeting was over, Jake stepped outside to get a breath of fresh air. He could see the upstairs lights of the hardware store where the Whiteheads lived. He could not see Laura's bedroom window from the street, but the longing to see her weighed heavily in his chest. He knew he would not be welcomed if he knocked on the White-head's door, but the only thing stopping him from trying to see Laura was his guilt. He could not face her, knowing it was his fault that she was hurt. The two men had followed him to send his father a message; Jake's cheek would have been sliced open whether Laura was there or not.

"She doesn't want to see you," Aaron's voice said with a touch of hostility. He stepped out onto the street closer to Jake. "You can forget about her because you'll never be welcomed around her again."

"Have you seen her?" Jake asked solemnly.

"Of course. I visited with Laura for a few hours today," he lied, just to let the words cut Jake deeper. "She despises you for letting those monsters do what they did to her. You were supposed to protect her, Jake. But she said all you did was cry." Aaron shook his head with disgust. "She said you were a coward." He added quickly with raised hands when Jake's eyes hardened, "Those are her words, not mine."

Jake felt like a shotgun had blown a hole through his chest. Guilt, heavy as a barrel of concrete, constricted his throat and tightened around his chest like an invisible python squeezing the life out of him. He gasped to get a breath. His eyes were watering heavily as he looked at his old friend. "Take care of her, Aaron. Tell her I'm...sorry," he barely got out above a whisper. He turned his head away from Aaron to wipe his tears. "I have to go."

Aaron wanted to smile victoriously at the sight of his old friend's breaking heart but remained stoic with an emotionless frown. "I'll tell her, but it isn't going to take the baby out of her belly, is it? That's your fault, Jake. It would be best if you moved to Branson or just disappeared for good because if she ever sees you, it's going to bring it all back again."

Jake didn't say another word as he stepped purposefully over to his horse tied along a rail and climbed into the saddle. He turned his horse and rode down a side street.

"Jake, where are you going?" his father shouted as he stepped outside with a group of men. Jake rode into the darkness.

"Aaron, where's he going?" Gunther asked.

Aaron shrugged his shoulders. "He didn't say."

Bode Thomas was Jake's oldest brother who had stepped outside with his father and others. "What did you say?" Bode asked accusingly.

"Nothing much," Aaron answered. "I just told him it won't do him any good to stand on the street like a statue staring at Laura's house. He's not welcome there."

"I'm *sure* that's all you said," Bode replied sarcastically.

"I just told him the truth. Laura doesn't want to see him."

———

JAKE RODE his horse behind the church before dismounting. He could see the stairs to the cellar and slowly stepped down each stair until he reached the door. It was locked with a padlock by the church to stop any more trespassing. Jake kicked the door just to the side of the lock and the short screws holding the clasp in place broke free, bursting the door open.

Jake stepped inside the dark cellar, wiping a spider web from his face as he entered. He felt along the shelves, hoping to find the lantern he had kept there. It had been moved, and the wick was unlit. He carried the lamp up the stairs to his horse and reached into a saddlebag. He felt around the saddlebag in the darkness until he felt a box of matches that he kept for starting campfires when he stayed out with the cattle. He lit the lantern's wick and carried it down the stairs before turning up the oil. The light burned bright, illuminating the cellar.

It felt like someone had punched him in the gut when he saw the bloodstain on the concrete floor where Laura had been pushed down. The cold air in the cellar brought a chill that his wool coat could not protect him from. The memory of Laura's face twisting in agony and the sound of her muffled screams haunted him like a ghost refusing to leave the cellar. He could not get the memory out of his head as it played over and over again. It was a heart-wrenching fact to live with, knowing he watched two vicious men ravage the lady he loved. He had never felt more helpless than knowing he could not stop them. He could not pull his eyes from where her blood discolored the concrete floor. He dropped to his knees with a loud sob that burst forth and collapsed forward onto the floor, sobbing uncontrollably.

With a loud and furious yell, Jake rose to his knees and threw the lantern against the shelves. It shattered the glass shade, but the sealed metal container held secure. Angry, Jake grabbed the lantern and uncapped the oil reserve. He poured the oil out, spreading it around on the floor and shelves. The wick still burned when he tipped it upside down and touched the flame to the oil on Laura's blood stain. It lit and before too long, flames burned the oil on the concrete and moved up to the shelves. The cellar filled with smoke, forcing Jake to retreat to the stairs to breathe fresh air. He saw his older brother Bode standing there watching him.

"Feel better?" Bode asked him. He stood with his arms crossed in a blue shirt like a statue, watching his brother. Bode was six feet tall, stocky, and muscular, with short dark-brown hair and a full-faced beard that he kept short. Bode was a handsome man with a square-shaped face and gentle brown eyes, but despite his easygoing nature, Bode was known to be one of the no-nonsense and more formidable men in the Hollister area.

"No," Jake answered while passing by his brother. "I'll feel better when I have Jesse Helm's scalp hanging on my wall."

"What's that supposed to mean?"

Jake stopped and turned around to face Bode. "That means Jesse Helms is still alive, and I'm going to kill him."

"First of all, you have no idea where he is. But what are you going to do if you find him? Do you think he won't recognize you?"

"I'm going to put a bullet in his gut! I want him to suffer for what he did to Laura. If I'm killed in the process, that's fine. But he's going to die for what he did. I won't be known as a coward, Bode. I won't!" He wiped his eyes.

"Coward?" Bode questioned gently. "No one has called you a coward."

"Laura did!" he shouted. "I have to do this to make things right. I'm leaving in the morning."

"Is that what Aaron told you?" Bode questioned.

Jake stopped at his saddle. "Yes." He lowered his head.

"There was nothing I could do, Bode. I tried. I'm going to kill Jesse Helms if it is the last thing I do. I'm not a coward!"

"I know you're not a coward. But dying isn't going to prove it to anyone. You won't find Jesse Helms, Jake. He's long gone. All you'll end up doing is upsetting Mother. And she's got enough issues without worrying herself to death about you. You're her baby. None of us can break her heart like you can. So you think about what you'll do to Mom before you go riding off." He motioned to the smoke pouring out of the cellar. "This fire is going to be hard enough to explain to her and Pa."

CHAPTER THIRTEEN

"Good morning, sir. My name is Tim Hazelton. I was curious if you're doing any hiring. I'm experienced with sales and know my way around a hardware store pretty well. My grandfather owned a hardware store similar to yours in Elko, Nevada. I worked for him all through my teen years until he passed a couple of years ago. My grandmother recently sold the house and store and moved to my aunt's place in Utah. There was nothing left for me in Elko, so I left to see what I could find, but now winter's coming fast, and I saw your store." He offered an innocent shrug. "I thought I'd take a chance and hope you had some work to keep me through the winter. I can do it all. There's nothing I can't do. And I'm trustworthy, sir. I won't steal, rob or lie to you. I just don't want to be stuck out in the cold anymore."

Mitch Whitehead looked the young man over. He was a respectable-looking young man with short blond hair with a touch of a red tint of about twenty-one or two. He was clean-shaven and appeared to be honest enough. Unfortunately, Mitch didn't need any more help. "I'm sorry, I don't need any help."

"I won't ask for much. All I need is a corner to sleep in and a meal. I don't need three squares, just one meal a day. I'll work for that. In the spring, if you feel like I earned it, you can pay what you think is fair. I'd just be thankful for the room and board through the winter. I'll follow every rule you have and if I become a burden, I'll leave. I'm offering you more than I'm asking for. Like I said, there's nothing I can't do and I'm good at sales too. I'll work hard and do you right, sir."

"I wish I could help you, but..."

"What's your name, sir?"

"I'm Mitch Whitehead."

"Mr. Whitehead, sir, I don't mean to be so forward, but I'm cold, hungry, and have nowhere else to go. You have nothing to lose by my free labor, sir. I don't eat much and that's all I'm really asking for. I don't drink and I don't carouse. If anyone breaks into your store, I could be like a guard dog and chase them away. I grew up working in a business just like yours, and like I said, you don't have anything to lose because I already know this business. I'll work hard and treat your store like my grandfather's, with the utmost respect."

Mitch hesitated. The young man was definitely a stranger in town but seemed sincere and kept eye contact when he spoke, which Mitch liked.

"Please, Mr. Whitehead. I have nowhere else to go. I have no family and no home to go back to. I'm just hoping to get out of the cold."

"What's your name again?" Mitch asked.

"Tim Hazelton, sir."

"Where are your parents?"

"They were murdered by outlaws when I was young. I was raised by my grandparents, who owned a hardware store in Elko. This seems like a nice town with good folks, and I'd like to stay if you allow me to. I could ask one of the ranches, but I don't know a thing about that. This,"—he waved around the store—"is what I know."

"What brought you way out here in the middle of nowhere?" Mitch questioned. Hollister was not a town people usually passed through without a reason.

"The road," he answered with a shrug. "I had been riding west for three days and sleeping in the cold. I hoped to find a place called Branson, but I think I took a wrong turn because I ended up here. You wouldn't have to train me. Sir, from one hardware store employee to another, I'm real hungry and appealing to your mercy for a meal at least. If I could?"

Mitch hesitated thoughtfully. "My family and I live upstairs. How about I introduce you to my wife, and you let us discuss it?"

"I don't have much money, but I could pay a nickel or two for the meal."

Mitch frowned empathetically. "We'll feed you for free. I meant, let me discuss hiring you with my wife."

Tim's eyes widened. "That's all I can ask for. Thank you!"

———

TIM RODE his horse several miles outside of town to where his small canvas tarpaulin was strung over his bedroll. He secured his horse's reins to a tethered rope stretched between two trees and joined his friends around a campfire that helped keep the October cold at bay. "I talked him into hiring me," he said to Jesse Helms. "I'm moving into their storeroom today. I told them I had to come gather my things from my camp."

"Good. Did you see her?" Jesse questioned.

Tim shook his head. "Nope. She was apparently taking a nap when I was upstairs in their place. I met Mrs. White-head though. She seems like a nice lady."

"Is she pretty?" Colin Kennedy asked. He was Tim's older cousin. Colin was in his thirties with long, unbrushed brown hair that fell on his shoulders like limp noodles. He stood over six feet with a thin and wiry frame. His face was diamond-shaped, with a pointed chin hidden under a long, scraggly beard and an untrimmed mustache that curled under his upper lip. Colin held the belief that people would like him or they wouldn't, and it didn't matter to him one way or another what they chose.

Tim shrugged. "I didn't think Mrs. Whitehead was that attractive, but you might. I doubt she'd be interested in you though. She's married."

Colin grinned, exposing his rotting teeth. "You never know."

"Hmm, I have a pretty good idea," Tim answered.

Jesse Helms's brow lowered. "So she's still pregnant then?" Jesse was of average height and had a thick, stocky, muscular body. He kept his brown hair cut close to his head and wore his goatee about three inches long. Jesse had a broad, square-shaped face with blue eyes that peered at the world with a menacing glare.

"I don't know. She was taking a nap when I was there.

I'll meet her at dinnertime and I'll find out. Anyway, I need to get back. I just came to get my things." He paused. "Well, while you all enjoy the cold nights, I'll be in the warmth of the storeroom. It's good to be young," Tim said with a laugh.

"If she's lost the baby, get back here so we can go home. If you're not back by morning we'll know the plan's still on. Tim." Jesse warned with his hardened stare, "Don't screw it up."

"I won't. Trust me, I'll do my part."

Byron Krall asked Jesse, "What is our part again? I don't remember us having a *part*."

Jesse ignored Byron and looked at his right-hand man, Rusty Wells. "I can't show my face in town, as you know, but I still owe Gunther Thomas for my friend Elliot Zook's death. Tomorrow, I want you and Byron to ride out to the Long T Ranch and size it up. Ask the old fat man about a job."

"Jobs?" Byron questioned. "Hell, if we're just coming here for jobs, we could have stayed at your parent's dairy and worked in the cheese room with the pretty Mexican women."

Jesse peered at Byron, annoyed. Byron had been complaining since they left Natoma. "Just do it."

"What about me?" Colin questioned. "What do you want me to do?"

"You're hanging out with me in case I need you. For now, though, go find some more firewood."

———

HOLLISTER'S ONLY DOCTOR, Wayne Anderson, had told Laura and her parents that the chances of Laura becoming pregnant from the rape were doubtful. The timing after her most recent menstruation put her toward the end of her ovulating cycle, but also the amount of bleeding from the forced intrusion would wash the unwanted sperm out of her. If there was any good news they could hold onto at the time, that was it. The weeks brought changes, but most were attributed to her exhaustion brought on by her restless nightmares and the lack of sleep. The nausea that other women experienced in the first months of pregnancy was the telltale sign that most women looked for, but morning sickness had never been a significant factor for Laura. She had vomited a few times, but she trusted Dr. Anderson's expertise and attributed it to a stomach bug going around or something she had eaten the night before that didn't settle right.

Laura never missed her menstruation cycle, though the unexpected bleeding was explained by the damage the men had done to her. To hear Dr. Anderson say the words, *you are pregnant*, hit her with the shock and terror of a pronounced death sentence. Now, after getting used to the shock of it, the disbelief, fear, and sorrow had run their course. She could accept that she was pregnant and no longer looked to find excuses for the fatigue and changes that were happening with her body.

Laura stepped out of her bedroom, feeling lethargic, bloated, and uncomfortable. Her stuffy head felt like it was floating on an unstable post during a windstorm. Her brow lifted with surprise to see a stranger sitting at their dinner table. He was a handsome, blond-haired young man with a touch of red to his hair. He pushed his chair back and rose. His eyes locked on hers with a respectable gaze as she entered the dining room.

Mitch spoke from his seat. "Laura, this is Tim. He'll be

working for us for a while. Tim, this is our daughter, Laura. She's not been feeling good today."

Tim stared at the pretty blonde-haired girl. He had never seen such innocent blue eyes. Jesse had told him and the others that she was pretty, but Tim doubted that Jesse had very good taste when it came to women. Laura was the prettiest girl Tim had seen in a long time.

"Hello," he said with a nod. "I'm Tim."

She sank into the chair, her shoulders sagging, and offered a faint smile. "Welcome to our home. It's nice to meet you. You'll have to forgive me; I'm not feeling well."

"I hope you feel better soon." He sat and placed his cloth napkin over his lap. "I thank you for the dinner. I haven't had a real meal in weeks. Thank you, Mrs. Whitehead. It smells great."

Helen smiled kindly, appreciating his gratitude. "You are welcome. So, tell us about yourself, Tim."

"Well, there's not much to tell. As I mentioned to Mr. Whitehead earlier..." A knock on the door interrupted him.

Mitch rose and answered it. "Aaron. What a surprise. We were having dinner. Would you like to join us?"

"If you got extra, sure." He removed his coat, hat, and gun belt and hung them on the mounted hanger beside the door. He entered the dining room with a fading smile when he saw a stranger at their table. He reached a hand out to shake as he approached Tim. "I'm Aaron. A friend of Laura's."

"Tim," he answered, standing to shake Aaron's hand firmly.

Mitch said, "Tim will be working in the store through the winter."

"Just for the winter? Will you be moving on in the spring?"

"That's my plan. Unless I take a liking to here and these fine folks are willing to keep me around. I'm just wandering until I find a home." He smiled with a glance at Laura.

The flirtatious glance didn't go unnoticed by Aaron. It sparked a touch of jealousy that burned down into his spine. "Where are you staying during your stay? The hotel?"

Mitch answered, "He's staying downstairs in the storeroom for now. We'll make up a little room for him. So what are you doing in town, Aaron?"

"I had to pick up a few items from the mercantile. Ma is sewing a new shirt for Pa's birthday, so I picked up the material she ordered. I thought I'd stop by and visit Laura for a bit. I hope you all don't mind?"

Helen waved a dismissive hand. "Don't be silly. You're always welcome."

"I suppose you folks heard that Jake broke into the church's cellar and caught it on fire last night, the shelves and stuff. Concrete doesn't burn," Aaron said.

"Excuse me," Laura said, standing and hurried to her room.

"Laura," Aaron said as he watched her leave. He looked at Mitch and Helen. "I'm sorry. I didn't mean to upset her."

Mitch sighed. "I thought it would be prudent not to mention it. But since you did, do you know if he was arrested for arson?"

Aaron gave a disgusted scoff. "The sheriff won't arrest him. You know that. Gunther said he'd replace the shelves, and the church is happy with that."

"That young man is trouble from the word go," Mitch said before taking a bite of his dinner.

"He came to the cattlemen's association meeting last night. It's the first time I've seen him since, you know."

"Did you talk to him?" Helen questioned.

"No. Look, I upset Laura, and I apologize. I think I'll skip dinner and go on home. Will you tell her I'm sorry? I didn't mean to upset her."

"Of course."

Laura stepped into the dining room. "I'll walk you outside." When they stepped outside on the top of the exterior stairs on the side of the building, she closed the door and asked, "Aaron, do you know why Jake burned the cellar?"

He lowered his head hesitantly. "I do, but Laura, I don't want to tell you because all it's going to do is hurt you."

"It can't hurt me worse than I already am."

Aaron hesitated. "Yes, it can," he warned.

"Tell me."

Aaron took a deep breath and exhaled. He lowered his voice. "I lied to your parents. I did talk to Jake after he caught it on fire. He said he had to burn away the memories of you." He paused hesitantly. "Laura, I know he's lying, but he's telling people that you invited those two men to do what they did. He said they didn't force you."

"What!" she exclaimed with a horrified expression. "No, Jake wouldn't say that?" she questioned more than she stated. Her eyes filled with thick tears.

"I know he's lying. Listen, he's not the same man we knew and loved. He's angry at the world and blames you for the scar on his face. If you haven't seen him, the scar has deformed his face enough that he keeps his face covered now. I know you love him, but he never wants to see you again, Laura. I didn't want to tell you that."

Laura covered her face with her hands and began weeping. "No," she said when Aaron tried to hug her. She quickly went inside and closed the door behind her.

The corners of Aaron's lips rose slightly. If he could convince Jake and Laura both that the other person never wanted to see them again, then when they did meet, they would not speak to each other, and that close bond they had would fade and leave room for him to step in.

CHAPTER FOURTEEN

RUSTY WELLS YAWNED AS HE RODE THE following day toward the Long T Ranch on the north side of Hollister. He and Byron had gone to the 1878 Saloon the night before and stayed a little too late. To avoid any suspicion, they brought their bedrolls and slept in the loft above the livery stable. They had spoken to a few cowboys about any open positions, and the only ranch that might need a hand or two was maybe the Pollard-Lee Ranch. They weren't too interested in finding a job but hoped to hear more about the Long T Ranch. They met a couple of hands who worked there, but the two men they met were more interested in talking with their friends than meeting them. It became apparent that Hollister was a close-knit community that wasn't too hospitable to strangers.

"I didn't sign on with Jesse to run errands," Byron Krall complained. "If he doesn't want to rob a stage or a bank, then what does this town have to offer us? You do understand all of this is to get some girl and to use us to get revenge for his old friend, who we never met. This whole trip doesn't benefit you or me at all. It is just a waste of time for us. As my pa used to say, time is money. And we aren't making any."

Rusty tilted his head in agreement. "I can't argue with you about that. Patience, my friend. We'll have our big payday next spring. Right now, let's help Jesse, and he'll do right by us."

Byron rolled his eyes. "We were promised we'd do better in Nevada than we did. I'm beginning to think he brought us up here to Oregon just to milk cows and make cheese for his family's dairy. Oh, and winterizing his aunt Mattie's house for her. We'll be doing more work than we'll get paid for. He was saying we're going to fix the roof on his aunt's house when we get back."

"She's an old woman who needs some help. It will keep us busy for a few days. I don't think Jesse has a bad idea about wintering in his hometown and letting things settle down in the Elko area. We have a warm place to stay, free food, and get to make a little money working at his parents' dairy. There's a saloon in town, and on the weekends, we can go to Branson for some fun. It's just a time to relax and stay warm and fed." Rusty paused. "I have faith in Jesse. He led the Sperry-Helms Gang for years, and you know their reputation. Heck, we terrorized Northern Nevada and they don't even know who we are. I think Jesse is doing all right by us."

Byron leaned to one side of his saddle and blew his nose by holding one nostril closed; he did his other nostril. "Jesse went into Matt Bannister's office and bragged about being free. Do you think the marshal is going to sit on his butt when that girl goes missing? It's my understanding that Jesse's cousin, Morton, was the leader of the Sperry-Helms Gang until the marshal showed up, and then he quit the gang and took a job as the marshal's deputy. If *that* doesn't tell you how dangerous the marshal is, nothing will. He scared Morton Sperry straight. And Jesse wants to keep this pregnant girl at Morton's mother's house?" he asked with an astonished expression. "Doesn't this sound like a suicidal plan to you? Because it sure does to me. I'm losing faith in Jesse. We should cut our losses and leave, Rusty." He waved a hand toward the road ahead of them. "This rancher he wants us to kill doesn't mean anything to me. Why are we getting involved and doing Jesse's dirty work? Do you think it's so our necks can get stretched and not his? I do."

Rusty listened to his old friend and considered his words. Byron and Rusty had been partners since their teen years and decided to join up with Jesse for the promise of more significant paydays. The paydays varied on the contents of the stagecoach strongboxes and passengers, but they had done well for themselves on occasion since teaming up with Jesse. Rusty spoke thoughtfully. "He's never asked us to do anything like this before. This is a special circumstance that Jesse didn't see coming. Let's do our part and we'll come out of it okay. We always do."

Byron gave a short, sarcastic chuckle. "We've never been asked to murder someone either. Do you think the murder of the president of their cattle association and a missing girl won't put Matt Bannister on our trail?"

"Relax," Rusty said. "Jesse's got family here, including the Crowe Brothers, who saved his butt last time. If worse comes to worse, and the marshal gets on your trail, just surrender. The Crowe Brothers will make sure Jesse and us are set free. We won't find that kind of loyalty anywhere else."

"Except the Crowe Brothers have no idea who we are."

Byron Krall was nearly six feet tall, with broad shoulders and a thick body build. He had brown hair that fell straight over his ears, which he had been meaning to have cut. His round face was clean-shaven except for a week's worth of stubble that was beginning to itch. His blue eyes scanned the surrounding area irritably. "This whole thing is bullcrap."

Rusty smiled. He knew his friend well enough to know that part of Byron's complaining was because he was hungry. "Jesse would get us out of jail. Let's just do what Jesse asked and get back to the Helm's Dairy. That one Mexican woman who works in the cheese room named Gabriela is pretty fine. I got my eye on that one."

Byron said, "I'd rather be back at the dairy milking cows for a wage than here risking my life for nothing."

"All we have to do is meet Gunther Thomas and take a look around. It would be nice to know how many hands Gunther employs before we kill him."

Byron spat out, "Why don't you just kill him and get it over with so we stop playing games? Jesse has us coming out here pretending we're cowboys and Tim spying on that girl." He shook his head. "We could go in there and get her, stab her parents, assassinate this Gunther fella and be done with it."

Rusty Wells was of average height and body build. He had dark-brown hair that he kept short and a horseshoe mustache that reached the chin on his oblong-shaped face. Rusty's brown eyes were both mischievous and deadly. "All I know is Jesse wants us to fit in and ask about jobs. And that's not too hard for us to do. It sure beats sitting in the weather out there at camp." He could see the Long T Ranch headgate above the driveway and a black buggy being driven by a young man. Behind him on the passenger seat were what looked like two ladies dressed warmly and covered with blankets to keep warm on their journey. "It looks like we have company. Be nice, smile, and let me do the talking," Rusty said as he and Byron stopped at the head gate to wait for the buggy.

———

JAKE DROVE the buggy with his mother and older sister Darra sitting in the back seat. They had been cordially invited to the home of Holly Fairchild for a noon luncheon. Jake didn't mind going, but he feared driving past the hardware store. He wanted to see Laura, but he was afraid to at the same time. It would be the first time he had to drive past the hardware store and the anxiety was upsetting his stomach.

Jake had gotten into some trouble for burning the cellar, but once the sheriff and the town's reverend learned why he did it, they understood. There was no real damage done, and Jake's father promised to replace the shelving. As Jake drove the buggy toward the headgate, he noticed the two men waiting. One of them waved a hand to stop the buggy.

"Good day, folks. I am curious, is this the Long T Ranch?" Rusty asked.

Jake pointed above him at the headgate that proclaimed the ranch's name. He replied, "Yes. Can I help you?"

"Are you the owner?" Rusty asked with a growing grin when he saw the scar on Jake's cheek. He'd have to remember to compliment Jesse for doing such exquisite knife work.

"My father is," Jake replied. He could see the man's eyes fixated on his scar.

The stranger stepped his horse closer and reached out a

hand to shake. "My name's Rusty Wells. That's my pard, Byron Krall. We heard you might be looking for a couple of hands."

"No," Jake said, with a shake of his head. "We have a full bunkhouse. You might try the Tall Double Tree or the Pollard-Lee Ranch. I hear they have an opening or two."

Rusty's eyes shifted back to the two ladies under a blanket in the back seat. "Ladies," he tipped his hat politely. "You must be Jake?" he asked. He traced a line up his cheek where Jake's scar was.

Jake's eyes narrowed suspiciously. "I am."

Byron spoke for the first time through a knowing smirk. "That's quite the scar you got there, young man. Did a horse kick you?"

"No," Jake answered, keeping his annoyance under control. "Gentlemen, I don't believe we're hiring. Good day."

"Mind if we check with the boss?" Rusty asked, waving his thumb toward the driveway.

"There's no need," Sasha Thomas's fragile voice answered from the back. She had a bad feeling about the two men. "You'll find your best opportunity for work elsewhere."

Rusty tightened his lips and nodded quietly. "We'll check elsewhere then. Ma'am, pretty lady," he nodded at Darra. "Have a good day."

Jake did not bother parting company politely. He clicked his tongue and loosened the reins with a quick shake to get the horse moving.

"I didn't like those men," Sasha offered. "They didn't feel right. They look like trouble to me."

Jake said, "I don't like them either."

CHAPTER FIFTEEN

HOLLY FAIRCHILD WORE AN ORDINARY BLUE DRESS with gray stripes when she opened the door. Her golden-blonde hair shined as it lay across her shoulders. Her smile was bright and genuine as she welcomed her guests into her home. "Please come inside and make yourselves at home. Sasha, it's so good to see you again," she said, taking a gentle hold of Sasha's hand.

Sasha said, "You have a beautiful home."

"Thank you. I had it rebuilt exactly the way it was. It's funny how it can look the same but feel so different."

"I can understand that." Sasha motioned toward Darra. "I brought my daughter if you don't mind. Her name is..."

"Darra," Holly said before Sasha could finish. "You're as beautiful as the first time we met. Welcome. I'm glad you're all here. Let's go into the sunroom and get acquainted over some tea before lunch. I haven't hired a cook yet, but Ross assured me he could make a fine soup and sandwiches. He's one of my guards, but he's actually not a bad cook," she explained as she led her guests to what she called the sunroom. It was a medium-sized room with a large window that looked out over the lake. Several plush cushioned chairs were in a semi-circle around the room facing the window yet made it easy for conversation. A large round table with a teapot and cups were in the center. A silver tray of white frosted pastries was on the table as well.

Jake sat in one of the most comfortable chairs he'd ever sat in while listening to the attractive widow Holly Fairchild talk with his mother and sister about a wide variety of topics ranging from sewing to Darra's dream of going to college, which was on hold so she could care for their mother. It had all been small talk for the first half an hour of tea and pastries, which Jake found to be delicious.

Holly hesitated before speaking to Sasha curiously, "You haven't questioned me about the canal I'm having dug or the woolen mill. I know you must be curious about those?"

Sasha smiled uncomfortably. "It's not a well-received subject around here. I have to admit you are not well-liked by a good portion of folks here."

Holly forced a small smile. "I suppose I'm not. But let me ask you. If the cattle market drops significantly, what are you and the other ranchers going to do? The cattle market supports everything you own, and if prices drop for any length of time, most of the smaller ranchers will lose everything. This community will suffer because it's built around the beef industry and has no other means of survival. I'm here to help because sheep are the future. All the hate for me right now will eventually turn to gratitude."

Jake scoffed. "Sheep will never replace beeves."

"No?" Holly questioned. "Beef will always be a commodity, but sooner or later, the price will fall, and you won't be able to sell a cow for half the price you bought it for. If you're lucky, you might break even. The market is bound to drop sometime. The benefit of sheep is that they provide wool, which is used for everything from socks to blankets. Everyone in America needs clothing. Unlike satin or silk, wool isn't a luxury; it is a necessity. That makes it a valuable market, and it will only grow. Sheep need to be sheared twice a year, and that's two good incomes a year."

"Yeah, but they'll kill the grass and ruin the water holes around here," Jake argued. "There won't be anything left for the cattle."

"The shepherds keep the flocks roaming so the grass isn't eaten too low, and the water is the same. I'm preparing for the future and although you don't see it coming, my husband did, and I do too. If the beef market drops, what will your neighbors and you fall back on? The wool market will still be strong and flourishing. Each sheep pays for itself ten times over and if you multiply that by hundreds or thousands, it's the best investment you can make. To protect your ranch, your home, and your family, I encourage you to talk Gunther into buying sheep as a precaution. And, just so happens, I'm in the sheep-selling business. If you want a thousand head, I can get them for you and reliable shepherds, too."

Sasha sighed. "Did you invite us here to sell us sheep?"

Holly laughed. "No, I did not. I invited you here because you struck me as an honest and upfront lady at the church bazaar. I respect that and I'd like us to be friends. Sasha, I'll never bring up sheep again if you're not interested. I happen to believe the wool market is the new gold, especially for those of us who get into it early. But no, I invited you here to get to know you all and to let you get to know me. I don't have any friends here, and I was hoping to find a few."

Sasha nodded her head the little bit that her fused vertebrae allowed. "That sounds nice. I would be disappointed if we were only here to hear a sales pitch for sheep."

Holly placed her hand on Sasha's. "No. I promise you that's not so. Jake," she said, shifting in her chair to look at him. "If I may ask you a personal question?"

"Sure," Jake said.

"At the church bazaar, I asked you about that young lady who was in the cellar with you, and that rude woman selling the pork seemed to want to answer everything I asked you."

Sasha said, "Her name is Claire Archibald. You will not find a nosier woman or louder gossip under the good Lord's heaven. I don't mean to interrupt or talk for my son, but that's who she is and you need to know that before you invite her into your home."

Holly grimaced. "I have no intention of inviting her into my home. I didn't like her." She put her attention back on Jake. "That young lady's name is Laura, right?"

"Yes," Jake said. The sadness in his eyes couldn't go unnoticed.

"Her parents won't let you see her? Is that what I'm to understand?"

He nodded.

"Claire said she was pregnant. Is that from that night?"

Jake took a deep breath as his eyes misted while his head hung downward. He nodded, unable to speak.

"You love her, don't you?"

Jake's eyes rose to meet Holly's. He sniffled as he said, "Yes."

Holly shifted in her chair as she stared thoughtfully at him. "Suddenly, I feel like Friar Laurence."

Darra chuckled at the comment.

"Who?" Jake questioned.

"You haven't read Romeo and Juliet?" Holly asked.

He shook his head.

"I'm afraid my library was burned, or I'd let you borrow it." He turned her head to face Darra. "You must have read Romeo and Juliet?"

"Of course. I own a copy of the book Jake can borrow, if he'll read it. Jake doesn't like to read."

Holly turned back to Jake. "Read the book when you go home. It's a play by William Shakespeare. It's about young love and feuding families. Please read it. How would you feel if I arranged a meeting with her here at my house without her parents knowing?"

Jake's eyes narrowed with interest. "How?"

"You leave that to me. I'll let you know when to come over. Is Laura really engaged to another young man?"

Jake shrugged. "He says so, but one of the cowhands who works for his family says that's not true. Aaron told me the other night that Laura blames me for what had happened to her, so she might not want to see me."

"If that's the case, then this community will hate me even more when they learn about a surprise meeting, won't they?" Holly asked with a nonchalant shrug of her shoulders. "This community has already hurt me as deeply as they possibly can. I don't care if I'm hated or not. But I'm a sucker for romance. Let's arrange a surprise meeting between you two and find out what happens." She turned to Sasha. "Is that okay with you?"

Sasha lifted her face as far as her curved back and neck

would allow. There was a mischievous glint in her eyes. "Yes."

———

TIM HAZELTON WAS busy counting different sizes of nuts and bolts as he took inventory of what products and how many were on the store shelves. He had been honest with Mitch Whitehead; Tim was raised by his grandparents and worked in his grandfather's hardware store. He would have liked to have inherited the store when his grandfather died, but his aunt and uncle came after the funeral and talked Tim's grandmother into selling the store and the house to live off the money. They convinced her to sell all her belongings, pack up her most cherished items and move hundreds of miles away to Utah to live with them.

Tim recognized it as a scam for his aunt's husband to get his grandparents' money, but despite his pleas for her to pass the hardware store on to him as his grandfather had promised, she sold everything before moving to Tim's aunt and uncle's. Tim was invited to go as well, but the long list of rules and expectations written out by his aunt's over-controlling husband were too strict for any average person to live by. From the list of rules Tim was expected to follow, it was clear that his uncle did not want Tim to move there.

Left alone, Tim found himself depressed and lonely until one night while having a few drinks in a local saloon, he ran into his distant cousin on his father's side, Colin Kennedy. Colin took Tim under his wing and introduced Tim to Jesse, Rusty, and Byron.

Tim enjoyed working in the hardware store; it reminded him of his youth working with his grandfather. Tim didn't mind doing inventory; it felt good to be doing what he knew best. He was enjoying himself and even hummed a tune or two while counting. He ignored most of the customers who entered the store, but his attention was drawn to a beautiful, tall, golden-haired woman as she entered the store, followed by two stern-looking men wearing suits and derby hats. The well-dressed woman and two men did not fit the customary mold of a cattle town's usual dress code. He knew immediately that the woman was different from everybody else in town.

"Mrs. Fairchild, hello. What can I do for you?" Mitch asked, clearly surprised to see her.

She spoke pleasantly. "Please, call me Holly. My husband is no longer here, and I'd prefer not to be reminded of that every time someone speaks to me. We've met once before when my husband was alive. What is your name again?"

"I'm Mitch Whitehead. So, what brings you in here today?"

"Two things. First, this is Wolfgang, the head of my security. He has a long list of items that I could order from elsewhere, but I want to help the local businesses in town. You'll have to order most of it, but you'll find it quite lucrative for you."

"Oh!"

"I will let you and Wolfgang go over the list. Mr. Whitehead, may I ask your permission to meet your beautiful daughter?"

"Why?" he asked, taken aback by the request.

Holly narrowed her eyes thoughtfully. "Her world and mine were both altered by what happened that one night. I think your daughter and I share that in common. I've thought about her a lot since then, and my heart goes out to her more than you could possibly know. If it's okay with you and your missus, I'd like to build a friendship with her because I believe we could help each other heal from that night. I'm sure you can understand that, I hope."

Mitch spoke uncomfortably. "I just want you to know, Mrs. Fairchild, that I didn't have anything to do with what happened to your husband or your home. I was caring for my daughter that night."

"Of course," Holly said without a doubt that Mitch stayed home with his family that night. "Please." She smiled. "Call me Holly. Being called *Missus* reminds me that I was married, and it saddens me to hear it. Would it be okay if I meet your daughter?"

Mitch nodded. "I don't see any harm in that. Tim, will you help this gentleman with his list while I introduce Missus, sorry, Holly, to Laura."

"Sure," he said, stepping toward the counter. He nodded to the attractive lady just as she smiled slightly at him and turned to follow Mitch to the stairs behind the counter that led upstairs to their home.

————

"HOLLY, THIS IS OUR DAUGHTER, LAURA," Mitch said, introducing her as he brought Laura out of her room.

Holly's smile was genuine when she looked at Laura. "It's nice to meet you."

"Hello," Laura said meekly, standing slightly behind her father. She had no idea why Mrs. Fairchild wanted to talk to her, but Laura feared Holly was there to blame her for the night that Holly's husband was murdered. Laura leaned backward to stretch her lower back, which was stiff and sore.

Helen spoke nervously. "Forgive the mess; we weren't

expecting company. We would have cleaned the house, and Laura would have dressed more appropriately if we had known you were coming." She felt a sense of insecurity about her appearance and home in the presence of the wealthy and beautiful lady in their family room. Helen quickly picked up a coffee cup that had been set on a side table that morning.

"No, don't worry about it. Your home is lovely," Holly said. "I am curious. Would it be okay if I spoke to Laura in private? Like I told both of you, it's a personal matter. I promise I won't upset her."

"I think that will be fine. Laura, we'll be downstairs," Mitch said as he and his bride went down to the store. Laura's eyes widened, surprised, as she watched her parents descend the stairs, leaving her alone with Holly. It was most uncommon for them to leave her alone with anyone like that.

Laura asked anxiously, "What's this about? What happened to your husband wasn't my fault."

Holly smiled reassuringly. "I know it wasn't your fault. Laura, you and I were both victims that night. I thought since we have that in common, then we might as well get to know each other. Maybe we can help one another. How about we sit and talk?"

"About?" Laura asked. She sat in the nearest chair.

"Is your back sore?" Holly asked, noticing Laura's stiff movements and how she stretched her back with a slight grimace.

"Yes. My back is always stiff and sore when I wake up. My mother says it's the pregnancy, but I think it's my bed. It's probably both. So, what did you want to talk about? My father said you wanted to talk to me?"

"May I see your bed? You have a long way to go before

that baby's born, and I want you to have a comfortable bed."

"You can see it, but why would you want me to have a comfortable bed?" Laura began to wonder if her parents had talked to Holly about adopting her baby.

"Will you show me your room? I may have some ideas to make it just a little more comfortable."

Laura shrugged, stood, and led the way through the hallway into her room. "Do you have any children?" Laura asked as she walked along the hallway.

"No," she said as she followed Laura into the room. It was a small square room with a bed on a metal frame, a dresser along one wall and a bedside table. A window looked out at the roofs of two of the smaller buildings across a narrow street and then the side of another two-story building, but it revealed little more.

Holly sat on the mattress to feel the lumpiness of the cheap mattress. "Yes. You need a new bed. How about I..." She paused when she saw the ceramic white grand piano music box on the bedside table. She continued slowly, "How about I buy you a new bedroom set? I mean a better bed with a headboard and matching dresser with a larger mirror."

"Why would you do that? You just met me."

Holly looked at her with a haunted expression. "Because that is what a friend does, Laura." She took a breath. "That piano, what is it?"

"A music box. I'll show you." Laura picked up the piano and spun the key at the bottom. The sound of bells played. "I don't know what it's playing, but I sure love it."

Holly's eyes watered as her breath escaped her lungs, leaving her breathless for a moment. She hesitated. "That is 'Canon in D Major' by Johann Pachelbel. When I was growing up, my parents took us to the symphony quite often, and that's where I first heard it. It was played by violins and I fell in love with it. It's my favorite. There's a belief that Johann Pachelbel wrote it for his best friend Johann Sabastion Bach's wedding. Or so one of the symphony conductors told my father. My father paid a quartet of violins to play it as he walked me down the aisle when I married Robert." Her heart began to pound, but she forced a sad smile, fighting her tears. "If I may ask, where did you get that?"

"Sheriff Emmerson gave it to me after that night," she said with a reluctance to speak of what had happened to her. "He thought it might help me."

Holly took a deep breath and swallowed to keep herself composed. "Did it help you?"

Laura nodded. "I listen to it all the time."

Holly forced a smile. "That's because you have good taste." Robert had the music box made for her as a first wedding anniversary gift. Of all the things Holly had owned, the piano music box that played Pachelbel was her most treasured item. To see her anniversary gift in Laura's hands was a stinging slap across her face.

"Thank you," Laura said of the compliment.

"Listen, I have to go. But I would like you to join me for lunch tomorrow. We'll sit down and talk. I'll let you look through the catalogs I have for a new bedroom set and a few dresses or whatever else you may need." She added, "I don't want anything from you, Laura, except for us to become friends. I want to bless you because I can. I'll get it okayed with your parents. Would you like to come to my house for lunch?"

"Sure."

"Good. If it is okay with you, can I have my two security

guards pick you up without me? I don't have a cook yet, and I want to make lunch for us. I'm asking because I know you probably don't trust men that you don't know, but I assure you they will protect you with their lives just like they would for me. Does that sound okay to you?"

Laura swallowed. "I think so."

"Good. If you come downstairs with me, I'll get your parents' permission and then introduce you to them before I leave. They are good men."

————

HOLLY ENTERED the sheriff's office with pursed lips and heated eyes. "Sheriff Emmerson, have you made any progress in your investigation into who murdered my husband?" The anger in her expression could not be hidden.

Pat Emmerson appeared to be struggling to stay awake as he sat behind his desk. He cleared his throat. "Mrs. Fairchild, you were just in here the other day, and I told you then that it was the sheep shooters that attacked your home. No one knows who was or was not involved in that group. It was kept highly secret from all of us. I'm sorry to say."

"Hmm," Holly grunted. Her blue eyes burned into him. "Then I'll just have to hire the Pinkerton Detective Agency to find out. I won't let Robert's death go unsolved any longer."

"Mrs. Fairchild, they won't find anything. You'll be wasting your money."

Holly offered a slight smirk. "Lucky for me, I have plenty of it to waste. The question is, how long can any one of those sheep shooters, their wives, or friends hold out when I'll offer a thousand dollars for every name provided that was involved in my husband's murder? If that doesn't bring any results, I'll raise the price to two thousand per name, three thousand, and four. The point is that money doesn't mean anything to me. I'm tired of waiting, Sheriff Emmerson. If you're not going to do something about it, then I will. And I'll hire the best detectives that money can buy to track each of those men down and offer as much money as I need to spend to break the silence. Have a good day, Sheriff."

Pat Emmerson felt a chill run down his spine. He stood suddenly. "Holly, you don't want to kick the hornet's nest again, do you? That canal and mill you're building is bad enough. If you start threatening people's lives, it could turn bad for you real quick. I'm only the sheriff, but what happens when I'm not around is out of my hands. I'd hate to see something bad happen to you."

Holly turned around and spoke freely. "I'm not trying to cause trouble. I am trying to do your job for you. And I assure you, I will learn the truth. I hope you weren't involved, Sheriff." She turned and walked out of the sheriff's office to climb into her coach.

Wolfgang had gone inside with her but had remained quiet until they were outside. "Holly, I know seeing that music box has you upset, but do you think it was a good idea to say what you did to him? That was almost an invitation for them to come back and get rid of you."

She spoke softly so she wouldn't be overheard. "The sheriff *is* one of the men who murdered my husband. That's why he can't name any of the others." She closed her eyes and sighed. "Maybe it wasn't a good idea after all. I'll go apologize to the sheriff."

She went back inside the sheriff's office and came back out shortly.

"That should appease him for now. I apologized for overreacting. I told him it's a woman's prerogative once a month at least." She looked at Wolfgang with a distasteful expression. "I despise having to apologize to him. I need to stop at the telegram office and send two wires—one to my young friend Jake and one to my friend Matt. Once we get back to the house, please send a message to the construction company to ask Kent Kruse to come see me. I may not trust him, but he was a Blackburn Marshal and, therefore, supposed to be good with a gun."

CHAPTER SIXTEEN

MATT BANNISTER GRIMACED AS TRUET DAVIS told him the story of how Matt's brother Adam got a small chunk bitten off his finger while trying to catch a rat. "Why would he want a live rat?"

Truet gazed at Matt with a dumbfounded expression. "Fishing bait."

"What?"

Truet grinned with his handsome smile. Truet kept his brown hair cut short and his square-shaped face clean-shaven. He had friendly, deep-brown eyes, which narrowed pleasantly when he smiled. Truet was a carpenter by trade and had a large muscular body that impressed both men and women, as many single and married ladies in Branson were attracted to Truet. However, Truet's devotion had been earned by Matt's sister, Annie. "Matt, he's your brother, I don't know. All I know is he trapped it under a bucket and tried to reach underneath to grab the rat so he could save it for fishing bait. Your uncle Luther talked him into going over to the Snake River next week to catch sturgeon. Adam thinks a live rat would be good bait to catch a big one. He figured he could just put a hook in its back and chuck it out in the river and let it swim back to shore."

"Hmm. He should've been wearing gloves."

"That's what Adam said afterward too. So now he has a pet rat for the next week."

"He didn't kill it for biting him?"

"No. He lifted the edge of the bucket just enough and let the rat try to squeeze under it. He caught the rat by the scruff of the neck, picked it up like a mother cat, and scolded it for biting him. He shook his bleeding finger in the rat's face and said, 'It's not nice to bite!' and then flicked it in the head as punishment."

"Well, it's *not* nice to bite," Matt said with a slight chuckle.

"I'm afraid once I marry your sister, Adam will drive me a little batty with his ideas. I think he was kidding, but I'm not so sure when he said he was going to have that big stallion of his stuffed when it dies and...no, I'm not even going to say it. All I'll say is your brother has some odd ideas."

Matt laughed. "Well, whatever he said, it was probably said just to see your expression. He may have stayed up all night thinking of something he could tell you to keep you bewildered. It humors him."

"I never know if Adam's serious or not. Your whole family's sense of humor is a little off, including Uncle Charlie's and Aunt Mary's."

The cowbell above the marshal's office door rang as a twelve-year-old boy stepped inside carrying a sealed envelope. He held the envelope up and looked at Matt. "I have a wire for you."

Matt's deputy, Phillip Forrester, pulled some change

from his drawer and traded the tip for the letter. He handed it to Matt.

"Thank you," Matt said to the youngster with a friendly smile. He opened the envelope and read:

> *Please come to Hollister. The house is rebuilt. I may have found a wasp nest. I could use your help before it stings me again.*
> *Your friend.*
> *Holly Fairchild*

"WHAT DO YOU HAVE THERE?" Truet asked, reading Matt's expression.

"Trouble in Hollister. Pack your saddlebags, Truet. Tomorrow, you, Morton, and I are going to Hollister. We'll leave Nate here in town."

"What kind of trouble?"

"I don't know. We'll be going into this one blind." He handed the wire to Truet.

Truet looked at Matt skeptically. "How do you know she's not talking about a literal bee's nest? If that's all it is, I'm going to be mad."

"No," Matt said thoughtfully, "I think she's scared of something. We'll find out when we get there."

———

KENT KRUSE DIDN'T GET the message from his boss that Holly wanted to talk to him until the end of the workday, which was shortly before the sun descended. The last time he had gone to see her, he had worn his filthy work clothes, and she sent him away like an unwelcomed vagrant pilfering her garden. Kent was determined to make a better impression, so he bathed and put on his cleanest clothes, which were still sweat and dirt stained. He combed his red hair back and trimmed up his red beard and mustache as nicely as he could with a dull pair of scissors and a straight razor. He didn't have a lot of time and in his hurry, he accidentally cut a bald spot in his beard when a man bumped into him.

The message he received was plain: Holly requested to see him. There was a growing anticipation, a longing and a hope that she wanted to see him with a more forgiving countenance than she had sent him away with before. He knew her well enough to know that Holly didn't linger on the same words for long, meaning she wasn't inviting him over to accuse him of cowardice and send him away again. He walked quickly with the hope that she missed the friendship they had made and wanted to restore it. His affection for Holly was sincere. He didn't just want her money; he was in love with her. He loved everything about her. If he were a praying man, he'd be on his knees praying for her to fall in love with him every morning, noon and night. As it was, he mentioned it enough to a god that he didn't honestly believe in.

To be summoned by her was a good sign, and it filled him with a hope he had not felt in a long time. Nervously, he walked the mile and a half to the Fairchild Estate, which all employees of the Dutch Construction Company were forbidden to go near. Darkness had settled over the land for an hour at least by the time he stepped onto the large porch and pulled the cord for the bell chime.

The same big, bearded man that had been on the porch the last time he came to the house opened the door. "You made it," he said, looking at Kent with a slight smirk, knowing Kent had cleaned himself up to impress Holly.

"Yes," is all Kent said.

"Follow me."

Kent was led into the sunroom, drapes covered the large windows, and two other men sat in the room with Holly. The two other men stood and approached him with outreached hands.

"Ross Hall." He shook Kent's hand firmly.

"Alessandro Baccari." He nodded sharply as he shook Kent's hand with an excessively tight squeeze.

"Kent Kruse," he said.

Holly remained seated in a comfortable padded chair, holding a cup of tea. "You've met Wolfgang."

"I'm Wolfgang Grubbs."

"Is that German?" Kent asked.

"No, I just think my mother didn't like me." He smiled. "Have a seat. You're welcome to grab some tea if you'd like."

Kent waved the invitation away while saying, "No, thank you." He sat down in a chair and looked awkwardly at the three men and Holly, who seemed to surround him in the room in the momentary silence. "What's this all about?" he asked.

Alessandro chuckled as he touched his jaw. "It looks like you cut a little too close there."

Kent forced a small smile, knowing he had cut a bald spot in his beard. "I know."

Wolfgang spoke. "Kent, I understand you were part of the security detail when Robert was murdered and the property was burned..."

Kent's hopes crashed before him like a bird shot dead in flight. His temper rose with the fierceness of being smacked with an insulting slap to his face. He spoke heatedly. "I was! And if any of you think you could have stopped what happened that night, you are dead wrong. I was unarmed and fell asleep out on the lake. There was nothing I could do except be killed myself if I had rowed to shore. If I had my rifle with me, I could have killed a dozen of them, but I didn't! Okay? I apologize for surviving, but it seemed the wisest thing to do at the time! I didn't just watch Mr. Fairchild being dragged away; I watched my friends being gunned down like pigs in a pen. So if you can sit here and think I didn't *want* to help..." He shook his head. "You know what you can kiss. Are we done? I'll go now." He stood.

"No," Holly said softly. "Sit down, Kent."

"I'm not going to keep talking about it, Holly. I've said all I have to say. I am sorry I couldn't save Robert or my friends. I have to live with that, and it's hard enough without you shoving it in my face every time I turn around!" He sighed. "I don't even know why I stuck around here anymore. You all have a good night." He stepped toward the door to leave.

"It may happen again, Kent. But this time, it will be her they're after," Wolfgang said with a slight wave at Holly.

"What do you mean?" Kent asked, turning around.

"Have a seat. I wasn't accusing you of anything. I do not doubt that all of us would have done the same thing you did in those circumstances."

Kent sat slowly, his eyes going to Holly. "What's going on, Holly?"

Wolfgang answered, "Miss Holly has learned that the sheriff was here that night. The evidence is convincingly so. That said, the sheriff hasn't been able to arrest a single member of the sheep shooters that are responsible...."

"Of course not; they are his friends," Kent said impatiently.

"Yes," Wolfgang replied slowly. "Well, Miss Holly threatened the sheriff that she would call in the Pinkerton Detective Agency and threatened to make a large financial reward for each name of every man that wore a hood that night. The financial reward was quite substantial, and no one in this town looks like they couldn't use that money. You probably know better than anyone how that might rile up the sheep shooters."

Kent lowered his head, rubbed his forehead, and then raised it to ask Holly, "You told the sheriff that?" He was dumbfounded by how naive she could be sometimes.

Holly twisted her lips with a slight wrinkling of her nose before answering. "I saw that piano music box that Robert had given to me in Laura Whitehead's room. It was given to her by Sheriff Emmerson the day after my house was burned down. Sheriff Emmerson gifted it to her."

"So you threatened him?"

She wrinkled her nose hesitantly. "Yes, I did. But I went back inside and apologized."

"Good. The last thing you want to do is make more enemies, Holly," Kent said.

"Yes," Wolfgang agreed. "But the threat is still out there. My fear is that group may not risk her bringing in outside forces or posting a reward to expose them."

"These are all the guards you have?" Kent asked, motioning toward the three men.

Wolfgang answered as Holly nodded slowly. "Ross, Alessandro, and I are former New York City policemen. We are experienced lawmen."

Kent grinned lightly. "I'm sure you are, but this isn't

New York City. Did you wire the Pinkertons or the marshal's office?"

"I asked Matt to come here."

Kent sighed. "Good." He looked at Wolfgang. "I'm sure you three are great policemen and tough men, but as you can see, this isn't a city. This is a different breed of people you're dealing with, and you'll be wiped off the face of the earth if they decide to come here." Kent leaned forward to speak sincerely. "Holly, you don't ever have to trust me again, but I could not live with myself if something happened to you. Please go back to Boston or New York for your own good."

Holly shook her head. "No. I'm building a woolen mill in Robert's memory. This is my home now, and I'm staying."

"You have three homes back east and could build a new one just like this anywhere. The people don't like you being here, Holly."

"They will eventually."

"No, they won't. You're a threat to everything these folks live for. Sheep are despised around here. Why is this place so important to you anyway? If I remember right, you don't care anything about sheep."

Holly closed her eyes. "It's Robert's legacy, Kent. This is all he wanted."

"Robert's dead. He'll never know if the woolen mill is built or not."

"But I will. I need to finish it for him. It was his dream."

Wolfgang said, "Kent, we invited you here to offer your old job back. Understand that I'm the boss, and what I say goes. That's the way it is, period. If you think you can get along with us, you're welcome to join us as part of Miss Holly's security detail."

Kent raised his brow. "I can agree to that. I'm willing to die for this lady. So, yes, I'm in."

"Good," Wolfgang said. "That said, there's one last point to make. I understand you have some strong feelings for Miss Holly. Keep those to yourself. She does not share them. You'll be an employee, and that's all. Agreed?"

Kent nodded in agreement. "I understand."

CHAPTER SEVENTEEN

IT WAS MID-OCTOBER, AND THE STARS AND MOON illuminated the darkness without a cloud in sight. As stunning as the stars might have been, it was too cold to enjoy them. Instead, Jesse Helms and Colin Kennedy threw more wood on the fire to create a larger fire than they usually would have to help keep them warm. A lone coyote yipped across the valley, not too far away. It was a comforting sound to hear as the silence was only broken up by the crackling of the fire and continuation of rambling stories of Colin's childhood, which Jesse didn't have much interest in hearing.

Rusty Wells and Byron Krall were staying in town, trying to make friends with some of the local cowhands who worked on the Long T Ranch. Jesse and Colin would have liked to join them in the saloon, but Jesse couldn't take a chance of being recognized. Colin looked too much like the menacing outlaw that he was, and with absolutely no experience with cattle, he would make a fool of himself and ruin everything. Colin was more useful in camp and staying out of sight with Jesse.

There was no one with a more important job to do right now than the one given to Tim. Jesse's plan was simple enough. He asked Tim to beg for a job at the hardware store and befriend Laura. When the opportunity arises, ask her to go for a ride and bring her to the camp. Jesse was thrilled to learn that Tim had gotten a job there and would be living in the hardware store's supply room. It was Tim's second night there, but Jesse was already growing impatient. It was getting too cold, and finding enough firewood on the ground to keep the fire burning was a growing problem. Waiting patiently and being cold were always two of Jesse's weaknesses. So was listening to a man's stories that had nothing to do with anything being told over and over again.

"Will you shut up for a while?" Jesse snapped as he placed his cold hands closer to the fire. "You told me that story the second day we met. I know all about this old flame of yours and how she broke your heart. You told me three or four times now."

"Have I? Hmm," Colin said. He was wrapped in a blanket, leaning against his saddle next to the fire. "Well, that was the only time I was ever in love, I guess. I really like your cousin Jannie. It was nice meeting her. She's fun," he paused, looking out into the darkness, thinking about something else to talk about. "Tim is still young enough, you know. He might just be swooned by this girl if she's fetching."

Jesse tilted his head, considering it. "From what I remember, she's pretty."

"Why do you want the kid if you're not going to raise it? If you don't mind me saying so, all this seems pointless if you don't really want the kid. I don't think this plan of yours is a good idea to begin with. So, why do it?"

"I want the kid for Aunt Mattie. I feel bad for my aunt. She's a great woman. She can be a bit gruff and to the point, but her heart is gold. She raised eight kids mostly by herself, and now they're all grown and gone, for the most part. Three of her kids are dead. She needs fresh blood to keep that fire in her soul. A purpose for living, that's what the baby represents to her." He kicked a chunk of wood into the burning coals with the toe of his boot. "Besides, Aunt Mattie said that's probably the only kid I'll ever have. She's right; it's a Helms baby and needs to grow up with family."

"What about the mother once the baby is born? Don't you think she'll go to the nearest law?"

"No. Aunt Mattie will keep her there to feed the kid, I imagine. She will chain her to the floor so she can't leave if need be. My cousin Alan's wife was chained to the floor for a short time after he was sent to prison. She eventually escaped, but it took a few years."

Colin gave a slight chuckle. "That's quite a family you have. And then what? Do you think this girl will just become part of the family?"

Jesse shifted on the ground to get more comfortable. He yawned. "Listen, I don't really care about the girl or what happens to her. The only thing I care about is getting that baby for Aunt Mattie. She's my second mom, and it's the least I can do for her if she thinks that will keep her heart pumping. It's my kid and that's all I care about. I guess I have as much right to it as she does."

"I wouldn't say that's true. She's the child's mother," Colin said and resigned to keep the remainder of his thoughts to himself as he leaned back to watch the flames.

He hoped he could get a better night's sleep once the flames consumed what wood they had left. The bitter chill would penetrate his blankets once again and make for another hard night of trying to sleep. A vague movement in the darkness caught his attention; he leaned forward to squint into the darkness to see more clearly.

"What is it?" Jesse asked, following Colin's eyes. He could barely make out two riders approaching their fire. "Is that Rusty and Byron?"

"No. The town's the other direction."

A moment later, an unknown voice called out, "Hello there. Do you mind if we approach? We're peaceful."

Caught off guard, Jesse answered, "As long as you're peaceful." His gun belt was just out of reach, and his rifle was beside his bedroll a short distance away. His heart began beating quicker, knowing he was in danger of being recognized as a former Blackburn Marshal or worse, as the man who attacked two of the town's youths.

"I don't smell any sheep," the voice responded from the darkness. "You must not be shepherds." Two men on horseback rode into the firelight. Both men had unbuttoned their coats and had their gun belts exposed. The older one who had done the talking Jesse recognized as the town sheriff, Pat Emmerson. His badge was pinned to his heavy flannel shirt under his coat and glimmered in the firelight. The younger man at his side did not wear a badge but was clearly a cattleman who worked on a ranch. He carried his rifle across his saddle as they approached the fire.

A cold chill slowly crept up Jesse's spine upon recognizing the sheriff. He could scramble for his revolver three feet out of reach or stay calm and friendly. "I wouldn't mind shooting some sheep, but that's about as close as I like to get to them," Jesse said with a friendly nod. He knew the citizens of Hollister did not welcome sheep. He continued before Colin could speak. "My name's John Upshaw, and this is my pal Mark Brown. We're just passing through on our way north."

"North?" the sheriff questioned. "To the mining camp about seven miles up the Deluth Gorge, by chance?"

"No," Jesse said, not risking the chance of falling into a trap. "We're hoping to make it to a little town called Loveland before the snow gets too deep."

"It's a little late in the year for that. The snow's already fallen up there. You'd be better off going the long way around. But if you think it's cold now, wait until you get up into them mountains."

"I know it's going to be a hard and cold trip. But my brother lives there. I haven't seen him in a while. Maybe you know him, Pete Upshaw?"

"No. I don't know him. You look familiar, though. Where are you two from?" the sheriff asked.

"We're from the Nevada way," Jesse answered, trying to think quickly. He could see the sheriff's eyes narrow as he tried to piece together where he knew Jesse from. "A place called Robin's Roost. It's a mining camp."

"Well, I'm Pat Emmerson, the sheriff of Hollister, a few miles that way. This gentleman beside me is Don Olson. His family owns the Olson-Westfall Ranch, which you gentlemen are camped on..."

"We had no idea. We'll be leaving in the morning if you can permit us to do that," Jesse said.

Don nodded. "That's fine."

"Gentlemen, have a good night." Sheriff Emmerson started to turn his horse but paused. He turned back to Jesse. "Are you sure we haven't met?"

"I'm pretty sure about that," Jesse said. "We've never been here before, Sheriff."

Pat slowly grinned, half-humored. "You've never been here before but you think you can find Loveland by crossing these mountains in the winter? We'll find you frozen solid in the spring. You better go south and stick to the main roads. It will add a hundred miles to your trip, but at least you might get there without freezing to death. I don't think you understand how high these mountains are or how cold it gets up there."

"That's good advice. We'll do that. Thank you," Jesse said.

Sheriff Emmerson jabbed a pointed finger at Jesse. "I know I've seen you before or someone who looks a lot like you."

Jesse shrugged. "My brother probably comes through here sometimes. We're twins, you know. He's the one who told us to come this way."

"That might explain it," the sheriff reasoned.

Without warning, Colin jerked his revolver from under the blanket, aimed, and fired at Don Olson, hitting him just below the collarbone. Don's horse reared up in fright as Don's rifle slipped from his hand and fell to the ground. He remained in the saddle as the spooked horse toe hopped away from the fire. Colin aimed at Don and fired a second time, hitting him in the lower back just above his left kidney. Don arched back and fell out of the saddle.

Sheriff Emmerson had turned his horse and given it a series of sharp kicks to escape. Colin turned his gun toward the sheriff and fired three quick shots, missing all three. He dropped his revolver and quickly scrambled forward to grab the rifle while Jesse quickly fired all six shots in the cylinder of his revolver toward the figure riding away in the darkness.

Colin aimed the rifle and fired once. The sheriff's horse collapsed to the ground. The sound of Pat Emmerson cursing and Don Olson's groaning in agony were the only sounds as silence quickly filled the valley.

Jesse emptied his spent cartridges and reloaded the cylinder. He cast a hardened glare at Colin. "They were leaving!"

"He recognized you," Colin said with a calm voice.

"He had no idea who I was!" Jesse shouted.

Colin retorted sharply, "But he might have figured it out when he went home! He's still alive if you want to let him go. I'll finish the other one off though. His horse is running home, so we better make this quick and leave. I'm not going to get myself hung because of your past crimes or your new plan."

Jesse cursed and walked into the darkness, carrying his gun in his hand.

Breathing heavily and sweating from exertion, Sheriff Emmerson tried to pull his left leg out from under the dead horse. His foot was still in the stirrup, and chances were his lower leg was broken. The pain was terrible, but the fear of being killed was overwhelming, comparatively. He struggled to pull himself free, but there was no chance of it. He could see one of the two men walking toward him, and the panic to free himself grew more desperate. He no longer had his revolver, or he would have killed the man that neared him. He had pulled his revolver while riding away and dropped it when his horse collapsed. He had no idea where his gun was. His rifle was in the sheath, but he could not sit up enough to grab the stock. He rested against the cold grass and felt a sob choke his throat when he heard the man's boots stop only a few feet away.

"Go ahead and kill me," he said, resigned to die.

"Do you know who I am?" Jesse asked.

Sheriff Emmerson lifted his head to look at Jesse. After a moment, he asked, "We've met?"

Jesse nodded slowly. "I'm Jesse Helms. Maybe it's better this way because I don't need you chasing after us."

The sound of Colin's revolver firing echoed in the valley; it put an end to Don Olson's groans. Colin shouted, "Hurry up, we need to go."

Pat Emmerson gasped while holding his hands out protectively. "My leg's broken. I'm not going anywhere. Listen, I'll say I had to shoot Don. I swear, no one will ever know I even saw you. Rob the bank or whatever you want. I swear I'll look the other way and never say a word. If you let me live, I'll keep my mouth shut. I swear it! I'll even pay you for letting me live."

"What if I take the girl that's carrying my baby? Same deal?" Jesse asked.

"Take her and go! I swear, you'll never hear me say a word. I'll make it look like she drowned in the lake. No one will ever know."

"I'm sure you would, but that's not a chance I can take." Jesse lifted his revolver just enough to aim at the sheriff's head. "You should have left us alone." He pulled the hammer back until it clicked.

"You don't have to do this. Let me live, and I...I promise won't I say a word!"

Jesse pulled the trigger, killing Pat Emmerson with a bullet through his head. The shot echoed through the valley. "You won't say a word now either."

Back at the fire, Jesse shouted, "I wanted this to go

quietly like ghosts in the night so no one would know we were here! Now, we're going to have to take her in the middle of the night and probably kill her family. That wasn't the plan, Colin!"

Colin was rolling up his blankets in his bedroll. "We didn't have a plan. They just showed up. You can't plan for surprises. You have to adjust to the circumstances. The sheriff recognized you. We had no choice."

"He had no idea who I was," Jesse seethed.

"Well, either will the people who find him. We have to adjust and move on. I think you should leave the girl alone, but if you're bound and determined to get her, let's go do it and go home."

CHAPTER EIGHTEEN

TIM HAZELTON WAS SENT TO THE WHITEHEAD family with devious intentions. However, working in the hardware store with the scent of coffee on the woodstove and linseed oil was reminiscent of his grandfather's store. The sound of clanging iron, the weighing of nails on the scale, and customer verbiage struck a forgotten cord of his heartstrings that longed for home. Home no longer existed as far as that word's definition went, but being in a hardware store was as close to home as he could be. It felt right, like he belonged there.

Mr. and Mrs. Whitehead had accepted him into their home, perhaps a little skeptical at first, but their warmth, fairness and honest friendship were as genuine as his grandparents were. Tim found a warmth and comfort that he had been missing in his life since his grandfather passed away. For the first time in a long time, he felt at home with the Whitehead family, even though it was only his second night there. It surprised him because he had never thought people could be so kind and welcoming as Mitch and Helen were.

It was getting late, but Tim's stomach grumbled when he thought of getting another piece of apple pie. He ascended the stairway behind the store's counter to the Whitehead's home. He was surprised to see the dining room lit brightly, and Laura sitting at the dining table eating a piece of pie.

It was his first time entering the Whitehead's home after everyone went to bed, and getting caught by Laura made him feel uneasy. "Your mother said I could get some food after they went to bed if I ever wanted to," he explained awkwardly.

Laura stared at him expressionless as she chewed her food and swallowed it. "The pie's good."

"That's what I came up for, actually. I wouldn't do so if I weren't invited," Tim reaffirmed.

"That's good to know," she said before taking another bite.

"Mind if I join you? Or should I take this back downstairs?" She motioned across the table to a chair. Tim sat and asked, "You couldn't sleep?"

"I wish I could. It's hard to sleep when your back aches. Tomorrow I'm going to Miss Fairchild's house to pick out a new bed. She wants to buy me a new one."

"You mean that tall blonde lady that was here today? I overheard her talking to your parents."

"I've never been to her house before, so I'm excited."

"Where does she live?"

"In the big house on the far side of the lake. She owns most of the land around the lake. It was a pretty big deal around here when her husband bought that land. The folks here were furious, and many still are. She's the one having the canal and mill built outside of town. That big camp of workers out there she is paying for."

"I haven't seen it or know where the lake is. Is she rich?" he questioned.

"I'd guess so. Holly's nice though."

Tim said, "I heard her mention that her husband died. She sure is a pretty lady. Are all the single men around here trying to court her?"

Laura shrugged. "I don't know. I'll ask her. I do know the ranchers don't like her and that's all that is around here."

Tim swallowed. "You look like her. I mean your hair, eyes, and things," he added awkwardly.

Laura's lips curved upward. "Thank you, but Holly's much prettier than me."

"Not really. How old are you?"

"Fifteen. How old are you?"

"I just turned twenty-one in June. Was that Aaron fellow who came over to see you, your beau?"

"No," Laura answered with a slight furrowing of her brow. "I don't have one. I thought I did, but I just found out that he isn't who I thought he was." She exhaled irritably through her nose.

A pang of guilt for his own deception swirled through Tim's chest. "I can understand that."

"I'm sure you're not as nice as you seem either," Laura said bluntly.

"Why would you say that?" he questioned. He swallowed nervously, fearing she somehow knew there was a darker motive for his being there.

She answered with a touch of fire in her eyes, "Because I thought I knew Jake, but I don't." Her eyes watered heavily as she breathed in emotionally. "I have nothing more to say to him. I'm beginning to understand why Christine's mother killed herself."

"Who?"

"Never mind. It's not important." She sniffled, forcing her tears away as best as she could. "Jake's lying about me."

"About?"

She shot a bitter glance at Tim. "That's none of your business!" She stood to take her plate to the counter. "Be sure to put your dish in the wash bucket. Good night."

"Good night. I'm sorry if I upset you."

"It doesn't matter," she said as she walked toward her room.

Tim finished his piece of pie and went downstairs to the back, where the storeroom was. Mitch and Helen had hung canvas tarps from the ceiling to give him a small corner where a cot and a dresser were set up. He had a lantern for light and was given a key to the back door lock so he could come and go at will and lock the door behind him. There were rules he had to follow, but none were more important than he could not have any guests and had to lock the door if he left. There was no drinking allowed, and although they were not going to make him go to church, Tim was invited to join them. The rules were reasonable and easy to follow, and there was a large part of him that wished his reason for being there was as sincere as he had pretended it to be.

He knew what had happened to Laura and Jake. Jesse had talked about it on several occasions with a sense of victorious pride. In fact, Tim probably knew more details about what happened than anyone else did, including who the father of Laura's baby was. Now that he had met Laura, talked with her, and witnessed the sadness and pain in her eyes, he could feel the weight of knowing more than he could say. What Jesse had done wasn't right and what Jesse planned to do was even worse. Tim liked the Whitehead family and the more he got to know Laura, the more empathy he had for her.

His maternal grandparents raised Tim to be honest and treat everyone the way he wanted to be treated. To honor a handshake and keep his word as a man of integrity. Now, lying on a cot in the storeroom of a wonderful family's hardware store, Tim wondered how his integrity had fallen so quickly into thievery, robbing stagecoaches, and lying. It didn't start that way, of course. After his grandfather passed away and his grandmother moved out of state, Tim had lost all he had known except memories of a happy home.

It began that one night, while trying to drink his sorrows away and saw his distant older cousin on his father's side of the family. Colin Kennedy had an infamous reputation as a local outlaw with a two-year stint in prison behind him and a number of dead men as well. Tim's grandmother said on a few occasions that she had no idea how Colin could be related to Tim's father, who was a fine Baptist minister. Tim was five years old when his parents were murdered by outlaws who were very much like the ones he rode with now.

Tim was an only child and had no other family that lived locally except Colin Kennedy. Colin introduced him to Jesse Helms and Tim found himself wearing a gun belt and learning how to use his new Smith and Wesson .38 caliber revolver. He had pointed it at people as they robbed stage-coaches, but he had never fired it at anyone.

Tim had slipped a long way from his Christian upbringing into Colin's ways, and he knew how disappointed his grandparents would be in him. His father, Reverend Eugene Hazelton, had kept a detailed journal and had written his hopes for Tim, or as he wrote, *Little Timmy* would follow in his footsteps into the ministry and achieve far greater things than the reverend ever did. Those written words had convinced his grandmother that Tim would go into the ministry, but he never felt called to it. He had no interest in ministry, but he believed in the Lord and went to church regularly. However, after his grandfather passed away, he thought the hardware store would be passed on to him. That's what his grandfather always told him, but when the store was not passed down to him, he felt betrayed, lied to, and lost when his grandmother sold it along with the house. He had nothing or anyone left to cling to. He had prayed so hard, and it had led to nothing. Discouraged and angry, he took up drinking and one day, Colin came into his life. Now, he was supposed to win a family's trust and betray them in the most heinous of ways and deliver Laura to the father of her unwanted baby. It would be a life of slavery until she was no longer needed, and then, as a rabid dog owner would do, she'd be put down.

It was an assignment that Tim did not want to do. He knew all too well that he couldn't tell Jesse Helms no. Colin was highly efficient with his gun and unafraid of anyone, but even Colin was reluctant to say no to Jesse. Tim was given a mission to devise a plan to deliver Laura to Jesse, but no plan was forming. The only thing forming in his mind was what a terrible person he had become. Shame filled him, knowing he was deceiving a family that was treating him like one of their own. Praying with the Whitehead family at meals and listening to Helen talk about the Lord was resurrecting something inside him that was filling the emptiness that he hadn't been able to fill since he walked away from the Lord.

He did not get onto his knees or bow his head; his eyes remained open as he lay on his cot staring at the ceiling, knowing directly above him was Mitch and Helen White-head's bedroom.

"Jesus," he prayed quietly, "it's been a long time since I've spoken with you. I don't even know if you can hear me anymore; it's been so long. I'm in trouble, Lord. I don't want to do what I have to do. If I don't do it, I'm a dead man. If I do, I don't think I could ever forgive myself, even if I got away with it. I don't know if you're willing to help me or not..." He gasped as the air left his lungs emotionally. His eyes burned with moisture. "I'm scared. I don't know if you are here or listening. I'm guilty of doing everything I was told never to do. I've sinned, Lord, and I ask you to forgive me if you can." His eyes watered heavily. "I like it here. I don't want to leave. I don't want to hurt this family. Please, Lord, give me a way out."

"Tim?" Laura's voice questioned as she came into the storage room carrying a lantern. "Are you sleeping?"

He wiped his eyes and sat up on his cot, wiping his eyes a second time. "No." He stood and stepped through the canvas wall of his makeshift room to speak to her. "What are you doing down here?"

"I wanted to apologize for being rude. Jake and I were supposed to get married next year. We were going to elope." Her eyes watered as she paused to swallow emotionally. "Aaron told me last night that Jake's saying I invited those men to...rape me." She swallowed. "He blames me for what happened. Like I wanted them to do it."

"That's not true though. Do you believe him?" Tim questioned gently.

"Who?"

"The fella who told you that."

"Aaron has no reason to lie."

"Unless he wants to court you. If I loved a lady enough to want to marry her and something like that happened to us, I would never blame her. It just seems the opposite of what love is supposed to be."

"They cut Jake's face up. I hear he's got a big scar now that he blames me for."

"Then he's a fool. I'd be knocking on your door every day, even with a scarred-up face. That should have drawn you two closer together, not torn you apart. That's just my opinion, but I'm not wearing his boots or yours."

"Jake can't knock on my door; my parents won't let him. And I can't go anywhere alone anymore."

"I'm sorry to hear that. You know, I'd ask him if he said what Aaron told you. I just don't see a reason why he would, but I can see Aaron having a motivation to say that."

Laura hesitated in thought. "If I wrote Jake a letter, could you find a way to take it to him for me?"

Tim shrugged. "Well, just as long as your parents don't find out, I can. I like it here, and I don't want to get kicked out into the cold."

"I won't say a word. I promise. Thank you, Tim. I think I'll go write him a letter."

"You do that. I'll see you in the morning."

―――――

JESSE HELMS COULD SEE a faint light in the small window of the storage room and peeked inside to see Laura talking with Tim. "There she is," Jesse quietly said with a slight smirk. "Prettier than I remember."

"Let me have a gander," Colin said, looking through the window. His brow lowered, and he shook his head. "She's just a kid, Jesse."

"Yeah, well, she's carrying my baby."

Colin watched his cousin talking to her for a moment. "She's too young for Tim too, but the young buck's feeling his oats, isn't he?" He chuckled.

"Not with my girl, he isn't," Jesse said with a narrowing of his eyes. "My baby is inside of her if you can believe that?" he questioned in wonder as he gazed at her. "I never wanted to get married, but maybe now I do. I could be a father to a few screaming brats with her, I think."

Colin scoffed with disgust. "Now you're sounding like a proud father," he said sarcastically. "Knock on the door and ask her to marry you. I'd like to see what happens."

Jesse's lips lifted upward. "My money says she'd say no. But that doesn't mean we can't have a few more brats once she's at my aunt's house. I'll keep her pregnant and in the kitchen."

Colin shook his head with distaste. "Like your own personal slave, huh?"

Jesse nodded slowly before pulling his head out of the window when she turned around to leave. "Dang, she's prettier than I remember." He watched her leave the storeroom and knocked gently on the window. It took a few knocks to get Tim's attention. He motioned toward the back door.

Quietly, Tim opened the door and tried to step outside

to keep them from entering the store. He was pushed inside by Jesse. "We can't be seen outside."

Tim motioned toward the ceiling. He whispered, "Mr. and Mrs. Whitehead's bedroom is right up there. Shh. What are you doing here? You can't be here. Laura just went upstairs." He looked nervously behind him to verify she wasn't in the storeroom.

Jesse spoke softly. "Listen, there's been a change of plans. We need to speed things up. We had to kill the sheriff and another man tonight. Pack your gear. We'll go upstairs and kill her parents and grab her. Is there any of that stuff in the store that makes people pass out?" Jesse asked. "They'll be searching for us tomorrow, so we need to get home tonight."

"Wait. Wait. Wait, what?" Tim asked louder than he intended to. He quickly realized he was in deeper trouble than he ever wanted to be in.

"You heard me. Listen, we're going to go upstairs. I need you to point out her parents' bedroom. Colin and I will use our knives to kill them quietly while you keep the girl quiet. Use your gun to knock her unconscious if you don't have...ether. That's what it's called."

"Wait, wait, wait," Tim said as his mind spun with the suddenness of Jesse's plan. In a panic, he spat out, "You don't need to kill anyone. She's going to the rich woman's house tomorrow by herself. That rich woman is sending her carriage for Laura at noon. You know where she'll be."

Jesse grimaced. "What rich woman?"

"I like the sound of a rich woman," Colin quipped. "We might ride out of here with some money after all."

"Tall, blonde hair, I forget her name, but she's apparently very rich. The one that lives by the lake." Tim's mind spun a thousand revolutions a minute, trying to save the family.

"Holly Fairchild?" Jesse asked.

"Yes! That's her name."

"Holly's back?"

"I guess. She's sending her carriage to pick Laura up tomorrow at noon. You don't have to kill Mr. and Mrs. Whitehead. There's no reason to. You can stop her carriage just like we did, stagecoaches."

Colin asked Jesse, "Is that the woman you told me about who married your old boss? The old rich man who brought sheep here?"

Jesse nodded. "It is. Noon, huh?" he asked Tim.

"Yes."

"How many guards does she have?"

"I only saw two," he said with the hope of convincing Jesse that he didn't need to kill the Whiteheads.

Jesse thought quietly while rubbing his goatee for a moment. "Why is she going to Holly's house?"

"I don't know, to visit."

"Are her parents going?"

"No. She'll be alone."

Colin suggested, "We could commandeer her coach and hide out at the rich woman's house for a while. Maybe get some money for the rest of us while you're convincing that young lady that you want to be a loving father. That would help make this venture profitable."

"This isn't about making a profit; it's about assuring I can keep my kid," Jesse answered, sounding annoyed.

"Kid?" Colin questioned. "You don't care anything about that kid."

"Well, now I do."

"You can fawn all over that kiddo as far as I'm

concerned. In fact, I think you should, it might change your life. But if that woman's rich, then she can afford to give us some money," Colin said. "Time is money, and none of us are getting paid to put our lives on the line for you. We want to help, but you're asking a lot from Rusty, Byron, me, and especially young Tim for nothing. We're helping you; why not help us out, too?"

Jesse twisted his lips and spat on the floor. "Too risky. I know she has guards protecting her. Probably a lot of them. We'll come back to Holly's at another time. Colin, go fetch a drink and tell Rusty to meet us in the alley so we can talk about tomorrow. This may work better yet."

CHAPTER NINETEEN

MORTON SPERRY AND TRUET DAVIS SAT IN THEIR saddles outside of Matt's house, waiting. They had saddled Matt's horse and brought it with them so they could leave early for Hollister. However, Matt took a little bit longer to say goodbye to his wife than Morton had. He shook his head impatiently as he watched Matt kissing Christine on the front steps for the fourth time. "I wish I could have held my wife like that before leaving her. I guess it pays to be the boss man, doesn't it?" Morton Sperry was the former outlaw leader of the Sperryy-Helms Gang. He was of average height, broad-shouldered and stocky. He kept his brown hair short and wore a thick goatee about an inch long. His green eyes and rough exterior were intimidating, but his reputation as a cold-blooded killer still followed him even though he had changed his life around.

Truet answered loud enough for Matt to hear. "Mort, you should know by now that when it comes to Matt, you're supposed to do what he says and not question what he does. He told us to hurry with the horses because we're in a hurry. You know that."

"I don't think two horses could pull them apart. For crying out loud, Matt, there are school kids walking by," Morton griped.

Matt laughed lightly as he broke the kiss with Christine. He glanced back at his friends. "One minute, fellas."

"It's been a few," Morton chided.

Truet kicked a leg up over the saddle horn and leaned back, tipped his hat over his eyes, and placed his hands behind his head and yawned. "As long as there's some sunlight left in the day, I suppose we have time to hurry." He closed his eyes to get a moment's rest. He lowered his voice. "However, if that were you, Morton, Matt would grab you by the hair and drag you to your horse."

"There wouldn't be time for me to kiss my wife. Matt did say we were in a hurry, didn't he?"

Truet reached over and tapped Morton's arm. "He did, but I think I could have slept in for another half hour. I'm beginning to wonder if we'll get to Hollister before dark, or should we wait until tomorrow?"

"Do you think they'll be done with that goodbye kiss by then?" Morton questioned.

Christine laughed with a reddened face.

"The doctor didn't sew lips together. I was beginning to wonder about that," Truet quipped.

Matt winked at his bride. "All right, fellas, I'm coming." He paused as he looked into Christine's eyes. "I'll be back in few days."

Christine did not want to let him go. "I wish I knew what was going on at Holly's. It makes me uneasy not knowing what kind of mess Holly has gotten herself into now. Promise me that you'll be okay." Christine's concern filled her expression.

"I'll be fine. I have those two looking out for me."

"And you wonder why I'm worried," she teased. "I love you, Matt." Her eyes watered. She despised saying goodbye when he had to leave town.

"I love you, Christine," he said and kissed her again.

"Oh, here we go again," Morton complained to Truet.

"Yeah. Wake me up when it's time to leave," Truet replied with a yawn.

Christine broke the kiss. "That place is making me hate sheep. Promise me you'll come home in one piece, Matt."

"I'll do my best." He turned and stepped to his horse and into the saddle. He put on his old misshaped Stetson that Christine wished he'd thrown away when she bought him a new one. Matt looked at his two deputies. "Are you two ready to go? We're in a hurry and have a long ride ahead."

"Mind if we swing by my house? I suddenly feel like I didn't do a satisfactory job kissing Audrey goodbye."

"I'm sorry, Morton," Matt said as they rode away from the house. "We don't have time for that."

Christine stood on the steps and watched the three men ride around the corner, out of sight. "Lord, Jesus, please put your protective hand over those men."

———

JAKE THOMAS WAS NERVOUS. His hands shook while he buttoned his shirt before looking in the mirror. His hair was combed, his face shaved, and he brushed his teeth with a bit of salt and rinsed his mouth with salt water. He was torn between the excitement and fear of seeing Laura for the first time since their nightmare in the church cellar. He was worried that Laura would shutter with disgust when she saw his scar, and at the same time, he had no doubt that he was unprepared to see her with a baby in her belly. His breathing felt restricted as his anxiety grew the closer the time came for him to leave the ranch and ride to the Fairchild Estate.

"Mother, how do I look?" he asked as he walked into the family room.

Sasha smiled proudly. "You look very handsome, son. You look nervous though."

"I am. I'm a little afraid she won't like what she sees." He touched the scar on his cheek.

"Jake, if Laura's love is so superficial that a scar scares her away, then you will be better off without her. We all grow old and lose our external beauty, but inside here,"— she touched her breast with her crippled hand—"that's where the true beauty in people lies. If she does not see that in you, then you're not losing the love of your life. You're saving yourself from a life of heartache."

"I know. Mother, I would marry her whether she's pregnant or not. What I'm afraid of,"—he swallowed nervously —"is Aaron told me that she blames me for what happened. She apparently thinks I'm a coward for not stopping those men," he said as water misted his eyes. He continued to change the subject. "Aaron also said they're engaged, but Ray, their ranch hand, told Bode that wasn't true. I don't know what to think anymore."

Sasha spoke with her fragile voice. "Claire Archibald is not a reliable source, and I wouldn't say Aaron is either. If he lies about one thing, he will lie about another. I wouldn't put a lot of stock into anything Aaron has told you." She hesitated with a slight frown. "What concerns me is how you will react when you see her carrying another man's baby. That news is true, Jacob. And I also heard she had been beaten up severely that night and now is missing a front tooth. I'm sure she will feel very much the way you do. I hear she doesn't smile like she used to."

Jake sat down in his father's chair. "That night was such a nightmare. I remember her bleeding and screaming, crying and all of that," he said as his voice broke into a higher pitch. He paused to get control of his emotions. "I didn't know she was missing a tooth. That breaks my heart." He exhaled heavily. "I should be the father of her child, not one of them."

Sasha gazed compassionately at her son. "Yes, you should be. But *should be's* are never promised and quite often are just a part of life. I *should be* able to hold a frying pan, but I can not. Your sister *should be* at college getting an education like she wants, but she is not. Bode *should be* taking an interest in sheep so he can start courting Holly Fairchild, but..." She hesitated and smiled. "I'm working on that. I do like her."

Jake smiled at his mother's unexpected wit. "He should be."

"Jake, *should be's* are only *should be's*. They are not always what we get in life. So please remember to always take what the Lord Almighty has given you and be grateful for it. You get to see Laura today without her parents knowing. This could be a wonderful day for you if you are honest with her. Leave nothing in here." She patted her breast. "Be courageous enough to tell her how you feel, share your fears, and be open and honest with her. If you do that, she will do the same. This day could be one of the greatest days of your life." She raised her brow. "I pray so anyway. You've been hiding away from everyone for so long and deep in your sorrow that I would like to see my son smiling again. And Laura's mother wants the same for her, I am sure."

Gunther Thomas stepped inside the house, speaking urgently to Bode, who followed him. "Grab my new Remington rifle. I'll tell Ma what's happening." He walked into the family room. "Jake, I'm glad you're here. Change your clothes and dress warm. Sheriff Emmerson and Don Olson were killed on the Olson's ranch. Someone was camped there and shot them. We're forming a posse to track the murderers down."

"Oh, no!" Sasha exclaimed. "How are Mick and Ellie doing?" she asked of Don's parents.

"Not well, sweetheart. Mick's a mess and I haven't seen Ellie. But we are going to find those killers."

"Were there any witnesses?" she asked.

"No. Let's go, Jake, come on!" Gunther growled impatiently. He was in his midsixties, average height with broad shoulders and heavier than most men, being a bit obese. He had black hair that refused to gray and small, steely brown eyes on his broad face that was kept cleanly shaven. Gunther's voice was deep, powerful, and domineering as he repeated, "Jake, get moving."

"I'm going to see Laura," he replied sheepishly. His father was a fair man, but it wasn't wise to disobey him.

"That can wait—"

"No," Sasha interrupted quickly, "it can't wait. You have enough men to search. Our son has something he must do for himself. It's important to him, Gunther."

Gunther paused and gazed at his wife. He was a bear of a man, big, powerful, and loud, but when it came to being overpowered, his disabled wife, with her fragile voice and hunched back, was the one person he could not stand up to. "All right. Jake…" He nodded with understanding. "I hope it goes well." He gave his wife a quick kiss. "We have to go. I'm leaving a couple of hands here at the house to keep you and Darra safe, but the rest are coming with us."

Bode Thomas entered the room. "Mother, I love you and we'll be back." He gave her a quick kiss on the cheek. He looked at Jake. "Little brother, go win your woman back," he said with a wink.

Sasha touched Bode's wrist to get his attention. "You should go with him and make sure Holly is okay. There are murderers out there and they might be attracted to her place."

Bode shook his head. "She has guards protecting her. She'll be fine."

"Yes, but she doesn't have you protecting her. That lady would make you a wonderful wife."

Bode laughed skeptically. "I'm a rancher, Mother. She would have no interest in a simple, uneducated, and uncivilized man like me. I have nothing to offer her. But I do have to go. Order me a bride from the paper if you want me to get married so bad."

"I will not!" she exclaimed adamantly.

Bode laughed as he walked out the door.

THERE WAS no lack of knowledge among the thirty or so men of the posse being led by Gunther Thomas and Phil Dawson. They were a rugged collection of cattlemen, farmers, and men from town, set on tracking the murderers of their two friends down and hanging them before the sun crossed the sky. They had gone to the Olson-Westfall Ranch, where the bodies of Sheriff Pat Emmerson and thirty-year-old Don Olson were found by Don's father,

Mick, that morning. It was clear that several men had camped there for a few days by the depth of ashes in the fire and a wide area of knocked-down grass. There were an estimated four or five horses tethered between two trees by the amount of manure, grazed grass, and tracks. There was nothing left of the camp except for empty cans of beans, human waste, and trails of knocked-down grass going toward town. The small valley they camped in was used for spring and summer grazing, and no one noticed the tres-passers on their land until Don saw the glare of a campfire and thought it might be shepherds with a flock of sheep on the other side of the hill. He told his parents that he was going to town to get the sheriff to speak to the shepherds to see if they were passing through or hired by Holly Fairchild before he roused the Hollister Sheep Shooters. Don's saddled horse had returned, but Don had never come home. There was no description of who the men were that they were looking for, but it had become clear that the murderers had come and gone to town several times. Gunther and Phil were convinced that the group of killers would be found in town or traveling the roads around Hollister.

Rusty Wells and Byron Krall had made themselves known in the saloons among the cowhands over the past three nights and had become the prime suspects once the trails leading to town were discovered. But the owner of the Hollister livery stable was able to verify that the two men had been sleeping in the livery loft for fifty cents a night. Rusty had told Jesse if they had to play the part of unemployed cowhands, then they ought to look like it to the locals. In truth, it was just a shorter distance to travel after a night of drinking and carousing with the painted ladies. Now that they had become suspects, Rusty thanked his lucky stars or lucky horseshoe or whatever that they had decided to sleep in the hay loft of the livery stable. If they had been going to a camp every night after leaving the saloon, they would already have nooses around their necks and dangling from a tree branch.

It was true they were riding out to the camp every day to chat with Jesse and to eat, but to anyone's knowledge that had seen them leave town, they were riding to a ranch seeking employment. The suspicion of them was quickly extinguished.

That fateful decision to sleep in the livery stable and spend their evenings in the saloon was an unexpected blessing as it was an extended hand of trust into the tight-knit circle of friends of the Hollister Cattle Association. They were still outsiders, but they all had the same goal and that was to find the killers and hang them.

Jesse Helms had a bold and dangerous plan that Rusty didn't think was wise at all, but it was Jesse's hide on the line and if Jesse and Colin were caught, at least Rusty and Byron could ride away and not look back. If Jesse succeeded in taking the girl and getting away with it, they'd meet Jesse and Colin in Natoma in a week or two without raising any suspicions. The safest place for Rusty and Byron to be was with the posse. If it came right down to it, Rusty and Byron both agreed they would be the first to kill Jesse and Colin to save their own lives.

As the posse searched the abandoned camp, Rusty suggested, "Whoever it was probably went north." He pointed a finger toward the towering snow-capped Wallala Mountains to direct the posse away from Jesse and Colin.

"What's your name again?" Gunther questioned him gruffly. He had met the two strangers when they came onto the Long T Ranch to ask about work and earlier when they were accused of being suspects, but he did not know who they were or where they came from.

"I'm Rusty, sir. You're Gunther Thomas, owner of the Long T Ranch and president of the Hollister Cattle Association. I met your boy Jake, wife, and pretty daughter the other day on their way to town before meeting you. You have a beautiful family, sir, if you don't mind me saying so."

Gunther licked his dry lips, ignoring the compliment. "You clearly have no idea what you're talking about. There's nothing north of here except fifty miles of the roughest and coldest mountains you've ever seen. They aren't going any further north. They came from the southwest, but they aren't rushing back south. They went to town. Alex," Gunther called to one of the men in the posse. "Anyone come into the saloon last night that seemed suspicious; strangers?"

Alex Bethard was a skilled horseman in his youth, but now that he was in his sixties and had broken more bones than most men could and still live, he drank his evenings away in the saloon to dull the aches and pains. He worked as a cook and barkeeper in the 1878 Saloon. "There was a stranger that came in kind of late. Long-haired, bearded man, ugly as sin, and wore a slinging gun. He had a few drinks and left. He didn't say a darn thing."

"He didn't give his name?"

"He didn't say anything. He just came in, ordered a couple of drinks, and left as quietly as he came in. I'd guess he was on the run. Never saw him before."

"I saw him. Yeah, he was rugged," Barry McCracken offered.

Rusty spoke. "I went out to the privy not long after he left the saloon. I saw him riding north."

Phil Dawson suggested to his friend, "Gunth, maybe we should scout around north of town. Those killers could be camped just about anywhere, even on one of our ranches." Phil owned the Dawson Lakes Ranch.

Rusty tapped Barry McCracken on the arm. "You know Barry, I had a bad feeling when I saw that guy riding north. It's almost like I knew he was bad news. And Alex is right; my impression of him was that he was a drifter, an outlaw. What about you, Byron?"

Byron grunted, "Hmm, mm."

"I suggest we go north and look for another camp," Rusty said to the others. "Let's find these murderers and string them up. It's the only reason that man would be going north."

"Amen," a few of the others agreed.

"I don't agree," Bode Thomas said. He hadn't said much of anything throughout the day, so when he spoke, the others took notice and listened. "They killed the sheriff and a local rancher. I don't think any half-witted idiot would stick around to risk hiding on another rancher's property. We all know that other than a few locals, the whole construction company's camp on the Fairchild Estate is full of strangers. I think we should ask them if they fired four or five friends recently or if a group that size asked about work. Whether these men are outlaws planning to rob our bank or drifters searching for employment, it might be wise to check out Holly Fairchild's property and let her know there are murderers around. If these men are looking for easy money, seeing her place would be a strong temptation."

"They can burn her place down as far as I'm concerned," Phil Dawson said unapologetically with a bitter toss of his hand.

A cowboy named Joe Bookman agreed, "Yeah, she's going to drain our lake. I have no compassion for her. I say let's let them kill her before we hang them."

"I agree," another one of the cowhands said.

"It would get rid of any threat of sheep destroying our valley," Aaron Longley said.

One of Sheriff Emmerson's deputies, Lenny Garvin, spoke. "She came into the sheriff's office and threatened the sheriff. Mrs. Fairchild said she was going to bring in Pinkertons to find out who killed her husband. Maybe she hired someone to kill the sheriff?" he suggested. "We all know why she would."

"Maybe we should string her up like we did her husband," Joe Bookman suggested.

"Knock it off, Joe," Bode said.

"I'm not kidding. It might be the only way to save our lake and our ranches when the sheep take over."

Gunther Thomas said, "Mrs. Fairchild did not hire anyone to murder Pat and Don. She might want justice for her husband, but she won't have anyone murdered. She's too good-hearted for that. And I won't listen to any more talk like that, Joe," he warned firmly.

"Aren't you too old yet to be taken in by her womanly charms, Gunther?" Joe questioned irritably. "I suppose since your wife is all crippled up and no good, that woman is young and pretty enough to compromise your vows, huh?"

Bode leaped from his saddle and stepped quickly past three other men to grab the back of Joe's coat and jerked him backward out of the saddle. Joe wasn't expecting to be pulled off backward and fell awkwardly onto his left shoulder on the hard ground. A searing pain shot through his arm and across his shoulder as he lay on his back with a painful grimace. Bode dropped a knee into Joe's sternum before straddling him and driving a series of furious right fists into Joe's face.

Stunned and unable to move his left arm without searing pain, it all seemed like a dream to see his friend's enraged snarl as Bode's right fist rose and fell with a powerful blow to Joe's face. Joe could feel the warmth of his blood running down his nasal cavity and could taste the blood in his mouth. Joe was dumbfounded and stuck in a weird dreamlike sensation as he gazed in bewildered wonder at the fury in Bode's eyes as he repeatedly hit him. Joe did not try to protect himself, let alone fight back.

"Break them up!" Gunther ordered; two of the men had already dismounted and reached for Bode to pull him off Joe.

Bode cursed and tried to fight the two men for a moment. He regained his composure as Aaron Longley handed Bode his hat. Bode pointed to Joe, who was still on the ground. "Don't you ever speak that way about my mother again! I swear, if I hear you say anything like that again, I'll beat you to death." He looked at his father. "You all do what you want. I'm going to warn Holly."

"Bring Jake home when you come back," Gunther said with an approving nod.

"Why's Jake there?" Aaron asked. He had been curious why Jake wasn't with the posse. He had asked Bode earlier and was told it was none of his business. His question went unheard as Gunther turned his attention to Joe.

"Joe, get out of my posse. I don't want to see you for a while, and when I tell Sasha what you said, well, you can take it up with her."

Joe was helped to his feet with a dangling arm from a dislocated shoulder and a nose that bled profusely. He lowered his head in shame as his blood dripped steadily. "I'm sorry, Gunther and Bode. I never should have said that about Miss Sasha."

"Tell it to her, not me," Gunther snapped, ill-tempered. "I'll expect you to apologize to her face to face, Joe. By the way, to answer your absurd question, Miss Fairchild has nothing over me. I'm faithful to my wife. Miss Fairchild is an honorable woman, and I stand by that. If any of you bother that lady, I'll have your hide stripped." He looked at Bode. "Go get Jake."

CHAPTER TWENTY

THE IDEA MADE IT SEEM EASY ENOUGH, BUT JESSE had neglected to consider that Gibbon's Lake was not quite a mile outside of Hollister, and the Fairchild Estate was perhaps another two miles on the other side of the lake. He had planned to stop the coach at the end of the Fairchild Estates long driveway, but he didn't know there would be men digging a canal and building the woolen mill close by. The men working near the driveway were potential witnesses, and the key to Laura disappearing without a trace was that there were no witnesses. It narrowed Jesse's plan of kidnapping Laura to the two-mile or so stretch of road between Hollister and the Fairchild Estate headgate. Unfortunately, it was also the main road leading in and out of Hollister, and the chances of being spotted or the sound of a gunshot or a scream could draw unwanted attention.

Colin Kennedy sat on his horse next to Jesse along the road and looked north toward town and then south. There was nowhere for them to hide as the open prairie of grass left few places to find cover. Worse, a hill to the south blocked any view of someone approaching the top of the hill. He coughed and sucked the phlegm from his chest and spat to the ground. "It would be just our luck if the posse looking for us came over that hill right in the middle of us taking her. I don't like this idea, especially not out here in the open like this."

"What other choice do we have?" Jesse snapped. He didn't like being in the open, either.

"The rich woman's house since that's where she's going. We could disarm her guards, gag your little angel, and slit the throats of everyone else if you want. We could even get some money to pay ourselves for this venture. I have to tell you, Jesse, no one's too happy about risking our lives like this for free. And I feel a bit exposed sitting out here in the open. We killed their sheriff, you know."

"I know," Jesse said with a harsh glare at Colin. "I don't need to be reminded that men are looking for us. And by the look of them we had, I'd say there's quite a number of them."

"Yeah. If they split up, we could be sitting ducks. I say we ride to the rich woman's house and see how many guards she has. Maybe we can get hired on as guards and wait for that baby to be born before you take it."

"No."

"How about I ride over there and find out? I'll say I'm looking for work. And look around. The worst they could do is ask me to leave."

"We don't have time for that."

"So you want to try to risk fighting the guards and her, because she's going to put up a fight right here out in the middle of the road?" Colin asked, not liking the idea.

Jesse sighed irritably. "The guards aren't going to know every rancher and cowhand around here, nor will they know all of the men building the woolen mill. That works to our advantage if we use it. I remember once Morton told a stagecoach we were about to rob that the bridge had washed out ahead. The coach was well-guarded and it was a narrow mountain pass with no place to turn around. They had to unhitch the team of horses, and we offered to use our ropes to keep the stage on the road. We lowered the back end over the edge of the mountainside to reverse the horses." He chuckled. "When the guards thought we were helpful pals, we pulled our guns and robbed the stage and the passengers. Morton cut the ropes and the stage plummeted to the bottom of the mountain. We were probably forty miles away by the time they walked back to town."

"Your cousin Morton Sperry did that? The deputy US Marshal?"

Jesse nodded with a reflective smile. "He wasn't always on the side of the law. We had our fun. We were accused of that crime, too, but our cousins, the Crowe Brothers, paid a visit to the district attorney one night, and it was dismissed. We've done the same for them a time or two. It's good to have family. I'm thinking we could do the same thing, more or less. Listen carefully because we have one chance at this, and if you mess this up, I'll kill you myself."

———

JESSE COULD SEE a black Concord Coach with gold ornamental trim being pulled by two horses, coming toward them in the distance. It was being driven by two men wearing derby hats and long wool coats over their suits. Jesse waited a moment for them to get further from town and then kicked his horse into a gallop. He and Colin raced toward the coach, not knowing if Holly Fairchild was inside the coach with Laura or not. He pulled the reins to a sudden stop, intentionally centered to the team of horses, to remain out of Holly's and Laura's sight if they peeked out of either door. He lifted his hands into a surrendering motion as he spoke frantically. "You two work for the lady Fairchild, right?"

"Yes," Wolfgang Grubbs replied. He had picked up a double-barrel shotgun upon seeing the two riders approaching. They looked like trouble to him.

"We work for the construction company. We watched some men ride past us and soon heard shooting and a scream. I don't know what's going on, but I was ordered to come find help. We can help you, but we don't want to be mistaken for the murderers who killed the sheriff last night. Are there more guards there because we heard some shooting?"

"One. I didn't know the sheriff was killed. So they went to the house?" Wolfgang asked as his chest began to rise and fall.

"We have to go, Wolf. Holly's in trouble," Ross Hall said with concern. "We can't take her though." He motioned behind him.

"We can't leave her out here," Wolfgang replied. The concern on his bearded face was quickly torn on what he should do with his passenger.

"Holly's life's in danger. We haven't got a choice!" Ross snapped.

Jesse suggested, "My friend James can take her home. His horse is faster than mine and I'm a better shot. I'll run back to the camp and gather a few more men. I'll meet you fellas there!" Jesse turned his horse and snapped at Colin, "Take her home, James!" He kicked his horse into a hard run back up the road before the carriage door could be opened. He was grateful that Holly wasn't in the coach, or he'd have to kill her along with the two men right there on the main road.

Wolfgang was hesitant. He gazed at Colin questionably. "You can take her straight home?"

Colin hesitated. "I don't have much of a choice. I'll hurry back after dropping her off in town. I'll make sure she's safe."

Ross climbed down from the carriage and opened the door. "Little miss, I apologize, but today's meeting is canceled. Apparently, the sheriff was murdered and the killers may be at Holly's. This gentleman is taking you home for us."

"What? I don't understand. Who is he?" Laura did not like the fierce looks of the man. Colin's uncared-for appearance frightened her.

Ross turned to Colin. "Who are you?"

Colin shrugged. "My friend told you. We work security at the construction site. I'm James...Kennedy," he couldn't think of a last name to use when answering Ross. He leaned on the saddle horn and spoke to Laura as she stepped out of the carriage wearing her nicest blue dress with a white collar and neckline. A long tan coat and a scarf around her head to help keep her warm. "Listen, miss, I'll take you wherever you need to go, but I have to get back. So, can we hurry, please? The rich woman is in trouble."

Wolfgang climbed off the carriage. "I'm sorry, Laura, but you have to go with him. Holly's in danger. We need to go." He closed the door behind her and walked her to Colin's horse. He warned, "Mr. Kennedy, you take her straight home."

"Will do." He stepped out of the saddle to help Laura step up into it. "Miss, I may not look friendly, but I'm just here to help you. Honest, I am. You two need to go now!" he told Ross and Wolfgang.

Wolfgang and Ross climbed onto the carriage bench seat and urged the pair of horses into a fast trot.

Colin held the reins, standing next to his horse as he watched the carriage hurry down the road. It was being jolted with each rut and hole as it sped along. He shook his head at the ease with which Jesse had pulled off the easiest job they'd ever done. He jumped up behind the saddle's cantle onto his bedroll, which gave him a softer seat. He put his arms around each side of Laura to take the reins in his hands.

"I live in town above the hardware store," Laura said uncomfortably. She did not like being contained in the saddle with the ugly stranger behind her.

"That's fine. I don't want to scare you, but I need to run back and tell my boss something real quick and then I'll take you home." He put his boots in the stirrups, turned his horse and galloped along the road up and over the hill and down the other side. He thanked his luck that there was no one else coming toward him. He rode past the Fairchild Estates headgate when he heard several gunshots. He kept riding past the mill that was being built to the bridge over the Lower Flint River. He crossed over the bridge, slowed, and turned off the road toward the east, and rode down the bank into the river. Colin turned west and rode under the bridge to hide his tracks in the swift water.

Alertly, Laura realized the stranger was taking her away from town, and panic seized her. "Let me off! Where are you going? Let me go!" Laura tried to jump out of the saddle when she realized she was being taken against her will, but his arms blocked her way as they tightened around her. Laura screamed.

Quickly, Colin covered her mouth with his right hand and hissed into her ear, "Stop it! I won't hurt you. No one is going to hurt you, I swear it! Okay? But if you scream again, I'll make an exception and I really don't want to hurt you!"

JAKE THOMAS WAS NERVOUS. He found it hard to swallow with a dry throat, and a glass of water didn't seem to help for long. His sweaty palms shook while his knees bounced. He was sitting in the sunroom looking over the blue water of the lake with the snow-capped rugged mountains behind it. He stood and began to pace around the comfortable padded chairs that were set in a half circle facing each other.

Holly Fairchild chuckled as she watched him with a pleasant smile. "I think it's cute how nervous you are."

Jake turned to face her. "What if Laura gets mad because I'm here? What if she sees my face and it disgusts her? I don't know if this is a good idea after all. Maybe I should go."

Holly spoke sincerely. "Jake, honestly, I think you notice your scar far more than anyone else will. If she loves you, that scar won't matter to her. I know you are a Christian, so what does the Bible say? God tells Joshua *to be strong and courageous* in much more frightening situations than this one. I don't think running away from problems is what God planned for his children. Do you?"

"Laura's not a problem. She's..." He hesitated. "The love of my life."

"Then tell her that."

"I have. But then this happened." He pointed at the scar on his cheek. "Aaron told me she blames me for not protecting her. I don't know if that's true or not, but what if it is?" He gasped. His shoulders slumped. "What if she hates me?" His voice softened to barely above a whisper, "There was nothing I could do."

For a moment, Holly hesitated as Jake's tone was reminiscent of when Kent Kruse said the exact words to her. He meant every word, and the helplessness was evident in his voice. She shook the thought from her mind and focused on Jake. "I don't know who Aaron is, but that's not the impression I got from her, Jake. From what I heard, she'd like to see you, but her parents won't let her. You're worried about her seeing you, but my guess is she'll be even more worried about what you think when you see her. She's getting to the point where she'll begin to show."

"I've heard." He took a deep, slow breath and exhaled. "I'm ready for that."

"I imagine she's expecting to see your scar, too. Well, not really, because she doesn't know you're here. But I think it will be a nice surprise. I hope so, anyway. If not..." She paused as a series of four consecutive gunshots sounded in the near distance. "Were those gunshots?"

Jake nodded. "Yes."

Holly's brow lowered before she stood and left the sunroom. Jake followed. "Alessandro, were those gunshots?" she asked, entering the kitchen where he was slicing a sausage to make lunch.

"Yes, ma'am. My guess is someone from the construction camp is hunting a deer again."

"With a revolver?" Jake asked skeptically. "That wasn't a rifle."

"You don't think there is any reason to be concerned, do you?" Holly asked Alessandro with a touch of anxiety.

"No. Your young friend is right; it was a handgun. So, whoever it was, probably shot at a rabbit or something. The other day, we caught one of those construction fellas skinning a deer not far from here."

"He was hunting deer on my property?" Holly asked, displeased.

"Yes, ma'am."

"I hope you told him not to. I like to watch the deer that come here. We need to put an end to that. When the fellas return, will you send Wolfgang to speak to the boss man over there about that? I don't want anyone hunting on my property."

"Absolutely. I'll have lunch ready in a few minutes."

"Thank you, Alessandro."

———

BODE THOMAS HAD LEFT the search party and rode out of town to the Fairchild Estate headgate and turned his horse onto the long driveway. He rode along, watching the distant construction of the mill for the first two hundred yards or so before he focused on the sound of the steam shovel and rising smoke as it dug the canal. The busyness of the men working and the sound of sledgehammers pounding spikes into the rail ties were fascinating for him to watch. It was a vast project that appeared well organized, and the question of how so much could be accomplished so quickly was answered by the number of men employed working together like a well-oiled machine.

He continued riding until he crossed a newly constructed bridge over the stone-lined canal. There was a concrete dam at the edge of the lake that was closed to keep the water at bay until the day it was opened to let the canal fill with water. The canal had angled banks that were cemented cobblestones, and a thick layer of river rock filled the bottom to stop any erosion and ensured the water would remain unsoiled as it left the lake, powered the woolen mill, and returned to the river. There were plenty of folks in town who criticized the canal being built, but upon seeing the work for himself and the expense that went into it, Bode felt a growing respect for the lady Fairchild.

He gave his horse a slight kick with his heels and moved forward. The road followed the hilly terrain surrounding the lake and rounded a bend along a steep bank that blocked the view of what was an S-curve around the shore of the lake. He gently pulled the reins back and stared as a cold chill ran down his spine. In front of him was Holly's Concord coach with the brakes locked. One passenger door was swung open like an empty barn stall. Two bodies lay motionless on either side of the concord. One man's eyes stared lifelessly toward the sky, with a narrow stream of blood slowly trickling from his head. The other lay crumpled, face pressed into the dirt. A twisted leg bent at an unnatural angle. The air reeked of a strange acidic odor that penetrated Bode's nasal cavity and left an acidic taste in his mouth.

Bode pulled his revolver from his holster as he dismounted and slowly circled the carriage. Both of the dead men were dressed in suits and armed. A big man with a beard lying near the hill wore a gun belt with his revolver still secured in the holster. His derby hat lay in the grass. He appeared to fall face down from the bench seat. A shotgun lay next to him that had not been fired. Bode rolled him over to see if he was alive. He was deceased, having been shot twice in the chest.

The other man wore a shoulder holster under his suit jacket. He was the only one who had freed his weapon but had not fired a shot. He had been shot twice as well. There was no trace of anyone else around the carriage, nor any blood or anything out of sorts inside it. There was a lone trail through the tall green grass from a single horse riding up the hill to escape across the open country to the south.

"Jake," Bode said with alarm and ran to his horse. He galloped quickly the rest of the way to the large house and jumped out of the saddle to run onto the porch. Afraid he would find his brother dead, Bode banged on the front door, yelling, "Jake!" He pounded on the door and tried to open it, but he found the door locked. "Jake!" he yelled frantically.

Alessandro Baccari came out of the kitchen carrying his revolver. The heavy pounding on the door made him uneasy and heightened his senses to be ready for anything once he opened the door. He peeked out the window to see a lone horse that he did not recognize.

"Jake!" the voice hollered.

"Who is it?" Holly asked as she came into the foyer, worried.

Jake answered, "That's my brother, Bode. Something's wrong."

Alessandro opened the door and allowed Jake to step in front of him. "Bode, what's wrong?" he asked.

Bode stepped inside the house, relieved to see that Jake was fine. He spoke to Holly. "I just found your carriage up the road with two dead men. I'm guessing they are your guards. They were wearing suits."

"Where?" Alessandro asked.

"Just up the road at the S-curve. Whoever did it rode up the hill to the south. I thought it might be the murderers we're looking for, but it appears it was only one rider that did it."

"They're dead?" Holly questioned at the shock of the news. "Laura, too?" Holly asked. Her eyes widened with the shocking news. Her chest rose and fell heavily, fearing the worst. "Where's Laura?"

Bode's brow lowered. "There was no one else there. Just two men."

Alessandro spoke to Holly. "Do you know this man?" He was suspicious of Bode and didn't know if Jake's brother was a friend or a stranger.

"He's Jake's brother," Holly said, shaken by the news. She sat heavily on a bench beside the door. "Laura wasn't there?" she questioned.

Alessandro was skeptical of Bode. "You said they are dead? Are you sure?"

"Yes, I am sure."

"How did you find them? Why are you here?"

Bode answered, "We were tracking the murderers of Sheriff Emmerson and Don Olsen and followed their trail back to town. I came out here to check on Jake and Mrs. Fairchild because we don't know where they are or who they are, for that matter."

"What about Laura?" Holly asked in a stronger voice to get an answer. "She wasn't in the carriage?"

Bode answered, "No. There was no one else there. Are you sure Laura was coming here?"

Holly's voice broke as she said, "They went to pick her up." Her large blue eyes grew moist.

Jake sat heavily on the third step of the staircase. "They took her. Someone took her."

"We don't know that, Jake," Bode said, trying to reassure his brother. "There was only one rider that I can tell. There was one passenger door open, but it looked like the smaller man was trying to use it as a shield to me."

Holly gasped. "We need to find out if she is at home or not. That's what I need to know."

"I need to go see if Wolf and Russ are really dead, but I can't leave you, Miss Holly," Alessandro said. "If there is an attack of any kind, I need to be here."

"Bode, are you sure my two security guards are dead and not hurt?" she asked.

"Yes!" Bode said. "They were both shot in the chest twice. I checked them both; they are dead."

"Those gunshots we heard," she said to Alessandro.

Alessandro nodded. "How many men were you looking for?"

"Four from what we could tell. Maybe five. They were camped out on the fringes of the Olson-Westfall Ranch. That's where the sheriff and Don's body were found."

Alessandro pointed toward the back of the house and said, "Jake, would you mind watching out back? We might have some visitors trying to get in from there. I'll grab some rifles. Holly, you had better grab your gun in case someone gets inside. Keep it on you," he emphasized.

Bode said, "I'll grab my rifle and watch the back. Jake, take my horse and ride into town to see if Laura is home. Then, find Pa and the posse and tell them to get out here. If Laura's been taken, we need to know it."

"No!" Holly said sharply. "Laura's parents can't know Jake was here. You're going to have to do it, Bode. I can shoot a rifle, and Jake can too, I'm sure, but please don't tell them Jake is here. Lord willing, Laura is at home and didn't feel well today. I don't want to ruin the trust they have in me if that's the case."

Bode waved a thumb toward the back of the house and spoke pointedly. "If they're coming, there's four or five of them!"

"We'll fight them off," Holly said, with her blue eyes burning into Bode's. "I already lost my husband and house once. I will not do so again! I'll fight tooth and nail to save it."

Bode smiled slightly. He admired her stout determination. She reminded him of his mother when she stood up to her father in her younger years. "I'm sure you will. But I hate to leave you here when there could be danger out there."

"I appreciate that," she said as she ran her fingers through her hair. "But we need to know if Laura was in that carriage and is missing or at home. I pray she is at home." Her large blue eyes blinked a layer of frightened moisture away.

"Me too," Jake said with a nervous swallow.

The sound of a lone horse galloping to the house caught Alessandro's attention. He peeked out a window. "That man, Kent, is here. Wasn't he supposed to be here this morning?"

The front door opened suddenly as Kent Kruse burst into the house shouting, "Holly!"

"We're fine, Kent," she said, surprised that he barged inside.

"I was on my way here and saw the carriage. Wolfgang and Ross are dead. Thank God you're okay." He holstered his revolver. "What's going on? And who are you?" he asked Jake, who was sitting on the stairs. His eyes moved to Bode and hardened with recognition. "I know who you two are; you're Gunther Thomas's boys. What are you doing here? Are the sheep shooters circling back? Holly," he pointed at Bode. "He's one of the ones who murdered Robert and burned your house down!" Kent took an aggressive step toward Bode, but Bode shoved him back.

Holly shouted, "Stop it right now, Kent! Bode, go now and hurry back to let me know about Laura."

Bode spoke heatedly to Kent. "I didn't kill anyone! I was with my brother that night. Wasn't I Jake?"

Jake nodded in agreement. "Yes," he lied. He knew his father and brother were involved in the attack on the Fairchild Estate, which led to the murders of Robert Fairchild, the Blackburn Marshals, and the burning of the estate. It was a secret that the Hollister Sheep Shooters and their families would take to the grave or be put in an early grave if they uttered a word to anyone about it.

Bode continued, "You were a Blackburn Marshal. I remember you."

Kent nodded, affirming it. "Yes, I was. How dare you even show your face around here. You and your brother are both liars. You are a murderer!"

Bode watched Kent with a bitter scowl. "Says a hired killer who admits he was a Blackburn Marshal. Think what you will, but I've never worn a hood to hide my face. I never needed to kill anyone. But if I did, I'd do it like a man and not poison a family's water well." Their mutual dislike for one another had filled the foyer of Holly's house with a dark tension everyone could feel.

Holly interrupted, "Bode was with his injured brother and had nothing to do with that night, Kent. If he had, he wouldn't be here. I don't think Jake would lie to me about that. Bode, please hurry, and find out about Laura."

"I'll let you know," Bode said. "Jake, come get my rifle."

He needed to make sure Jake understood the importance of keeping their secret. He did not doubt that Kent would try to pressure Jake into admitting that Bode and their father were involved in the murder of Holly's husband.

Once Jake followed Bode outside, Kent said, "He was here with his father. I know it."

Holly was in no mood to hear it. She snapped, "Did you see their faces, Kent? Because you told me before that you didn't recognize anyone."

"No. But I know..."

"Don't accuse my friends of that again! You were in a boat way out in the lake and couldn't identify anyone. If you accuse Bode of something so heinous again, I'm going to ask you to leave and never come back. That's the only warning I'm giving you."

Kent scoffed as he peered at Holly, perplexed. He was supposed to be her friend, not the Thomas boys, who were the enemy a few months before. "Fine. But I know what I know."

Holy's eyes burned into Kent. "We have more important things going on right now! Either help us secure this house or leave!"

MITCH WHITEHEAD WATCHED Bode enter the hardware store. "Afternoon, Bode. Did you fellas find Pat and Don's murderers?" he asked as Bode approached the hardware store's counter.

Bode removed his hat and shook his head. "No. Mr. Whitehead, is Laura at home?"

Mitch sighed with annoyance. "Listen, Bode, I won't let you give her a note from your brother. I've said it a dozen times; she doesn't want anything to do with Jake, and I won't let her even if she did. So, you can take the note or whatever you have to say right back to your brother and tell him to shove it! Tell Jake to move on and ruin someone else's life. He's done enough to ruin my daughter's—"

Bode's patience was thin. "Is she, or is she not here?"

"That's none of your business!"

"Yes, it is. Because if Laura went to Mrs. Fairchild's place, she's been taken. Is she home or not, Mr. Whitehead?"

The color faded from Mitch's face. "What do you mean taken?"

"I found Holly Fairchild's carriage. The guards were dead, and the carriage was empty. I told Holly, and she sent me here to ask if Laura was here or in the carriage."

Mitch gasped, unable to breathe. His voice shook. "It was empty? Where's Laura?"

"I'm asking you! Is she here?" Bode nearly yelled with frustration.

"No," he gasped. "Laura left with them."

"Oh, Lord," Bode said as he suddenly felt sick to his stomach. "I'll gather the posse back together and start looking for her."

Mitch's knees buckled as he grabbed onto the counter to steady himself. He couldn't speak as the news took his strength away. His eyes filled with tears. "She's missing?" he gasped.

Bode reached across the counter to put a reassuring hand on Mitch's shoulder. "We'll find her, Mitch. We'll bring her home."

"P...p...please do. Oh, Lord." His bottom lip began to quiver.

"We'll do our best. I promise." Bode cast a glance at Tim and then walked out of the store.

"Please do," Mitch said weakly and turned away from the counter to ascend the stairs and tell his wife that the murderous group of killers had taken their daughter.

Tim Hazelton's lips had suddenly gone dry. He had been hoping Jesse and Colin would change their mind or would be fought off by the two guards, but Laura was gone. Tim was fond of Mitch and Helen, and within moments, he heard Helen begin to wail. His heart sank deep into a pit of guilt's bottomless mire that brought a heavy weight of shame. A part of him wanted to tell the truth about what he knew, but if he did, it would lead to the death of his cousin. Colin was the only family he had left anywhere within hundreds of miles. He suddenly wished he had gone to Utah to live with his aunt and uncle. Tim would have had to follow their absurd rules, but at least he wouldn't be feeling the ton of weight crushing his spirit. He didn't know what to say to the Whiteheads or if he should say anything at all. He approached the counter to fill in for Mitch.

PART THREE

CHAPTER TWENTY-ONE

Matt Bannister, Truet Davis, and Morton Sperry stopped along the main road to gaze at the construction of the Fairchild Woolen Mill. It was a large factory two-story structure made of flat-walled red bricks, except for the thick row of bricks that extended outwards, spelling the words Robert F. Fairchild Woolen Mill on the sides and a smaller version above the front door. The concrete floor and brick walls were completed, and the trusses for the roof were in place. The employees worked to finish the roof before the coming snow. The sound of hammers pounding, saws and clanging of boards filled the air as the busy crew worked inside and out to complete Robert Fairchild's dream of opening a woolen mill.

"They've come a long way in no time at all," Matt said to Morton. He was impressed by the amount of work that had been done since he was last there.

"Holly said she was going to build it. She keeps her word, doesn't she?"

"I'll bet this might have something to do with the urgency of her wanting us to come here," Matt replied.

"You think?" Truet asked with a sarcastic roll of his eyes. He had spent several days over the past year in Hollister trying to settle disputes between the ranchers of the Hollister Cattle Association and Robert Fairchild's determination to graze his thousands of sheep on public land. He waved toward the woolen mill. "This is like carrying a hive of free-roaming termites onto a sea-going wooden ship. It's a disaster just waiting to happen."

They rode forward and turned onto the Fairchild Estate driveway. They stopped on the new bridge and admired the canal for a moment before riding around the S-curve. The three men dismounted when they came to the abandoned concord, still harnessed to the team of horses, with two dead men lying on the road.

"Do you know them?" Truet asked.

"No," Matt replied. "But I'm guessing they were hired to protect Holly." He checked the inside coat pocket of a large, bearded man and noticed his billfold was intact with some money. "They weren't robbed." He looked around and noticed fresh horse tracks in the dirt going to and from Holly's residence and a trail riding up the hill. "Let's go."

Matt climbed into his saddle and rode quickly the rest of the way to Holly's home. He was expecting the worst and waved Truet and Morton to go around the sides of the house. Matt dismounted, keeping his horse partly between the windows and himself. He approached slowly, watching the windows for any sign of movement. He released the reins, drew his revolver, and ascended the three steps onto the porch.

Suddenly, the door was jerked open and Holly stepped quickly out onto the porch with widened arms that wrapped around him. "Matt, I'm glad to see you! My guards were killed. Laura was supposed to be with them, but I'm praying she wasn't."

"You're going to have to explain better than that. What's happened?" Matt asked while she released her embrace. Truet and Morton joined him on the porch.

"Come inside. I'll explain everything."

———

HOLLY TOLD him about seeing her music box in Laura's room and learning that Sheriff Pat Emmerson had given it to Laura after Robert was murdered and her house burned. She knew then that the sheriff was one of the men who murdered her husband. In the heat of the moment, she confronted the sheriff and made some heated threats that she feared would cause the Hollister Sheep Shooters to attack her home and kill her. It was that concern that forced her to contact Matt with an urgent message to come to Hollister.

However, since then, she explained, Sheriff Emmerson and a local rancher's son were murdered by unknown bandits. A posse was formed that morning and could not locate the men they were looking for. Since Holly had invited Jake to her house for a surprise meeting with Laura, Bode Thomas came to her home and discovered the dead bodies of Wolfgang Grubbs and Ross Hall. Holly didn't know if Laura was taken or at home not feeling well.

As they spoke, Kent Kruse came inside through the back door and was surprised to see Matt and his deputies sitting with Holly and Jake in the sunroom. "Matt," he greeted him with a handshake. "I didn't know you were around here."

"I just arrived," he said, standing to shake his hand. "You're back working for Holly or..." he questioned with a curious glance at Holly. He knew Kent wanted to court her the last they met.

"Yes," she answered quickly. "Kent's just employed by me."

"I am just working," Kent answered awkwardly. "I rode the property, and there was no sign of anyone. In fact, I saw no sign of more than one rider. I followed that trail to the river. I can't tell if he went upstream or down, but he didn't cross it. There is no one around here."

Matt questioned aloud, "Why would one person risk killing two of your guards if robbery wasn't the reason? He might have wanted to kill you, Holly, but you weren't there. Certainly, they wouldn't mistake Laura for you if she was there. It could have been the sheep shooters whittling away your guards to make an attack easier, I suppose, but having the Blackburn Marshals here didn't slow them down any. I doubt three men would either. Something about this seems odd to me."

Truet shook his head. "An assassination attempt that went wrong, sounds most probable."

Morton took a drink of coffee. "Being a former outlaw myself, I can tell you that the men that killed the sheriff and the rancher's son camped out on that ranch to stay hidden. They didn't want their presence known because they're planning something big like robbing the bank or you," he said to Holly. "One of those guards didn't have a chance to pull his gun, so you know we're dealing with an experienced, cold-blooded gunman to kill two men like that without missing a shot. I do think it's one of the men that killed the sheriff, but if there are four or five of them, where were the others? That's what doesn't make sense to me."

Matt reasoned, "There is the possibility that we could have two things going on that are not related. We know the sheriff wasn't too upright, so maybe he pushed some folks too hard, and they had to defend themselves. The killing of Holly's guards could very well be a lone sheep shooter, but Morton's right. I think it was done by a professional gunman, considering most people would miss at least one shot. All four wounds were to the chest, killing shots. Whoever did it was not looking for money, or they would have searched those two men's pockets. It could be that he wasn't expecting a young female witness and didn't know what to do with her, so he chose to take her with him rather than check for money." He looked at Holly. "Whoever the shooter is, and however it happened, he sat there and waited to ambush you."

Alessandro offered, "I don't want to make any accusations, but Kent was supposed to be here this morning, but he wasn't. He didn't show up until after they were dead."

Kent scowled. "Why would I kill Wolf and Ross?"

"Jealousy. Holly told us you wanted more from her than friendship, and you're supposedly a gunman."

Kent grimaced with a loud groan. "Oh, go to hell! Of course, I wasn't here! I got my final paycheck from the construction company and took it to the bank. Then I went and bought some new clothes and to the barbershop," he said, rubbing his hand down his new suit. "You can go to the bank and store and ask them. I have no reason to kill them."

Alessandro said, "Somebody killed Wolf and Ross. I'm not counting anyone out right now. Everyone is a suspect until I know better. And right now, the only people who I know didn't do it are Holly, Jake, and me."

Kent stammered. "I'm here to protect her." He pointed at Holly. "I'm not going to kill two men who have the same goal as me."

"Kent didn't do it," Matt said calmly. "It's not doing us any good to sit here either. I'll take my deputies and follow the man's trail to the river and see if we can't pick it up where he came out of the water. We know that's the man we're looking for." He stood.

"Horses," Alessandro said, hearing the trotting of what sounded like a herd of horses out front of the house. He left the sunroom to check out front. Kent, Matt, and the others followed.

Bode Thomas was already on the front porch, along with eight other men. Bode spoke as soon as Alessandro opened the door. "Laura's gone! She was in the carriage. They took her. Marshal Bannister," he said, taking notice of Matt. "Sir, we could use your help to find her."

Holly gasped and took a seat on a small bench beside the door as the strength left her body, horrified by the thought of what could have happened to Laura. "I'll never forgive myself if anything happens to her. Oh, Lord, please be with that child."

Matt asked Bode, "Are you sure Laura was taken?"

A man behind Bode named Wyatt Reeves, was quick to speak. "Yes. Her father said she went with Holly's guards. He watched her get into the carriage."

"How was Mr. Whitehead acting?" Matt asked Bode.

"How was he acting?" Wyatt questioned. He owned the General Mercantile in town and was Mitch's close friend. "How do you think? He was upset. Mitch's daughter was kidnapped!"

"I'm sure he is," Matt replied. He asked Bode, "When you first told him, what was his reaction?" He had not forgotten about Mitch Whitehead's wanting Laura to have an abortion. It would horrify him to learn that Mitch had hired someone to kidnap his daughter and force her to have an abortion, but it was a possibility he could not afford to overlook.

"Shocked," Bode answered. "I told him, and he was upset. Why? How would you expect him to act?"

"Terrified. Did he look *terrified*?" Matt emphasized.

"Why are you asking that?" Wyatt questioned impatiently. "For crying out loud, the man's daughter is already traumatized, and now it's happening again! How do you think he's going to act?"

"I didn't ask you!" Matt snapped sharply. "Unless you were there when he first heard his daughter was missing, you have nothing more to say about it. How did he act, Bode?"

"He looked like he was going to cry and went upstairs. His wife started wailing. He was scared," Bode said affirmingly.

"Thank you. My deputies and I are going to follow the murderer's trail and bring her home."

Bode said, "My father and the others are already doing that. They followed the trail from the carriage."

Matt closed his eyes and exhaled. "Oh, crap. How many of them?"

"Oh, at least twenty men. I got eight with me just in case those killers try to take Holly. I figured it might be their plan."

Matt ran his hand over his hair. He knew the trail he needed to follow was now buried under twenty other horses. "The killer was alone, and he wasn't after money. He was after something else, probably Holly."

"Well, they got Laura," Wyatt said.

Matt spoke to the other men with Bode. "You all can spread out on the property or go home." He knew most would be leaving, if not all. "Bode, will you come inside so we can talk?"

Bode entered the house while the men behind him left to join the posse to find Laura.

Matt closed the door and explained, "Holly contacted me, fearing reprisal from the sheep shooters. What do you know about that?"

"I told you!" Kent exclaimed while pointing a finger toward Bode. "I told you he was a sheep shooter, Holly."

Bode shook his head. "I'm not a part of that group, nor do I condone what they've done in the past. But I can tell you no one from around here took Laura. Undoubtedly, some of the men in the posse are sheep shooters, but right now, finding Sheriff Emmerson's and Don's killers and finding Laura are their biggest concern, Marshal."

"So you don't think they have anything to do with Holly's guards being killed or an attempt on her life?"

"No! My father is the president of the cattle association and he's told everyone to leave Holly and her property alone. He has made that very clear, and if anyone disobeys him, they'll be kicked out of the association and held accountable. I can assure you, this has nothing to do with anyone affiliated with the sheep shooters."

"What about a sheep shooter working alone to save your community—a lone wolf per se?" Matt questioned.

"That's possible, but I doubt it. No one from around here is going to take Laura."

"We were just on our way to trail the man who took

Laura, but now there won't be a trail to follow because of the posse trampling it. Luckily, Kent followed it to the river, so we know that much. Bode, you know this country better than anyone else in this room, if you went into the river, which way would you go to escape the law?"

"Personally, I'd go east from here to Scroggins Creek and ride it up our property. But there's nothing up that way except mountains. If they wanted to go anywhere else, downriver. The Lower Flint River goes all the way to the Modoc River, you know."

"I know, it borders the Big Z Ranch." The Upper Flint River drained from the Wallala Mountains into Gibbon's Lake and the Lower Flint snaked its way from Gibbon's Lake to the Modoc River between the towns of Willow Falls and Natoma.

"It's open country for the next twenty miles or so, just grass, shrubs, and a lot of hills until you reach Jessup Valley. There's a few small farms and ranches bordering the river, but there's nothing between here and there after Erickson's farm."

"How far downriver is Erickson's farm?"

"Eight miles or so."

"I can't imagine people sleeping on the ground would want to go to higher elevations, so I'm betting they went downriver. We're going to try to pick up their trail. The posse is going to confuse things a bit, but they'll either find the man and bring him in or lose him. You're welcome to come along with us if you like?"

"Yeah, I'll ride with you. Mind if Jake comes along?"

"I won't stop him as long as he can follow directions and keep quiet. Just so you both know it could be dangerous."

"I know. Let's go find Laura."

———

As Matt had expected, the original trail was buried under two dozen men on horseback, leaving a swath of downed grass to follow to the river's edge. Some of the men in the posse turned upriver, others turned down river and some crossed the river to go in both directions. At the edge of the flowing water that was about three feet deep at its deepest, Matt surveyed the landscape and then said, "Tru, how about you and Morton cross the river and spread out wider than the posse? One of you ride about a hundred yards or so further out and the other along the bank. We'll do the same on his side until it gets dark. At that time, find the tallest hill and look for a fire. We'll do the same on over here."

An hour later, Morton spoke loudly from across the river, "Matt, do you see that creek by the Willow tree?"

"I do," he said, looking downriver a few hundred yards.

"When I was leading the Sperry-Helms Gang, we did exactly what the man we're looking for is doing after we robbed the bank. Maybe I shouldn't say that too loud," he added with an awkward chuckle. "We were acquitted of that."

"Go figure," Matt replied. "Crowe Brothers?"

"Yeah. That was back when the district attorney was Tony Harrison. He moved."

Matt said, "The next time we arrest one of your family members, I'll be staying at district attorney Jackson Weather's house."

"Jesse is long gone, so there shouldn't be too many of them left except my nephew, Tad. I don't think my cousins would bother coming here for him. Anyway, we rode up that stream for a few miles to get away from the posse."

"Are you going to ride up it?"

"I'll be looking for tracks. Seeing the willow tree just reminded me of it. That was about eight years ago."

Truet called, "Matt, Mort," he pointed up a long hill where two riders were riding down the center of the stream. Matt whistled to the two Thomas brothers, who were riding a hundred yards away from the river. He turned his horse to cross the river.

Truet had raised his rifle as the two men rode toward them. "Try anything, and I'll blow you out of the saddle!" he shouted.

The two men raised their hands in surrender. "We don't have any money," one of the men said. He narrowed his eyes to focus on the badges of the two men nearing them. "Thank goodness you're lawmen. I thought you might be the bandits we're tracking."

Matt spoke. "I'm US Marshal Matt Bannister. These are my deputies, Morton Sperry and Truet Davis. I wouldn't try anything if I were you; you won't live through it. Now, who are you?"

A chill ran down Rusty Wells's spine. He swallowed nervously as he answered before Byron could, "I'm..." He paused. He saw Bode and Jake Thomas riding closer behind Matt. He was going to use a fake name just in case there was a reward for him, but now he knew he had to take a chance since he had been using his real name since coming to Hollister. "I'm Rusty Wells, Marshal. This is my pard, Byron Krall. We are part of the posse looking for the sheriff's murderers. Hey, Bode," he called with a wave and a friendly smile. "We checked this creek for about two and a half miles or so and found nothing. Not a single track, except deer and coyote." Jesse had told him the night before how to recognize the creek they would take Laura up to escape. Byron and him needed to cover any tracks along that creek before anyone else in the posse could. Rusty knew Jesse's plan had succeeded because they were looking for the girl, and he'd seen Jesse's and Colin's horse tracks in the soft soil along the rock creek bed. Rusty had taken the time to hide the tracks once the posse left him and Byron behind.

"Do you know him, Bode?" Matt asked, his hand was near the butt of his revolver. Morton held a shotgun loosely.

Bode answered as he joined Matt and Morton, "I don't know them, but they've been around looking for work lately."

"Are they part of the posse?" Matt asked, not taking his eyes off the two men.

"They are. But I don't know why. They didn't know the sheriff, Don, or Laura."

Matt's curiosity was raised. "You're not local?" Matt questioned.

"No, sir," Rusty answered, trying to keep his calm composure. "We came looking for some work cowboying and our luck might be changing. We've been talking to Phil Dawson; it looks like the Dawson Lakes Ranch might be our new home once we find those outlaws."

"Where are you from?"

"Nevada. We worked the Triple R for the past three years or so." He made up a ranch name to make it sound convincing.

"I'm not familiar with it. Are you?" Matt asked Bode.

"Never heard of it," Bode said. He had been suspicious of the two men from the beginning.

Rusty raised his brow. "Well, it's not a vast ranch. You know, most folks down there have never heard of the Long

T or the Dawson Lakes Ranch either, but that doesn't mean men don't work there. We didn't know any of the ranch's names when we came here. We just heard it was cattle country with several ranches that might be hiring."

Matt asked, "Have you ever heard of the Big Z Ranch?"

"No, sir. I haven't heard of that one."

"It's where I grew up, southwest of here. Why are you two part of the posse if you don't know anyone?"

Rusty looked at Byron before answering, "Because it's the right thing to do. You don't have to know a man to know his murderer needs to be brought to justice. But I don't have to tell you that, Marshal. Your reputation is well known, sir. It's an honor to meet you."

Matt spoke to Byron. "You must be the quiet one, huh?"

Byron smiled. "Rusty does enough talking for both of us." He looked at Morton and said, "I've heard of you. You led the Sperry-Helms Gang."

Morton nodded. "I did."

"Your cousin is in Nevada, causing trouble with a new gang. I hear he's robbing stagecoaches."

"Jesse or the Crowes?" Morton asked.

"Jesse Helms. He's causing some trouble down there and has people talking."

Morton shrugged a shoulder. "Jesse will be caught soon enough. He's not intelligent enough to not get caught. His time will come."

"You were the brains of your gang, I take it?" Rusty asked.

"I can't say we were never caught, but we were never convicted."

"That's because the Crowe Brothers always threatened the jury or lawyers," Byron stated.

"How do you know that?" Matt asked.

"Everyone knows that," Byron answered.

"No," Morton corrected. "Not everyone does know that. How do *you* know that?" He shifted the shotgun in case he had to use it.

Byron could feel his face beginning to redden. He had spoken too much and knew Rusty would have some chosen words for him if they could escape the Marshal and his deputies. He lowered his head with shame. "There was a time a few years back when I was not so upright in my thinking and mixed with some bad men. Auggy August was one; Colin Kennedy was another. They got me into thieving and a bit of rustling. We were caught and thrown in jail. There was a man in jail who was talking about you all and the Crowe Brothers. He apparently knew them. That's where I heard it. But I learned my lesson and never want to go back to jail again, so I live on honest wages now."

"What was the man's name?" Morton asked.

Byron shook his head. "I never spoke to him myself. I overheard him talking. I don't know his name."

Rusty added, "I didn't know Byron back then. But I do know he walks a firm line now. We're law and order from sunrise to sunrise, seven days a week. Hence, we're helping with the posse." He pointed west where the posse was coming back toward them. "I hope they found the girl."

A moment later, Gunther Thomas pulled the reins to a stop. "Marshal Bannister. What brings you out this way? Laura was just taken today, so I know it's not her."

"Nothing that takes priority over finding her. Did you find anything?"

"Not a damn sign. We rode downriver several miles and nothing. Thought we'd come back and check on these two and the others searching upriver and along creeks." He asked Rusty, "See anything?"

Rusty waved behind him. "We went up the creek to the bridge you told us about. Nothing. I was hoping you all found her."

Gunther said to Matt, "I don't know what brought you here, but I'm glad you're here. We definitely could use your help. I thought we'd be able to track them, but clearly not."

Matt asked, "These men say they might start working for Phil Dawson. Is that true?"

Gunther looked at Rusty and Byron. "Phil's riding north on the river, but you could ask him. I do know they were talking to him about it. What came from it, I don't know."

"It's true," one of the men in the posse said. "I was riding with them when Phil said he might have room for them on the Dawson Lakes."

"I wouldn't lie to you, Marshal," Rusty said.

Matt nodded after a short hesitation.

Gunther spoke to the group of riders. "It's getting dark and we can't do anymore today. We'll pick it up again tomorrow morning. We'll meet at the cattle association. Marshal, do you want to ride with me and tell me what brings you to town?"

"Well, it's an honor to meet you, Marshal Bannister," Rusty said. "Those murdering fools don't have a chance now."

———

LAURA SAT against a juniper tree that was one of several in a thin grove at the base of a hillside hidden within a narrow ravine protected by rolling hills. She held her legs tightly tucked together under a wool blanket that she clung tightly around her. It was cold and getting colder as the day's sun was beginning to set. The man who had taken her was strangely quiet as he waited, often looking in the distance for an unknown reason.

He was a frightening man, tall, lean, with long hair and a long, scraggly beard. His eyes lacked emotion and were like two stones that had no life within them. He looked fierce, mean, and dangerous. He had not said too much except to scare her enough to remain seated and not to move. He often glanced her way to verify she was there.

"Cold?" he asked.

She nodded.

He went to his tethered horse and untied his bedroll, a piece of eight-foot square canvas that was folded and rolled up tightly with blankets and a thin pillow inside. It was tied behind the saddle's cantle. He had already unrolled his bedroll once to give her a blanket. He pulled another gray wool blanket out of the bedroll and tossed it to her. He then rolled the canvas tight and retied it to his saddle.

Laura didn't know if it was so cold that she couldn't get warm or if the fear that ran through her veins was making it worse. More than staying warm, the extra blanket helped her feel more protected from the man who took her. She quickly wrapped the second blanket around her and held it tucked tightly under her chin.

"They'll be looking for me," she offered, hoping he would let her go.

Colin's lips rose slightly without a hint of concern. "That's why we don't have a fire. We won't be here long."

His words sent a chill down her spine. Her voice trembled as she said, "It's getting dark. Where are you taking me?" Her throat had become so dry that it felt like she was going to choke every time she swallowed.

He turned his head from the hillside to gaze at her. "I'm taking you home, young lady, just like I promised. There is just something I have to do first, okay?" Colin said to keep her calm.

Laura exhaled with relief. "Then why did you bring me out here?"

Colin smirked but hesitated to answer. "Because I didn't have a choice."

Before too long, a lone rider appeared in the distance and rode quickly downhill toward them. A light gray scarf covered his face as he rode into the grove of trees. He stepped out of the saddle and pointed at the hill behind him. "We'll have at least a two or three-hour head start. If Rusty does what I told him to without blowing it, then we should be in the clear. But I don't want to be anywhere around here when the sun rises."

Laura recognized the man's voice from earlier that day in the carriage. It stirred an uneasiness within her. He stepped closer and knelt in front of her. He lowered his head, removed his hat, and unwrapped the scarf from his neck, which covered part of his face. He looked up at her and smiled. "Hello, again."

Laura's eyes widened in terror. A sudden, terrified scream filled the valley. She pushed herself back to escape the man in front of her, but the tree blocked her attempt. She stood, scraping her back on the rough bark. Her eyes were wide, frantic, and locked onto the cold and menacing eyes of Jesse Helms. He laughed pleasantly at her reaction. Petrified, she stood paralyzed against the tree, staring at one of the men who haunted her dreams and caused her so much pain. Tears streamed down her face as her heart pounded in her chest. Her breath was choked by the sobs that she could not stop.

Jesse reached a hand out to touch her shoulder, but at the feel of his hand upon her, Laura screamed and began to run frantically and tripped on the blanket wrapped around her legs. She fell to the ground. "No! No! No!" she wailed.

Colin said, "She's going to scream that baby right out of her if you don't calm her down. Make it deaf, at least."

Jesse grabbed Laura, forced her to her back, sat on her abdomen and hovered over her, glaring into her eyes. His hardened scowl showed no mercy, very much like it did the night he forced himself on her in the church cellar. "Shut up!" he hissed and covered her mouth with his hand. "I'm not going to hurt you unless you make me. But if you make me, I'll hurt you bad. Now, shut up!"

Laura's sobs were uncontrollable. Gradually, only being able to breathe through her nose, the sobs quieted as she stared with panicking eyes at the man above her.

After a moment, Jesse removed his hand from her mouth. "Stay quiet, and you won't get hurt."

She spouted fearfully, "I'm with child! Don't! I'm with child!" She feared he'd force himself upon her again.

"No one's doing that to you again. Not ever again." Jesse leaned back slowly, revealing his empty hands. "Calm down. Just stay calm so we can talk." He slowly stood and stepped back with his hands raised to show he was no threat.

Laura quickly scrambled to her feet, dropped the blankets, turned, and ran screaming for help. Jesse cursed and sprinted forward to tackle her to the ground, only to have her scream and start wailing again. He forced her to her back, pinned her wrists to the ground, and once again hovered over her.

"I'm trying to be nice! Shut up!" he exclaimed. He released her left arm and slapped her across the face to stop her screaming. It stunned her for a second, but her wailing continued. Jesse shouted, "Shut up!" Enraged by her screams echoing through the valley, Jesse's hands went around her throat and began squeezing to silence her. Laura's face turned red, her eyes bulged, and she gasped for air, but the rage-filled snarl on Jesse's face revealed no intention of stopping until she was dead.

Colin said, "Hey, hey, that's enough. Jesse, that's enough!" he shouted.

Jesse's hands continued to squeeze like a python crushing a rat. Colin ran forward and dove the last few feet to tackle Jesse with enough momentum to force Jesse off Laura and end the death grip that was strangling her.

Jesse pushed Colin off him when they hit the ground and reached for his gun as he got to his knees.

"What are you doing?" Colin shouted as Jesse escaped his grasp. "She's carrying your baby!"

Jesse paused and took a deep breath. He nodded and turned his attention to Laura. She was leaning on an elbow, coughing, gagging, and crying as she tried to catch her breath and breathe normally. Her throat hurt.

Jesse holstered his gun, scooted across the ground behind Laura, and snuggled against her back while forcing his arms around her, entrapping her arms tight against her breast as he pulled her close to him. He spoke gently into her ear, "Now, maybe you'll listen to me. I don't want to hurt you, but you made me. I don't want to risk hurting my baby, so stop forcing me to hurt you. I'm going to take care of you, and we'll raise our baby together. You and me."

Her sobs grew louder and more desperate.

"Shh. Screaming and crying aren't going to do you any good. You're my woman now, and you'll learn to like it. I'm taking you home."

"I want my mom!" she bellowed. "Mommy..." she sobbed. "I want my mom."

"Well, Mommy is not here anymore. So stop bellowing like a baby and get used to it! Now, I'm going to put you on my horse, and we'll talk all the way home. We'll be there late, but I'll keep you warm. You can't escape, so don't fight me. I don't want to hurt you to make you obey me, but I will."

To feel Jesse's breath on her ear and lay in his arms repulsed her. It was frightening enough to be taken by a stranger, but to see Jesse Helms was terrifying; she knew how badly he could hurt her. But to know there was no help and no one to save her from an unimaginable nightmare was defeating and utterly hopeless. She could feel her spirit dying as her future, which was made bleak by her pregnancy, had suddenly become blacker than any darkness she had ever experienced before.

CHAPTER TWENTY-TWO

MITCH WHITEHEAD WAS SITTING IN THE FAMILY room searching his Bible for what comfort it could give him. Somewhere within the sixty-six books of the Bible, he hoped to find a verse that he could hold on to that promised his beloved daughter would be returned home safely. Mitch begged the Lord to show him a passage that he could cling to with a firm grip to reassure him that God, the creator of the earth and of man, would protect his little girl while in the hands of a group of murderers. Mitch was scared and quickly growing frustrated as he closed his eyes and randomly flipped the Bible open to wherever the Lord opened it and placed his finger on the page. He didn't find the comfort he desired in the Book of Job when he read about the death of Job's children. He didn't find the comfort he desperately needed when he flipped the Bible open to the book of Ezekiel and read about God telling Ezekiel that his wife was going to die.

He closed the Bible, closed his eyes, flipped it open and put his finger randomly on the opened page. Opening his eyes to see where his finger landed, his heart sunk deeper. The genealogy of the tribes of Isreal in the Book of Numbers didn't satisfy his desperation any. Frustrated, he closed the Bible and intentionally placed a finger near the end of the Bible where the New Testament is and opened it. To his despair, he opened it to the Book of James and read the words:

Brothers, as an example of patience in the face of suffering, take the prophets who spoke in the name of the Lord. "As you know, we consider blessed those who have persevered. You have heard of Job's perseverance and have seen what the Lord finally brought about. The Lord is full of compassion and mercy."

Mitch slammed the Bible closed irritably and set it on the table beside his chair before standing and beginning to pace the floor. He spoke irately, "I was just looking for some nugget of hope to hold onto in the Bible and all I got was God telling Ezekiel his wife was going to die. And then all I got was *Er and Ornan were sons of Judah, but they died in Canaan.* Oh, and a list of Judah's descendants through Shelah or something like that." He shook his head irritably. "Where's God when you need him, huh, Helen? All I wanted was some kind of a promise that Laura would come home." He shouted, "I can't even get that!"

Helen looked up from her crocheting a small stocking cap with three shades of blue. She asked calmly, "Did you lick the bottom of your shoe?"

He grimaced irritably. "What is that supposed to mean? Did I lick my shoe? Is that supposed to be a joke, Helen? Our daughter is out there somewhere and you want to tell jokes? I'm in no mood for your stupidity!"

Helen paused her knitting to gaze at her husband. "Certainly, you have heard the phrase a lick and a promise.

Maybe if you lick the bottom of your shoe, you'll find a promise."

"Shut up, Helen! I'm in no mood for your foolishness. I should have known not to try to confide in you."

Helen lowered her crochet needles and spoke bluntly. "Then let me speak clearly. A lick and a promise means giving a half-assed effort. The only time you read the Bible is when you're worried about something. Sure, it sits on your table for people to see, but you don't *read* it. And what are you doing? Flipping the Bible open and hoping the Lord is going to speak to you? Is that what you're doing? Are you hoping to find some hope in the random landing of your finger? Well?"

"The Lord can talk to me that way if he wants to," Mitch replied.

"Half-assed. Maybe you won't be so worried if you actually sit down and read the Bible every day. Then, you would know what God promises without having to flip back and forth and try to find a promise that may not even apply to you. Better yet, you'd have the confidence to know the Lord is with her."

"Like he was in the cellar? You can't tell me you're not worried about Laura."

She exhaled heavily. "God was with Laura in that cellar, and I thank the Lord every day that she is still alive. Cass Travers would be alive and well today if he and Jesse had killed her and Jake. And you don't know how the Lord is going to use that baby. Someday, that baby you despise so much could make you the proudest grandfather on earth. But to answer your question, I am scared to death. But I have given it to the Lord. I'm trying to keep myself busy, so I'm not fretting myself into a tight ball of nerves. I know the Lord is not surprised by what happened, nor is he sitting on his throne, biting his nails, fearing for Laura. He's right here with me and he's right there with Laura. The Lord knows what's happening. He knows how it's going to end too. One promise you might keep in mind is that he promises never to leave his children, not in good times and certainly not in times of trouble.

"You were once a Godly man but have slipped down some slope that must have a glacier frozen on it because it's not reaching your heart anymore, not like Jesus used to. There was a time when you read the scriptures like you were devouring them. Now, Mitch, you don't even read your Bible. You play the motions and act the part, but your heart has gotten hard. What happened to Laura back in July wasn't God's fault. Nor was it Jake's."

"It was Jake's fault!" Mitch shouted. "Now my baby girl is carrying some outlaw's wicked spawn and I'll never forgive Jake for that! Jake is probably the one who took her today."

"Jake didn't take her. He was with the posse, looking for her. I watched them ride back into town. He saw me in the window and waved. Jake looked absolutely devastated."

"Good! He deserves it."

"Mitch, God can't forgive an unforgiving heart. Keep in mind the parable of the unforgiving servant. Sometimes, we do things that are hard to forgive, too. I'll remind you of last week when you wanted to force Laura to drink that poison and kill her baby. And if that isn't bad enough, you beat her and me with your belt. Those were evil actions that you chose to do. Jake didn't choose what happened to Laura."

"I was drunk!" he exclaimed with a raised voice.

"Well, that just makes it so much better. That's the perfect reason to want to kill our grandson." She held up the blue knit cap she was making to show him what she was doing. "You beat your daughter and wife worse than you would an animal."

"What is that, a hat?" His eyes narrowed bitterly at the sight of the small knit cap.

"Yes. I'm making a blue one for a boy and a pink one for a girl."

"Not in my house!" He ripped the little hat out of her hand and walked hurriedly toward the woodstove. The balls of yarn were pulled out of the wicker basket beside her chair as a long line of yarn trailed behind him.

"Ouch! My finger was in the yarn; you imbecile!" she shouted as she jerked her finger free from a loop in the yarn. "Mitchell Whitehead, don't you dare!" she exclaimed, rising from her chair as he neared the woodstove.

He opened the closed door and tossed the half-completed hat into the fire before slamming the wood stove's door closed.

"You had no right to do that!" she shouted with angry tears filling her eyes. "Do you think it's easy for me to be her mother and see her go through this nightmare? I decided today that if she comes home again, I'll be thankful for her and that baby for the rest of my life. You can leave if you can not do the same, but I honestly thought you were accepting her situation. I don't think it's in you to be compassionate for her. I think you're so wrapped up in your bitterness that you'd rather see Jake suffer than your daughter live. I want to see Laura smiling again and I want to see her playing with that baby! I don't care who the father is. I want to see and hear Laura laugh like she used to. I will not allow you to ruin my peace because you are lost in your own sorrows. My relationship with Jesus is my peace. I know his promises, and I'm holding onto them to the best of my ability. That's all I have to hold onto. Read your Bible, and maybe you can learn to handle moments like this without starting a fight to make yourself feel better. As for me, I'm going to make my grandson or granddaughter a cap to keep his or her head warm."

"I'll just burn it," he muttered under his breath.

"That says more about your character than anything else, Mitch. I'm so proud that I married you," she barked loudly and sat in her chair.

"You know we have a guest downstairs, right?"

"Yes. Tim is a nice young man. God forbid he learns you're not the man you claim to be in public."

There was a knock on the exterior door on the side of the building. The knock startled both of them, as it was after dark and getting late. Mitch hesitated a moment and walked to the door. He opened it. It took him a moment. "Marshal Bannister. Come in. Did you hear about Laura?"

Matt stepped inside the home and removed his hat. "I did. I spent the afternoon looking for her. We haven't found her yet, but I promise you I will. I won't stop looking until I do. And those who took her will pay the consequences for doing so."

"Thank you. Was it the men that killed the sheriff who took her?" Mitch's fear was evident in his voice.

"I'm not sure. There were four or five of them according to Gunther and the others in the posse. Only one man took Laura. That's the man I'm looking for. I wanted to stop by and let you know if it's humanly possible to save her, I'll bring her home to you. And whoever took her will get a bullet or a noose around his neck. I'll be at his side every step of the way to make sure it happens. That's the only promise I can give you, but I do promise you that."

"Thank you," Mitch said, relieved to hear Matt's words.

Mitch could feel an undeniable sense of strength, security, and peace coming from Matt. It wasn't his physical strength, but something internal that Mitch suddenly realized he did not have.

Matt offered Helen a kind yet comforting smile. "Mrs. Whitehead, rest assured, I'll find her. You folks have a good night."

"Marshal, thank you for rushing here to help find her," Helen said.

Matt shook his head just slightly. "My deputies and I didn't come here for that, but I'm thankful we are here. I'll find her and bring her home to you if it is humanly possible. That I promise you."

Mitch closed the door and was strangely quiet. He looked at Helen. "Matt Bannister is here." His eyes began to water.

Helen took a deep breath and exhaled, feeling a sense of relief. "The providence of God works in strange ways, Mitch. Now, quit half-assing it and *read* your Bible. God keeps his promises. Every time I see a rainbow in the sky, I am reminded of how faithful God is, even when some folks don't know why the rainbow is there or what it represents. I know that it's God's only visible representation of his faithfulness to keep his promises. I don't doubt the Lord, Mitch. The question you have to ask is, why do you?"

———

MATT SAT at a table inside the 1878 Saloon with his two deputies, Truet Davis and Morton Sperry, having a fine steak dinner with baked potatoes and boiled broccoli mixed with chopped carrots. It was one the finest meals Matt had ever had in a saloon. Across the table from them sat Gunther, Bode, and Jake Thomas.

The conversation revolved around Laura and the plan to spread out the following morning to find the man's trail that had taken her. Speculation had gone nowhere as there were no suspects other than the two new faces in the saloon belonging to Rusty and Byron. No one had seen anyone suspicious except for a tall, ugly man who had come into the saloon the night before.

Bode said, "Matt, have you talked with the young man who's working at the Whitehead's store? I've never seen him before until today."

"No."

Bode called to a nearby table, "Artie, what do you know about the new man working for the Whiteheads? Anything?"

Artie Hope lived across the street from the hardware store. "I don't know much. Marlene had lunch yesterday with Helen, and she mentioned that his name was Tim. He's wintering here. I understand he's staying in the store-room. I hear he is doing a good job. That's all I know."

Hearing that an unaccounted-for young man was living in the same residence as Laura caught Matt's attention. "No one told me about him. I'll speak with him in the morning. Well, gentlemen, I think we should get back to Holly's in case there's trouble there. Tomorrow, can we keep four or five of your most trusted hands at the Fairchild Estate to protect Holly just in case the outlaws we're looking for circle back around?" Matt asked Gunther.

He nodded. "Yep. I'm sure Bode's mother would like him to volunteer. She has Holly in her mind to make Bode a good wife. And we don't argue with her, do we, son?" Gunther asked with a broad smile.

Bode shook his head slowly. "Like I told Mother, I have nothing to offer her that she doesn't already have."

Matt stood from the table. "You're half right, Bode. Holly doesn't need anyone to provide for her. But even the most beautiful women like to be listened to, cared for, and loved. They want someone to love them all the way through the good and bad, to be faithful and committed to only them. Women like to be heard, held, and comforted, and to be protected. They want someone to share their life with. Holly is no different. Everything Holly wants or needs doesn't cost a thing. You have more to offer her than you know. You might want to take a chance tomorrow to get to know her. We can track Laura without you." He looked at Morton, who remained seated. "Are you coming?"

"I'll be along shortly. You two go ahead," he said to Matt and Truet.

Bode said, "I'm just a dumb ranch hand. What would anyone like Holly see in me?"

Matt tapped his chest. "A man with integrity and heart. I just told you what she wanted. It doesn't cost a thing except the investment of taking a chance of letting her get to know the real you."

––––––

WHEN MATT and Truet left the saloon, they were quickly followed by Gunther, Bode, and Jake Thomas. Morton carried his chair and set it down at the table where Rusty and Byron were sitting with Barry McCracken and an ex-employee of the Long T Ranch by the name of Fallen McArthur, who now worked for the Dawson Lakes Ranch with Barry.

"Mind if I join you?" Morton asked while taking his seat.

Barry answered before anyone else could, "I don't see why not; I don't think any of us have broken any laws yet today to make us fear a deputy US Marshal joining us."

Morton grunted. "Heck, I've done more wrong in this world than all of you combined."

"I'd say so," Byron volunteered, feeling the alcohol's effects. "Morton led the Sperry-Helms Gang for years. How many banks and stagecoaches have you robbed in your life-time? Thirty-some stagecoaches and six or seven banks?"

"None that I was convicted for," Morton said with a wry smile. He had lost count of how many stagecoaches he and his cousin had robbed, but he had robbed six banks in his outlaw career and guessed thirty-some stagecoaches. The accurate guess of both and the other things Byron seemed to know about him was uncanny and made him suspicious. He continued as if he had not taken notice of the accurate numbers. "But I'm on the other side of the law now, not to say that I'm a little more lenient than my boss would like occasionally. I still have my moments where the law is negotiable. Don't tell Matt I said that," he finished with a friendly smile to put the others at ease.

Barry McCracken asked, "Matt doesn't have much mercy for people, does he? Outlaws, I mean."

"It depends on the situation and what you would consider mercy." Morton looked at Rusty to explain, "He's merciful to those who come clean and want to walk away from the outlaw life. Those who don't, well, many of them are in their graves."

"I heard you killed innocent people. I don't think you were one who understood mercy," Rusty said to change the direction of the conversation.

"Me?" Morton asked, widening his eyes. "I killed my share of folks. I wish I hadn't, but I did. I live with that. But what I didn't know then that I understand now is that human life is precious, and how we choose to live it is what we are going to sow in the end."

Rusty chortled. "So you became a lawman and a philosopher?"

"No. I just don't want to live my life in fear, anger, and hurt anymore. How many outlaws do you know that can honestly say they're joyful people? I don't know of any. Joyful people want to encourage others, not terrorize them. It's as simple as this: I want to enjoy my time on earth and live peacefully with a wife who loves me and children who respect me. You don't have that living as an outlaw. When I was running the Sperry-Helms Gang, all I knew was the fear of being caught, always looking behind me to see if I was being tracked by the law or someone looking for revenge. The only thing in my future was planning the next robbery because money never lasts, and then I was looking behind me again. How to use a gun, violence, intimidation, and crime were all I knew, but it didn't fill anything in here." He tapped his chest. "Everything I did lacked honor and integrity, and yet I still called myself a man." He shook his head. "Honor doesn't lie, cheat or steal. An honorable man doesn't hurt others for selfish gain. A dishonorable man does. I want to live my life as an honorable man the best that I can so that the children I raise will have something positive and good to look up to and learn from in this lifetime. I'm getting a late start in life, but now I sleep well, and there's nothing I'm afraid of anymore; not one thing. I'm free of my past and the wrongs that I caused to others. That doesn't mean the past may not come back and haunt me when a son, brother, or father puts a bullet in my back, but in here,"—he tapped his heart again—"I'm right with God, and I'm right with me. For the first time in my life, I feel good about being me. And that's something that no outlaw that I've ever known can honestly say."

"Even though your family wanted you dead?" Byron asked quizzically.

Morton's eyes narrowed slightly. "Even so," he answered. All four of the men he sat with had their hands on top of the table. He was tempted to ask Byron how he would know about that but resisted. "The only ones worth worrying about in my family are my cousins and none of them have come for me. Nor has anyone else, so I'm guessing what little bounty they're offering isn't worth the risk of dying. What are they offering anyway, a goat?" He chuckled.

Rusty frowned. "I don't think Jesse Helms is anyone to take lightly."

Morton nodded with a raised brow. "Well, that's true. But I know Jesse better than he knows himself. He's good with a gun, dangerous, and intense, but he's also as stupid as the dullest thinking sheep in the flock."

"He seems to be staying ahead of the law down south," Rusty argued. He was offended by the insult toward his friend.

"Until he gets caught," Morton said with a nonchalant shrug of his shoulders. "And he will. Jesse doesn't think plans through. He reacts to half-thought-out ideas, and now I'm not there to rein him in and think plans through. He'll hang himself before long, rest assured. Anyway, I'm calling it a night." He stood and hesitated. "Oh, Byron, how did you know my family put a bounty on me?"

Byron felt a chill run down his spine as his eyes widened. He had no answer other than the truth of Jesse telling him so. He could see Rusty's eyes harden as they stared at the tabletop. "I ah...I...ah, I heard that man in jail say so. Remember, I told you about overhearing that man in jail?"

Morton could see the surprise of the question written in Byron's expression and hear the struggling thoughts take form in the pattern of his voice. It was a lie. "Oh. Well, that makes sense. I sure wish I knew who that man was. It makes me wonder if he rode with us or how I might have known him. Well, you all have a good night."

Rusty glared at Byron for a moment after Morton had left. He wanted to tell Byron what a fool he was, but there were other men at the table. "I wouldn't want Jesse Helms looking for me if I was him," Rusty said.

Fallon McArthor picked his nose, pulled a booger out on the tip of his finger, and wiped it on the table's edge. "Jesse Helms won't ever come around here again."

Rusty smirked knowingly. "I think you're right about that." Morton could say whatever he wanted to about Jesse, but Jesse had planned and gotten away with taking Laura. Now, all Rusty and Byron had to do was play along for a few days and decide to leave.

———

THE HOURS HAD PASSED, and it was all Laura could do to stay warm as the night was bitterly cold. Her inner upper thighs burned from a rash that was forming from the hours of riding in the saddle. Exhaustion weighed heavily upon her as she struggled to keep her eyes open. Jesse sat behind the saddle's cantle, sharing a wool blanket wrapped around them both. She had no idea where they were, but Jesse was taking her far from her home.

Laura had wept, prayed, and tried to run away while urinating but was quickly caught and placed back on the horse. The wool blankets and Jesse's body heat helped, but the dress she wore was not meant to keep her warm, and every light breeze that crept up her legs brought a chill. Opening her eyes, unclear if she had slept momentarily or not, Laura tried to peer into the darkness to see if she could locate anything that might reveal where they were, but all she could see after hours of riding was darkness and the outline of trees, hills, and an occasional owl flying overhead. She had no idea what time it was when she could finally see the outline of buildings take form in the darkness. They were entering a small town without a single lantern burning in a window when suddenly Jesse's mouth moved close to her ear. He whispered, "We're almost home." The warmth of his breath on her skin sent a chill down her spine.

They turned left on a road that led out of town, entered a forested area beside a mountain, and eventually approached an isolated large home that looked as black as night in the darkened shadows of a large mountain.

Laura was gently helped down from the horse and led inside the dark house. Jesse disappeared to wake an old woman who appeared to have an angry and harsh expression in the dim lantern's light that she carried. Her long gray hair was loose and fell behind her sloped shoulders. She was a stocky woman who whispered to Jesse in the kitchen before having him grab a bottle of something from the back of the highest cabinet. The old woman quietly cursed so as not to wake anyone else when Jesse spilled the liquid on the counter. After a moment, she and Jesse approached Laura, who was held in place by Colin's firm grip on her bicep. The old woman held the lantern in front of Laura's face so she could see her clearly. "Hmm!" the woman grunted. "She's pretty. And young enough to give you twelve sons before she's used up. Good. Well, good night, little lady."

Jesse slipped behind Laura and suddenly placed a rag soaked in ether over her face. Laura tried to fight him, but she was quickly contained and growing faint as she breathed the fumes in. Her body went limp as she passed out in Jesse's arms.

Mattie Sperry glared warningly at her nephew. "You may be her husband, but you leave her training to me, Jesse! You know where to put her; just make sure she has plenty of blankets. You and your friend can sleep in Henry and Bernice's old room tonight."

CHAPTER TWENTY-THREE

LAURA'S HEAD ACHED AS IT DREW HER OUT OF A deep sleep. Her eyes opened to see the darkest blackness that she could ever imagine. Confused and disoriented, she could feel the weight of blankets covering her, but the darkness was thicker than the purest shade of black paint in her father's store. Panic struck like lightning, illuminating the sky without a moment's warning. Afraid of the dark, she sat up quickly and hit her head on an unseen barrier about a foot above where she lay. A knot began to form on Laura's forehead. Her hands reached out in the darkness to find cold wooden walls surrounding her, trapping her in a wooden box without a hint of light. Terrified of being buried alive, her heart raced, and her breathing quickened with shallow breaths. Incoherent whimpers rose to terrified screams, though no words could be formed through the wailing of a panic-stricken terror unlike any she had known before. She screamed as loud as her vocal cords could reach and pressed against the lid with all her might but was unable to budge it.

"No, no, no. Mommy! Help me, Lord," she screamed. "Someone help me! Mommy! Help! Help! Oh, my Lord, please help me," she sobbed between screams. Her feet kicked at the other end of the box while her fingernails scratched at the wood above her. "Let me out! Let me out! Please, God, help me! Let me out!" she cried as a fingernail dug into the wood and was pulled out of the nailbed. Oblivious to the pain, she kept trying to dig frantically through the wooden plank above her while desperately crying out as loud as she could for anyone to hear.

———

VINCE SPERRY WAS twenty-seven years old. He was of average height and overweight, with a large belly that fell over the waistline of his trousers, which were held up by suspenders. He had brown hair that fell straight to reach his earlobes. He had a round face that had been recently shaven and green eyes. He stood beside his mother next to the chicken coop that was set over an underground box they used to conceal anyone hiding from the law. Usually, the hiding box was not covered by a lid, but they placed Laura within the box and set the tongue in groove lid on top before adding several unsplit rounds of oak firewood to weigh it down so Laura could not budge the lid. They had slid the chicken coop back over the hole to conceal it for the night. Mattie had been patiently waiting for Laura to wake up.

"Now, Ma?" Vince asked his mother. They could hear Laura's desperate wailing coming from the ground.

Mattie shook her head with a bitter scowl. "Not yet."

"She's terrified, Ma." Vince had woken up that morning to the news of a new house guest sleeping in the hiding box. He had experienced something very similar before when his brother Alan was sent to prison and his wife Rachel wanted to take her children and leave the Sperry farm. Mattie had used her bottle of ether to put Rachel to sleep and let her wake up in the box with no way out. Rachel's response was similar to this woman's, but this young woman was more hysterical. The screaming and anguished cries coming from under the chicken coop were haunting. "How much longer, Mother? I think she's had enough."

"Shut up!" Mattie exclaimed. "I don't want her to hear you talking. She has to experience this to understand what will happen if she tries to leave. I should have done this to Morton's wife as soon as she got here, but I didn't. I want that fear you hear to soak in deep so she comes out of that pit broken like a horse ready to be ridden."

Tad Sperry walked out back, rubbing the sleep from his eyes. "What's all the noise? Who is in the hole?" He yawned.

"Jesse's bride. The pregnant one," Mattie answered.

"Jesse's back? He brought her here, really? I saw her at the doctor's office that day. She's pretty, I thought. Bring her up; let's see what she looks like."

Mattie turned her hardened gaze toward Tad. "You leave her alone! I won't have another son of mine stealing someone else's wife like your uncle Morton did. Grandson, either."

Tad lowered his brow. "I just want to see if she's as pretty as I remember her being. I only saw her for a moment."

Through the sobbing and frantic cries, Laura called out frantically, "Help! Somebody help me! Lord, please...." She sobbed, choking on her uncontrollable breaths.

Colin Kennedy briskly walked out of the house and shouted, "Get her out of there! Can you not hear that she is terrified?" He did not wait for Mattie's permission; he braced his arms against the chicken coop to push it back from the hole it covered.

Mattie's lips tightened into a slight snarl. "Vince, help him push the chicken coop back and pull her out."

They slid the chicken coop back, exposing a hole that looked like a grave with a casket inside with three pieces of unsplit firewood resting on the lid. "Just a minute, and I'll have you out," Colin said as he began tossing the heavy, unsplit rounds of wood off the lid. Laura's pounding on the lid and efforts to push it off barely moved the heavy plank lid.

Colin lifted the lid, allowing the bright gray clouds in the sky to chase the darkness away. Laura, wild-eyed and frantic, crawled frantically out of the box onto the ground covered with chicken manure. Her hands clenched the hardened soil and manure, like a sandy beach after a week lost at sea. She wailed uncontrollably.

Mattie grabbed her by the hair and jerked Laura to her feet forcefully. "Hush!" she shouted, shaking Laura's body by the hair. "Hush your babbling, or I'll put you back in there until you stop crying! We don't cry around here. Stop blubbering!"

Laura was not able to calm the panic that consumed her. She had been afraid of the dark since the night Jesse and Cass Travers attacked her, but terrified of being put back in the box, she tried to gain control of her sobbing.

Mattie waited for her to quiet down while holding a secure grip on her hair. "Are you going to obey me?" she asked, jerking Laura's head forward to keep her eyes downward.

Laura's lips trembled as she tried to nod affirmingly.

"Good. I am your new mother now, and you'll call me Ma. Do you understand me?"

Laura's lips tried to speak, but her voice was raw and low. "Yes."

"What's my name?" Mattie demanded to know with a jerk of Laura's hair.

"M...Ma."

"Good. I don't know what your name is, but from here on, you'll go by Alice Helms. Your new name is Alice Helms. You are going to be Jesse's wife and you're going to learn to like it. We are your family now. Who am I?"

Laura could hardly breathe from the nightmare that was quickly transforming in her life. "M...Ma."

"And your name?"

"My name's Laura," she screamed defiantly. Mattie quickly jerked Laura toward the hole by her hair. "No! No! No! Alice! I'm Alice!" Laura screamed desperately and began sobbing with loud wails at the sight of the box.

"Alice, what?" Mattie shouted into her ear.

"Helms!" Laura sobbed. "I'm Alice Helms. Please, don't put me back in there. I'm begging you," she pleaded through her tears. She dropped to her knees and collapsed to the ground, sobbing uncontrollably.

Mattie smiled just enough to show she enjoyed the power of seeing the young lady beg for mercy. "Now, stand up like a Helms and give your new momma a hug. And then we'll get you cleaned up." She smiled broader as Laura slowly stood and hugged her obediently. "We have a baby to deliver in a few months, and I don't want you getting so upset that you lose it. I'll show you to your room. You are going to love our family, aren't you, Alice?"

Laura sniffled as she allowed herself to be led into the house. "Yes," she said weakly.

"Yes, what?" Mattie asked. Her tone was as sharp as a thorn.

"Yes, Ma."

Tad nudged Colin's shoulder as they stood by the hole, watching. "I bet you she's my wife within the year. Jesse never sticks around for long. Grandma and I will have her trained in no time. Just wait and see."

"I think you and your family are a twisted bunch of people," Colin said before going to the privy.

———

HOLLY FAIRCHILD HAD her blonde hair tied back with a red ribbon and a bow above her forehead to hold her hair back as she cooked breakfast for her guests. She wore a plain brown dress and an apron to keep the dress clean. She fried eggs and bacon in one frying pan, diced potatoes in another and had biscuits in the oven.

Holly was heavily burdened and had not slept well. Her eyes were red and puffy from weeping. The loss of Wolfgang and Ross was reminiscent of losing her husband and brought the past back to life. What haunted her the most was Laura missing and she felt the heavy burden of being partly to blame.

Matt, Truet, and Alessandro all three offered to make breakfast so she could rest, but Holly insisted the men go sit down so she could busy herself with cooking.

It was just after seven in the morning and Matt was looking out the window at the lake while eating thoughtfully. "We had to have missed something yesterday. Gunther may have had good intentions leading the posse, but they ruined any sign that was left behind." It wasn't anything Truet didn't already know. Matt was talking primarily to himself. Kent Kruse and Alessandro went to the Dutch Construction Company's camp to ask Dutch if he could spare a few men with guns to watch over Holly's house until the bunch of outlaws were caught. Holly had gone back upstairs to lie down.

Truet answered, "She could have been taken by someone local and tied up in a house just around the corner, as far as we know." He took a bite of his bacon. "Whoever it was didn't disappear. There must be a trail somewhere."

"I'm afraid there's a lot of trails now that the posse rode all along the river. If we had a good identifying track of the man's horse, that would help, but we don't even have that. I hate to say it, but this is turning into the proverbial looking for a needle in a haystack."

"Morning," Morton said as he came downstairs. He looked tired and immediately poured himself a cup of coffee before sitting down.

"Did you get drunk?" Matt asked with a disappointed expression.

"No. I couldn't sleep." He yawned. "After you two left, I joined those two cowboys looking for work, Rusty and Byron. I was curious and sat down to talk with them. I didn't get much, but I know they're lying. What I can't figure out is how they know so much about me. Byron knew my family had put a bounty on me, but the way he said it was past tense. I asked him how he knew that, and he said he heard it from that man he was in jail with. But yesterday, when he told us that story out on the river, he said that was three years ago."

Matt listened with interest. "So, how would he know?"

"I couldn't sleep because I asked myself that question all night long." He held up two fingers. "Two things came to mind. When we ran into them, they were coming down Daphanie Creek and said they didn't find anything. I told you when I led the Sperry-Helms Gang that we robbed the bank here in town, and that was our escape route. We stayed in the river and went up that creek. It's marked by a willow tree, so you can't miss it. The creek has a rock base, so it was perfect for us."

Truet asked, "What are you getting at?"

Morton's eyes hardened as his face grew somber. "You two were in the office when Jesse came in to tell me my family's so-called bounty was gone. That makes it past tense, but his last words were a sarcastic mockery; I thought about me getting married. Remember, he said something about finding a wife."

Matt's fork slowly lowered to his plate as he considered the words he had just heard.

"You can't be serious. You think Jesse took her?" Truet questioned.

Morton held up a single finger. "I thought about it all night long. It's the only thing that makes sense. How could Byron and Rusty know so much about me and what I did? He knew how many stagecoaches and banks I had robbed. It wasn't a lucky guess. I know Jesse, and if it is him, he used the same escape route I made when we robbed the bank. The only difference is I think he had Rusty and Byron stay here to make sure no one followed his trail up that creek."

Matt said, "We'll ask Gunther if he sent them or they volunteered to check that creek. I would hate for you to be wrong while Laura is still missing."

"Matt, I think Jesse has her. There are too many coincidences. I'm not that famous. The only way they would know how many stagecoaches and banks we robbed is if Jesse told them. That's the conclusion I came to overnight."

"Jesse wouldn't risk showing his face in town, would he?" Truet asked Morton.

"No. He'd stay out of sight, which explains the sheriff being killed way out yonder somewhere. Remember those two saying Jesse was in Nevada, causing trouble? Where did they say they were from? Nevada. He's got his new gang here working for him. That's the conclusion I came to overnight. And I promise you that Rusty and Byron are outlaws, not cowboys. I recognized that right away. That's why I went to talk to them."

"How would he know Laura was going to Holly's? As far as we know, those two men had nothing to do with Holly or Laura's family," Truet pondered. "They were with the posse when she was taken."

"That I don't know," Morton admitted.

"I think I might," Matt said, remembering there was a new employee at the hardware store who was wintering there. "We're going to town."

———

MITCH WHITEHEAD'S hands shook with troubled nerves as he busied himself, pouring a cup of coffee while Tim continued to take inventory. Mitch sipped the hot cup of coffee. He had not slept more than an hour at most overnight. "Tim, don't forget about the items out front."

"I already counted them, Mr. Whitehead."

Mitch nodded his approval. "I'm going to leave the store in your hands today, Tim. I don't think Helen should be alone today." He had said the words, but he knew he was more emotionally compromised than Helen was.

Tim swallowed. "I hope they find Laura and she's okay. I really do."

"Me too, Tim. You'll never know the depths of fear a father can feel until you are one. I hope you never have to go through this in your lifetime. It would have been easier if we found her dead body. At least then, we'd know where she was." His lips squeezed tightly together as a well of emotion moistened his eyes.

Tim lowered his head, unable to look Mitch in the eyes. Shame, like a twenty-pound sledgehammer falling from the sky, cut a hole through his soul, leaving a whirlpool for what was left of his integrity to drain away slowly. "I'm sorry, Mr. Whitehead."

"Mitch," Helen shouted down from the stairs behind the hardware store's counter. "Will you come upstairs, please."

"I'll be right there, Helen," Mitch replied. He ascended the stairs, and a few moments later, he came back downstairs and said, "Tim, will you come here, please."

Tim hurried upstairs, opened the door, and stepped into the Whitehead home. "Yeah, boss?" he asked. He froze when he saw a man standing in the room wearing a federal marshal's badge pinned to his lapel. The man reached his hand out to shake, masked with a stern expression. "I'm Matt Bannister. What is your name?"

"Tim, Sir. Tim Hazelton." He shook Matt's hand, feeling a chill creep through his spine, knowing the man whose hand he shook had killed more outlaws than most outlaws kill in their short lifetime. He swallowed nervously.

"Have a seat," Matt said, nodding toward a chair. "I'll let you know now that my deputies are watching the front and back doors of the building, so you have nowhere to go…"

Helen Whitehead was troubled by Matt's sudden change of tone and abruptness with their young guest. "Do you think it's necessary to be rude, Marshal? Tim doesn't know anything about Laura's disappearance."

"Forgive me," Matt said to Mrs. Whitehead. He turned his attention back to Tim, who sat in the chair Matt had nodded toward. Tim's hands fiddled nervously before wiping his sweaty palms on his pants.

"What…what's this all about?" Tim asked with a quivering voice.

"I think you know," Matt said calmly, watching him carefully.

He shrugged and shook his head. His muscles were tight and his eyes danced around the room. His breathing was growing more shallow and quicker. "I don't know. I mean…I stole a handful of candies from the bowl downstairs. I'm sorry, Mitch. You can take it out of my pay."

"That's fine, Tim," Mitch replied. He asked Matt, "Marshal, are you accusing Tim of something? He was here when Laura was taken and when Sheriff Emmerson was murdered. Helen and I can both assure you of that."

"Yes, we can," Helen agreed.

Matt ignored Mitch and Helen, grabbed a dining room chair, set it in front of Tim, and sat down. He spoke softly. "I'm going to be reasonable with you, Tim, and I suggest you be honest because I can become unreasonable very quickly. What do you know about Laura's disappearance?"

Mitch exclaimed in a raised voice. "I just said he doesn't know anything! How about you leave him alone and go find my daughter."

Helen added, "Marshal Bannister, I think you're wasting

your time. He can't tell you anything that he doesn't know."

Matt closed his eyes as he took a deep breath. He could see Tim's confidence rise with the support of the White-heads. Tim answered, "I don't know anything like they said."

Matt placed his fingertips together as he leaned over his knees, watching Tim. He explained calmly, "Mr. and Mrs. Whitehead, I am trying to find your daughter. You're not making it any easier. Please, let me talk to Tim. That's all I ask. Okay?"

"But we've both told you he was here the whole time," Mitch argued.

Matt nodded. "I do not doubt that. I'm not accusing him of taking her. I know he didn't, but that doesn't mean he didn't tell someone when she was going to Holly's house. You knew the day before, right?"

"We all knew. It was planned," Helen answered.

Matt shouted unexpectedly, "Let him answer! Shut up and let him answer for himself." His harsh glare penetrated Helen's soul, and she took a step backward, afraid to speak again. Matt turned back to Tim. "You knew the day before, right?" he demanded to know.

Tim stuttered before answering, "Yes, sir. As she said, we all did."

"Who did you tell?" Matt asked calmly.

Tim shook his head, beginning to panic. "No one. I don't know anyone here. Who am I going to tell?"

Matt hesitated to make Tim just a bit more uncomfortable under his knowing gaze. "How about Rusty? Byron? Jesse Helms, by chance?"

Tim's eyes widened as the panic sent a sharp wave of horror through his body. He didn't know how, but the marshal knew what he had done. He looked at Mitch and Helen, knowing he had betrayed them and couldn't stand to face them or admit his wrong. He looked for a way out, but the marshal was too dangerous to try to fight and too close to run past him. The front and back of the building were being watched; he was trapped.

"Nonsense!" Mitch shouted. "How dare you mention that man's name in our home? You better leave my house, Marshal. I swear, I've never heard a more ridiculous accusation in my life. My daughter is out there somewhere and you're harassing an innocent young man over something he doesn't know anything about!"

Matt stood and turned his head to peer at Mitch. He spoke in a calm but authoritative voice. "We have reason to believe Jesse Helms took your daughter, and he is a part of it."

"There is no way..." Mitch began to say. He stopped when Tim took off sprinting down the hallway into Laura's bedroom and slammed the door behind him. Matt turned and ran down the hallway and burst through the bedroom door just in time to see Tim pushing the window up so he could crawl out of it. The drop to the ground was a good fifteen feet into a narrow alley.

Matt shoved Tim onto Laura's bedside table, knocking everything off it as Tim collided with the wall, coming to rest on the tabletop. Matt grabbed Tim's ankles and dragged him off the table, dropping him onto the narrow space of floor between the bed and the window. Tim hollered, trying to kick his legs free of Matt's grip. Matt released his ankles, jumped to the side, avoiding the flailing legs and slammed his right boot down on the young man's chest before sliding it to Tim's throat and pushing down to choke him. Tim's hands grabbed at and hit Matt's boot and lower leg, but he froze when he saw Matt's .45 caliber Colt being drawn and aimed down at his head.

Matt eased the pressure off Tim's throat as he pulled the hammer back until it clicked. His eyes were hardened with the mercy of cold steel as he asked in a firm voice, "Where is she?"

"His aunts! He's taking her to his aunt's house," Tim spouted quicker than a frightened piglet squealing after being kicked. He began to whimper as the crotch of his pants grew dark with urine. "Don't...kill...me. I'll tell you whatever you want to know. Please, just don't kill me."

"Who did you tell?" Matt demanded to know.

"Jesse...and my cousin." He whimpered as he wept.

"Who is your cousin?"

"C...Colin."

"Colin, who?"

"Colin Kennedy. He's with...Jesse."

"Jesse Helms?"

"Yes," Tim admitted and squeezed his eyes shut as his body jerked with quiet sobs.

"And Rusty and Byron? Are they involved?"

"Yes."

"What are they doing here? Was their job to cover the escape?"

"They're supposed to kill Gunther Thomas. That's all I know." He wept.

Matt could see that Tim was done trying to fight him and was willing to answer questions. He removed his foot and pulled Tim to his feet. Matt took notice that the ceramic piano music box that had belonged to Holly Fairchild had fallen to the floor and broken a leg off. He turned around to see Mitch and Helen at the bedroom door with dumbfounded expressions.

Helen removed her hand from covering her mouth. She whispered, "He has my daughter? Why?" she gasped. Her tear-filled eyes were gazing at Tim like an injured deer, longing for an answer to why the hunter wounded it.

Mitch found it hard to speak. "Y...You did this, Tim? You knew she was going to be taken by Jesse Helms? We took you in. We fed you. I trusted you. We were friends."

Tim gasped, unable to squeak out a word in return. The shame that had filled him came to the surface, and he lowered his head, crying. "So-orry," he got out in two broken breaths. "I..."

"Where is she?" Mitch shouted, suddenly angry. He stepped forward with a tightened fist to strike Tim. "Where is Laura?"

Matt put his hands up and pushed Mitch gently backward to stop him from hitting Tim. "Mr. Whitehead, I'll find her and bring her home. But it won't do any good if you break his jaw and he can't talk, now will it?"

Mitch turned and hit the wall with an angry scream. He turned to face Tim with an enraged snarl. "We treated you like family, Tim! How could you do this to us? I trusted you!"

"I'm sorry," Tim said as he wept. "I'm sorry. I'm so sorry," he repeated through his tears.

Matt said, "I'm taking him to the jail for the night. You can talk to him there." Matt said to Tim, "And if you are sorry, you can help by telling me the truth. That's the least you could do for these folks."

Helen's tears slid slowly down her cheek as she placed a hand on Tim's chest as Matt led him out of the room. "Please help us get Laura back."

Tim closed his eyes, nodded, and wept as Matt led him downstairs and out of the building.

CHAPTER TWENTY-FOUR

"MARSHAL BANNISTER, WHAT'S GOING ON?" THE deputy in the sheriff's office asked. He was surprised to see Matt bring Tim into the jail by the scruff of his neck.

"Throw Tim in one of your jail cells for me." He turned to Morton, who followed them. "You were right. It was Jesse who took her. Tim says he's taking her to your mother's house. Let's go collect Rusty and Byron before we go to Natoma."

"My mother's? Why?"

Tim answered, "Because Laura's having Jesse's baby. He wants her to raise it with your family."

"How would he know that?" Morton questioned.

"Someone named Tad told him. He found out at the doctor's office, I guess. Or something like that." He paused. "Marshal Bannister, will I be hung for what I did?" Tim asked nervously.

Matt shook his head. "Not likely. But you should ask yourself if you should be for the pain you caused the Whiteheads and the suffering you are putting Laura through. You cut them deeper than a sharp blade could. Throw him behind bars and lock that door. Tim, you and I will talk when I bring Laura home."

———

GUNTHER THOMAS STOOD in front of a large blackboard placed in front of the Hollister Cattle Association's meeting room, where the thirty-some men joining the posse were seated. The men were anxious to get in the saddle and start searching for one of their own citizens. Gunther had drawn a rudimentary map of the area and a line representing the river. He had broken the men up into three groups and planned a strategy to cover the most ground while remaining in earshot of a fired gun.

Matt, Truet, and Morton waited at the back of the meeting hall for the meeting to end. They remained pressed against the wall as the men in the posse left the meeting room until Matt saw Rusty walking toward him with Byron.

Matt waited for Rusty to step past him and drew his weapon, grabbed Rusty around the neck from behind and placed his revolver against Rusty's head. He pulled the hammer back until it clicked. "Don't move!"

Truet and Morton immediately pulled their revolvers and aimed them at Byron, who froze immediately and slowly raised his hands.

Morton holstered his weapon and removed Byron and Rusty's revolvers. He then secured Byron's wrists in a pair of shackles before moving to secure Rusty's wrists.

"What's this all about?" Rusty questioned. "You got the wrong man, Marshal. I don't know what you think you're doing, but we haven't done anything wrong."

There were a number of local cattlemen watching and most remained quiet, but Fallon MacArthur questioned why his new friends were being mistreated.

Gunther Thomas asked, "What's happening here?"

Rusty declared his innocence. "We're being arrested for something. I don't know what. We're just a couple of cowpunchers looking for a job," he said to the crowd of men.

Matt replied, "You should have taken one then. You two are under arrest for aiding and abetting Jesse Helms in his kidnapping of Laura Whitehead."

"What?" Rusty shouted. "I never even met the man. Gunther, you have some pull around here. Tell him to let us go."

"Matt, what kind of evidence have you got against them?" Gunther questioned.

"The kind that's going to save your life, Mr. Thomas. These two were sent here to kill you for Jesse Helms. I have Tim in the jail already. He told us everything we need to know. I imagine we'll find Jesse and Laura in Natoma, right?" he asked Rusty.

"I don't know!" Rusty seethed.

"Yeah, you do. Take them away. Truet, make sure they are not put in the same cell as Tim. I don't want them together."

Matt looked at Bode. "We're leaving. I imagine Jesse will be more than happy to surrender before we can kill him, so I'll be taking him to Branson. Someone will have to bring Laura home. We could use your help."

Jake Thomas volunteered before anyone else could, "I'm going! I'll do it."

"No, I will," Aaron Longley said while pushing his chest

out and stepping close to Jake to try to intimidate him. "She wants nothing to do with you, Jake."

Jake threw a right cross that hit Aaron in the jaw. The punch knocked Aaron to the floor. "I don't care if she wants anything to do with me or not. I love her. I'm going! If you try to interfere, I'll bust your head wide open!"

Bode said, "Jake and I will go. No one else."

———

THE FINGERNAIL on Laura's right index finger had been torn off, leaving the flesh exposed and throbbing with acute pain. Three other nails on her hands had been lifted from the nailbed just enough to make them sensitive to the touch, and one had a tear partly up the nail. Her misery wasn't just from her aching hands, but her inner thighs burned from the rash from the hours in the saddle. The longer she sat quietly on a dining room table chair set next to Mattie's rocking chair in the family room, the more her lower back began to ache. She shifted uneasily to find a more comfortable position, but the annoying ache could not be eased by repositioning. A wave of nausea was followed by a strange rise of heat that flushed her cheeks while Laura listened to Jannie Sperry's raspy cough while she coughed several times into a towel. Jannie wiped her mouth and laughed as her eyes went to Colin Kennedy. He had made a joke about her tattered stockings that showed under her poorly sewn woolen dress. It was an ugly gray dress that appeared to have been made from a wool blanket or something of the sort.

"Excuse me," Jannie said and coughed into the towel with another laugh. "I got a bug in my throat."

"From what I hear, you have more than that. But what

the hell? We all have to die sometime. I still think you're one pretty lady," Colin said. He had taken a liking to Jannie from the first time he met her the day they arrived from Nevada. But his feelings had grown for her throughout the days they stayed in Natoma.

"I'm not dying for years yet. I'll beat this, or my name isn't Jannie Sperry. We Sperrys are tough mountain folks. No little bug will beat us. Isn't that right, Ma?"

Mattie nodded. "Damn straight." She patted Laura's arm gently. "You better listen and learn. Helm's blood runs deep in all of us, Sperrys, and since you're marrying into the family, you had better toughen up, or you'll be eaten alive by this family of mine. I didn't raise pansies. I raised tough kids who can stand tall in this harsh world, and they won't back down to no one. That little boy inside of you is going to be the toughest of them all. I can tell you that right now."

Jannie peered at Laura and raised her brow questionably. She said with a wave of her dismissive hand, "She's just a teary-eyed little wench, Ma. There isn't nothing tough about her except maybe her hands after a few weeks of hard work here."

"She'll toughen up. Won't you, Alice?"

"Yes, Ma," Laura replied, feeling sicker to her stomach every time she said the words. She looked over at the kitchen table and saw a kitchen knife lying beside a loaf of bread. The longing to grab it and stab her stomach to kill the baby and herself was becoming more and more appealing the longer she sat with the repulsive Sperry family in their dirty home.

Tad Sperry tossed a small piece of bark from the wood-stove at her. "Hey, Alice, do you have a sister my age?"

Laura shook her head quietly. The annoying ache in her

back was slowly increasing. She shifted uneasily in the chair.

Mattie patted Laura's arm. "Answer him," she said firmly. "Around here, young lady, the wife answers to her man first, but any man in this family that speaks to you deserves an answer."

"No, I don't," she said softly. The fear of being thrown back into the hiding box terrified her.

"Cousins or friends?" Tad pressed. "Come on, you must have an attractive friend that we can take for me."

Laura shook her head. "No."

Tad rolled his eyes. "I need a woman. I'm old enough now."

Mattie replied, "I'll order one for you soon enough, Tad. In the meantime, you just leave Alice alone. By the way, Alice, tonight you and Jesse can sleep in Morton's old room. You'll need to consummate your wedding."

"What? What wedding?" Laura asked with a cold chill running up her spine.

"This afternoon, you two will marry the Sperry way. I'll say you're married, we can get drunk, and you'll start acting like a loving wife to your husband. If you have a problem with that, the hiding box will be your home until you can agree to be a loving wife."

Laura swallowed and silently cried out to the Lord. Her breath was squeezed from her chest. "May I use the privy?" she asked.

Mattie snapped, "May I use the privy, *Ma*! Don't forget that again, or you'll go back in the box! Do you understand me, Alice?" Her green eyes were ferocious.

"Yes, Ma," Laura whimpered.

Mattie nodded her head toward the back door. "Tad, go with her."

Outside, Tad walked beside her toward the privy. "You know Jesse is my favorite cousin. But when he leaves you, I'm claiming you as mine."

"You don't have to walk me to the door or wait outside it for me to relieve myself. I saw you peeking in on me when I bathed, and I don't appreciate it. You can wait here and see the door just fine. I want some privacy, please?" Laura spouted impatiently. She had learned that it was Tad who she had seen in the doctor's office. It was his fault that Jesse knew that she was pregnant. Laura could not stand Tad and did not want to look at him.

Tad grabbed her hair and yanked her head back forcefully. He drew his face close to her ear and hissed, "If I want to listen to you in there, I will! You better learn who the boss is when Jesse's not here. Do you think he's going to stay here and be your perfect husband? No, he won't. You'll be my woman soon enough, rest assured. I'll go in there with you if I want to!" He released her hair and slapped the back of her head. "Get in there and do what you have to do."

Laura closed the privy door and twisted the block of wood on a nail to lock the door. She sat on the bench seat and bent over to cover her face with her hands. The tears came quickly and she tried to weep quietly. With barely a whisper, she cried out desperately to the Lord, "Jesus, please help me. I'm scared. I want my mommy and daddy. Help me to get away from here, Lord. I want to go home. Help me...get back...home." She wept.

"Are you crying?" Tad bellowed from the other side of the door. "What did my grandma just say to you? You better toughen up before she beats the tears out of you with a switch and throws you back in the box."

"I'm not crying!" Laura shouted. "Go away!" The privy

was the only place where she could be alone, even for a short moment.

Tad yanked on the door, unable to pull the nail from the block. "Hurry up!"

Laura looked up at the roof of the privy and whispered, "Lord, you're my only hope. They always say you're faithful. Please help me. I want to go home."

Tad beat on the door. "Hurry up, I said!"

"Tad, back off!" Colin shouted as he neared the privy. Jesse had gone to town with Vince to pick up some food for the wedding ceremony. "Young lady." He paused at the door. "I can use the barn. Take your time." He pointed to the house and snapped at Tad, "Get back to the house. You can watch her from there."

Laura wiped her eyes and peered upward. "I don't want to stay here, Jesus. Please help me."

———

"So it was Jesse Helms who took her? It wasn't anyone after me?" Holly asked to reassure herself. She had been living on pins and needles, wondering if her life was in danger since her guards were murdered. She had sent word for more security guards, but as of yet, men from the construction site were her only protection aside from Alessandro and Kent Kruse.

Matt shook his head. "Jesse wasn't after you. He came here planning to take Laura and he did. We're on our way to get her back. I suspect we'll be there before dark, but I wanted to let you know that and wish you well, and I hope to see you again sometime."

"Of course. I'll come visit you and Christine before long. Matt, please find Laura and bring her home."

"Bode and Jake will be bringing her home."

"Good. That will give Jake and her time to talk. I hope she's okay. So, I have nothing to worry about here?"

"No."

"What about the sheep shooters?" she questioned nervously.

"Bode?" Matt deflected the question to him.

Bode cleared his throat nervously. "My father and I won't let anything happen. We're not part of that group, but they are part of the cattle association. I give you my word that you are in no danger living here."

She exhaled with relief. "Thank you. I imagine your word is as good as gold."

"I like to think so. Holly, my mother told me what you said about the sheep and the cattle market. I don't see the market dropping, but if it does, you might be right. There will always be a market for wool. My mother told me to keep an open mind. So I will. Maybe when I get back, we can talk about sheep?"

Holly watched Bode's eyes and knew he was being sincere. "I'd like that. Let me know when you return, and we can meet and discuss it over lunch or dinner, whatever works best for you."

"That sounds good. I'd like that."

Kent Kruse could feel his cheeks flush with a rising jealousy that swelled within him. He asked, "Matt, could you use another gun hand? I'm pretty handy with mine."

"Kent, if I know Jesse, there won't be any shooting. He'll surrender like last time. I don't need you."

Holly stood. "Matt, I don't want to rush you. But please go find Laura. The sooner she is back at home, the better I'll feel about this situation. I blame myself for what happened." She looked at Bode. "Please bring that young lady back home."

———

RUSTY WELLS SAT on the cot in his jail cell, rubbing a spider bite on his leg. "I don't think with the marshal's gun pointed at my head, I would have done any different, Tim. It's all right. You, Byron, and I didn't do anything wrong."

"I did," Tim said with a sorrowful voice. He was sitting on the bottom bunk in a cell to himself. "I should have been honest with Mr. and Mrs. Whitehead and protected Laura. I should have warned that lady's guards that Jesse was going to attack them. Maybe they'd still be alive, and Laura would be at home. I could have stopped it."

Rusty scoffed. "Maybe, but Jesse would have hunted you down and killed you if you had not done what you were told to do. Look at the bright side: you saved her parents' lives, and maybe she'll be brought back alive, too. At most, you'll get a month or two in jail, if that. You can claim that you had no choice due to fearing for your life. Byron and I did not break a single law, so we'll be out of here just as soon as we talk to the judge or can reason with the marshal. But if they want to arrest us, that's fine. Jesse's cousins will get us out of jail. We'll be free enough in no time."

Byron groaned tiredly. He was lying on the top bunk, staring at the ceiling. "I'm thinking as soon as I get back to the Helm's Dairy, I might take up residence and just work there. I kind of like those Mexican gals that work in the cheese room. It seems I could make more money milking cows and cheddaring cheese than I am robbing stagecoaches. Besides, I kind of liked the way it felt riding with that posse instead of running from one."

Rusty smiled. "Yeah, it had a particular enjoyment to it. It might have been more exciting if we were actually looking for someone. I might try settling down with that Gabriella gal. She's pretty enough to make milking cows worth it."

"Yeah," Byron agreed. "Well, I said from the beginning that this was a terrible idea. All it proves to me is that I don't want to ride with Jesse anymore. I'm grateful that we never tried to do what he wanted done. And as I said all along, we never earned a penny. Thank you, Jesse."

The sheriff's office door opened, and several men dressed in long black coats with white bags over their heads barged into the office carrying guns. "Get up and get ready to meet your makers!"

Rusty stood immediately and reached out his hands protectively. "Wait! Wait! Wait! We didn't do anything! We're innocent!"

One of the masked men unlocked the cell door; as others stepped inside to get control of Rusty and Byron, despite their pleas and fighting, they were tossed to the ground, and their hands were tied behind their backs.

"We didn't do anything!" Rusty continued to cry out for his innocence.

"Exactly," one of the men agreed. "Take them to the barn and grab that one, too," he said, pointing at Tim.

Tim stepped back against the wall. Terrified, he couldn't form any words as he was roughly grabbed and slammed against the bars. His arms were wrenched behind his back, and his wrists tightly tied together. As he was being led out of his cell, his high-pitched voice squeaked, "Rusty?"

"He can't save you, son. You should have chosen your friends better. Let's hang them, fellas."

Twenty minutes later, the dead bodies of Rusty and Byron hung by their necks in the livery stable from a rafter. Tim sat on a horse with a flour bag pulled over his head with a rope tightened around his neck. His breathing was rapid, and he wondered why he had been saved to be the last. He had urinated his pants and wept with the fear that filled him.

"Any last words, son?" an unrecognizable deep voice asked.

Tim tried to speak, but his throat was dry. "J...Just... tell...Mr. and Mrs....Whitehead I'm sorry. I...never wanted to do it. I wish I hadn't. I pray Laura is rescued. And maybe...someday, they can forgive me. That's...all. Jesus, Lord, I messed up and ask your forgiveness for what I've done." He sniffled.

Gunther Thomas nodded to Aaron, who held the horse's reins. Aaron released the reins. Gunther whipped the horse with a switch, and it ran out from under Tim, allowing him to fall three feet to his death as the noose, perfectly placed, snapped his neck. His body swung back and forth from the horse's momentum.

Gunther nodded to Mitch Whitehead, who had removed his hood. "There is some justice for you, Mitch. Now we'll wait to hear from the marshal and pray he has good news."

Mitch glared hostilely as Tim's body slowed its swinging momentum. "It's not enough. I don't feel any better about it."

CHAPTER TWENTY-FIVE

JESSE HELMS LOOKED AT HIS REFLECTION IN THE mirror. His hair was combed over and he had shaved the scruffy week's worth of growth off his face except for his goatee. He had put on some clean clothes and rolled his eyes with a touch of annoyance. It wasn't a real wedding and his aunt Mattie certainly wasn't an ordained minister to make a wedding license official. Jannie's eight-year-old daughter Louise had drawn a heart and Jannie wrote the words marriage license along with Jesse and Alice's names.

The ceremony was ridiculous and Jesse had no desire to go through with it other than Mattie was his favorite aunt and it would make her feel good. Jesse did not necessarily like the name Alice, but Mattie had chosen it to rename Laura to keep any suspicions of neighbors at bay when news came of a girl named Laura being kidnapped. Everything that Mattie did had a purpose. The box had broken Laura Whitehead's fighting spirit, and now she was being trained to become Alice Helms, the bride of Jesse.

Jesse wasn't in love and he didn't care about the girl in

one way or another. All he cared about was the baby being raised in his family. The foolish wedding ceremony that Aunt Mattie was so excited about was something that he just wanted to get through. There would be no actual consummation of the marriage because he feared hurting the baby.

"Hey," Colin said, "do you think your aunt will let me marry your cousin today? You know, like your wedding."

"What?" Jesse asked with a surprised scowl. "You mean a fake wedding?"

Colin shrugged. "Sure. I can believe it's real. Your aunt thinks you'll be married in God's eyes. I suppose I can, too."

Jesse chuckled as he shook his head. "I don't believe in God. This play, and that's all it is, a play, is nonsense. It's just something women do, like little girls playing house, but Aunt Mattie and Jannie are grown-ups. I don't understand it; I'm just doing it. It means nothing."

"That doesn't matter. Do you think she'll marry Jannie and me?"

"Jannie's dying, Colin. Don't you know that? She's got consumption."

Colin frowned. "I know. I wish I would have met her years ago. I think she's beautiful."

Jesse grimaced. "You're the first I ever heard say that sober. You need to ask Aunt Mattie, not me."

———

JANNIE PATTED the bed in Laura's room. "I bet you're excited to get back in here tonight, aren't you?" she asked, raising her eyebrows repeatedly. "You'll be a married woman."

Laura looked at Jannie and wanted to burst into tears. No one in the house seemed to understand that she was not impregnated by choice. She was not there by choice either and she had no desire to get married, even if it was fake as a dirt clod passed off as money. It sickened her stomach to think about going through the motions of marrying Jesse Helms. She utterly despised the man and what he had done to her.

What choice did she have though? It was either quietly play along or being forced back into the casket in the ground where the darkness was consuming. There were nightmares she'd have of Jesse returning and she'd wake up terrified and sobbing. She could no longer sleep in a dark room in fear of not seeing her surroundings when she awoke from the nightmares. Suddenly, her life had become a nightmare and it was hard to fathom where she was and how quickly life had changed. Yesterday she was riding in a plush comfortable carriage to her new friend's house and now she was the so-called bride of the man of her nightmares. The knife beside the loaf of bread was becoming more appealing the longer she remained with the Sperry home. She was, for all practical purposes, a slave to the foulest family she had ever met.

Jannie coughed and repeated to cough in her hand. "You're so lucky. Jesse is a great man. Maybe he'll even love you someday. Treat him right tonight." She started to laugh, but it ended in a fit of coughing.

"I'm with child," Laura said without any emotion.

"That doesn't matter. So was I, many times. Just think, we can raise our children together. You know, I lost my sister a few months back and I'm glad you're here. You remind me of Daisy. She was young, nice, and sweet too. I think we're going to be close." She quickly hugged Laura and left the room.

Laura sat heavily on the bed and tried to control her rapid breathing. "Lord," she whispered with tears burning her eyes. "Take me home, please." The aching in her back had worsened and moved into her abdomen. She had been constipated and figured it was gas working its way through her bowels. A slight cramp and dull ache were becoming more uncomfortable.

"Alice, get out here and marry your man," Mattie called down the hallway.

CHAPTER TWENTY-SIX

IT WAS ALL LAURA COULD DO TO KEEP HERSELF from bawling. She and Jesse stood in the family room facing each other while Mattie stood like a preacher. The rest of the family sat to watch. A chill crept through Laura's body like a thousand creeping spiders when Jesse took her hands in his. She felt sick to her stomach, and the room spun around her as a slight layer of perspiration moistened her forehead as a wave of warmth overtook her. The dull ache in her lower back had moved to her lower abdomen with a sharp sting of pain that struck like lightning and then disappeared, leaving a constant but dull pressure.

Mattie held a closed Bible in her hands as she said, "Today, we gather to celebrate the joining of two lives into one household." Her eyes hardened as they glared at Laura's downturned face and quivering lip. Her voice was as stern as an iron rail. "Weddings are joyous occasions and I expect you to enjoy your wedding, young lady. Look at me, Alice! Are you enjoying your wedding?" Her tone was threatening.

Laura nodded quickly and sniffled. "Yes, Ma. I'm just so...happy." The hiding box was intentionally left open for her to see before the ceremony began.

"Good. Look at your husband and smile then."

It was all Laura could do to look at the face of the man who attacked her, beat her, and hurt her. It was all she could see when she looked at him. Fear and anguish all swirled around inside her. Another sharp pain made her cringe. She felt hopeless and tried to think of nicer memories with her parents and Jake as she let her eyes focus on a spider on the wall behind Jesse. She'd rather kiss the spider than the man holding her hands.

"Where was I?" Mattie said. "Oh, yeah. So, we're all gathered here today to commit Alice Helms to serve and satisfy Jesse Helms. Alice, will you prepare his meals, clean up after him, and keep a good house for Jesse? Do you agree to be faithful at the cost of your life? Do you agree to do as he tells you for the rest of your life? And finally, do you vow to love him as his obedient wife, quietly and respectfully, for all time? Well, do you agree to all that?"

Laura swallowed and hesitated. Her throat went dry.

Tad warned, "You better say I do. The box is waiting."

"Shut up," Colin replied with a scowl at Tad. He did not like Tad at all.

Laura's lower lip quivered as she choked out, "I do."

Mattie nodded approvingly.

Jesse grinned and said, "You know I just found out consummating our wedding won't hurt the baby after all, so it's going to be different this time. You'll see."

"Hush it, Romeo," Mattie said with a slight smile.

"Jesse, do you vow not to harm her too bad when you're mad? Do you promise to be a husband and wear a ring?"

"I can do that."

"Then, with that. I pronounce you man and wife."

"You forgot the rings, Ma," Jannie said.

"Oh, yeah. Jesse, do you have a ring for her?"

He shrugged. "Found a washer out by the barn." He pulled a large metal washer for a half-inch bolt out of his pocket. He stuck the washer on her small finger, wedging it between her other fingers until she gasped in pain.

"Tell her you'll marry her," Mattie said.

"Yeah, I'll marry you for now."

"Alice, do you have a ring for him?"

Laura winced in pain as her fingers reached into a small pocket on her dress. She pulled out a ring that already belonged to Jesse and clumsily placed it on his finger.

"Tell him how much you love him," Mattie instructed.

"I...excuse me, I'm going to be sick." She moved quickly to step out the back door around the corner and bent over to vomit up her lunch. She dropped to her knees as her stomach forcefully contracted.

Jesse grimaced as he listened to her vomit. "I'm not kissing her when she tastes like puke."

"Ah, you don't have to kiss her now. Well, I already said it, so you're husband and wife. Congratulations."

"Let's celebrate!" Jannie shouted, followed by a fit of coughing. "Open that bottle, Vince, and let's get drunk."

"Wait, wait, wait," Colin said, standing. "Miss Mattie, will you marry me and Jannie like that? I bought a ring today." He pulled a thin golden ring from his pocket. "I bought it from the hotel. I'm serious. I want to marry your daughter for real."

"What?" Jannie asked with her mouth agape. "Seriously? For real, for real?"

Colin kneeled before her. "I just met you recently, but mail brides do it all the time. I think you are beautiful and you make me laugh. What more could I want?"

"A wife that ain't dying," Mattie said bitterly. "What's your game, life insurance?"

"My mom isn't dying. She'll beat this," Tad said defiantly. "We're Sperrys."

"No, Miss Mattie," Colin said, not taking his eyes off Jannie. "There's no game, con, or lie. I just think we're made for each other."

"Ohh," Jannie moaned with moistening eyes. "I feel the same..." She began to cough and quickly brought the towel to her mouth.

Mattie grimaced. "Listen to her." She pointed a finger at Jannie. "You can tell she isn't getting better. Why would you want to marry her when you know she hasn't got long? A year, maybe two at most, the doctor said."

Colin placed a supportive hand on Jannie's leg. "Because what little time we do have will be worth it. I can take her to a drier climate and maybe prolong her life. I don't know. But for today and tomorrow and so on, I'll enjoy just being with her."

"She's a drunk!" Mattie exclaimed.

Colin grinned. "So am I."

"She's got four kids by three different men. And several miscarriages by only god knows who."

"Oh, Ma," Jannie groaned and buried her face in a pillow with humiliation.

"I'm not so pure, either. My question is, why are you so intent on telling me all of her faults when I only see her good? Why shouldn't her last years be happy years? I will do everything I can to make her comfortable and happy. I'll even raise her children as my own."

"Ohh," Jannie moaned, gazing at him affectionately. "I will marry you whether my mother gives you her blessing or not."

Colin grinned. "Then, sweetheart, we don't need her." Still on his knees, he took her hand in his. "Marry me, Jannie. I'll make you a great husband. I'd have to because you deserve one."

"Yes." She laughed. "Yes! Oh, my! Mother, I'm getting married. You always said I never would, but I am!" She began to cough into her hand.

"Not for long," Mattie said lightly. "Where is that puking breath girl? Get in here, you little puke!" she shouted at Laura, who was sitting on the back doorstep holding her belly. "Now that you're family, I expect you to start acting like it. There's still enough time in the day for you to wash some laundry to hang on the clothesline. You better get to it."

"It's her wedding day, Ma," Jannie said. "Let her enjoy it. The clothes can wait until tomorrow."

Jesse stepped outside and put a hand on Laura's shoulder. "Where's your ring?" His tone was stern.

Laura looked at her left hand to see the washer was gone. "It must have fallen off." She was not feeling well.

"Find it and wear it. You're my wife now and I'll put a bull ring in your nose if I see that ring off your finger again," Jesse said with a cold glare.

"It doesn't fit my finger. It's too big," Laura explained anxiously. The washer had a half-inch hole that was far too big to stay on her finger. The outside diameter of the washer was just over an inch, which hurt her other fingers when she wore it.

Jesse's lips pulled upward at the corners into a devious smirk. "I don't care. Put it on and keep it on, or you'll suffer the consequences. That's your only choice." He picked the washer up from the ground near her puddle of vomit and shoved it back onto her finger, wedging it between her pinky and middle finger, forcing them to the side.

"Ouch!" she cried out with a grimace.

"No man's wife should be without a ring. If you want a real one, you'll have to earn it. After we eat, we'll go into the room and celebrate our marriage the right way."

———

IT WAS all Laura could do not to break down crying as she sat at the table with a bowl of soup and a piece of overcooked bread in front of her. The soup was made by boiling a whole chicken until the meat separated from the bones. The women left the bones in the soup to add flavor and added flour to thicken it, as well as a few carrots, potatoes, salt, and pepper, to the water. It was one of the foulest meals Laura had ever been forced to eat.

Her pinky and middle finger ached from the edge of the washer pressing into her bones, but she dared not move her left hand as it set flat on the tabletop. Jesse sat beside her and laughed, talked, and joked with his family members. Laura was overcome by a hopeless sensation that filled her very soul. If she was not found, this would become her new home and family. Laura was too afraid to say a word without being spoken to, let alone ever trying to escape. She had no idea where she was or how far away help could be. What she did know was how scared she was of being placed back into the box in the backyard. Mattie

scared her. Jesse terrified her. Tad and Jannie both frightened her. It was a house full of fearful people that she
didn't want anything to do with. She had been taken
against her will, and none of them saw the wrong in it.
They were celebrating a wedding that didn't exist, and she
was the unwilling and helpless bride.

Jannie leaned over the table and tapped Laura's hand.

"Ouch!" Laura cried out and pulled her hand back. Janie
had tapped her exposed nailbed.

Jannie laughed. "Sorry. You better eat up. You're going
to need your energy tonight. Colin and I will be in the
room next door celebrating our honeymoon, too," she said
as she sat back and kissed Colin at the table.

"I can't wait," Colin said as he broke the kiss. His arm
was resting over her shoulder.

Mattie gazed at Laura expectantly. "Aren't you going to
say it?"

"Say what?" she asked nervously.

Mattie slammed her fist onto the table with a loud
bang. Her expression was furious. "*Ma!* How many times
do I have to tell you to address me as Ma?"

Laura's chin began quivering with emotion as she tried
not to start bawling. "Sorry, Ma. What am I supposed to
say, Ma?" She cringed with a sudden cramp. What she
thought were gas pains were feeling more like menstruation cramps. She'd have to excuse herself from the table to
visit the privy soon. She could feel the warmth of bleeding,
but she was too afraid to ask for a rag at the dinner table.

Mattie's harsh eyes glared at her as she snapped, "That
you can't wait to take your husband back to your room for
your honeymoon."

"Of course, Ma," she said slowly, with a sickening repul-
sion churning her stomach. A wave of warmth swept over

her. She knew she needed to say something before she left a blood spot on the chair she sat on, but she was too afraid to. "I...I have to eat first," she said. She carefully picked up her spoon with her painful fingertips to take another bite of the soup. Her entire body winced at the thought of sharing a room with Jesse, and she was thankful that her monthly menstruation was starting. However, it didn't feel right. Her mother had told her women didn't have menstruation cycles during pregnancy. Her breathing quickened with the approaching nightmare of having to mention it to Mattie very soon. If she could find a bone in her soup to choke on, she'd swallow it and hope they could not save her because the nightmare she was experiencing was getting worse, as she feared she would be thrown back in the box for starting to bleed.

"Horseys," Jannie's youngest daughter, four-year-old Eve, said, pointing out the front window. Tad got up from the table to look.

Tad's eyes widened, and he spoke with alarm, "Jesse, Uncle Morton is here with the marshal and three others. They all have rifles pointed at the house!"

"Oh, no!" Jannie said, leaving the table to look out the window. "No. No. Jesse, please don't let them take Colin," she said with her eyes watering heavily as she gazed at her cousin. "We're getting married, Jesse."

Jesse rushed to peek out the window and cursed. He turned his gaze toward the dining table where Laura was seated. "Our honeymoon has to wait a week or so. Your ride home is here but enjoy your parents while you can because when I come to get you, it will be the last time you see them."

Colin grabbed his gun belt and hitched it around his waist before joining Jesse at the window. "I suggest we run out the back and take the fight to the hills to keep the women and children safe."

Jesse glanced at his friend with a slight chuckle. "No. We surrender. My cousins will get us out of jail." He waved a hand toward Laura. "Then we will kill her parents, take her, and go where they won't find us until the baby is born. The dairy has milk, so we can do away with her, bring the baby back here for Aunt Mattie to raise, and no one will know where the baby comes from or can prove who the mother was."

Colin peered at Laura, who was holding her stomach with a sour expression on her pale face. He shook his head. "I like the surrendering part, but I won't help you kidnap her again. I asked Jannie to marry me. Once I'm out of jail, I'm taking Jannie away from here and making an honest effort to go straight."

"What do you mean you won't help me?" Jesse asked with a threatening tone. "Let me put it to you this way; you're facing the gallows if I don't get you out of jail. You owe me your life, and you'll either help me take her and come with us, or I'll leave and let the marshal hang you from the gallows. Either way, you can forget about that walking death trap of a cousin of mine. She'll just end up killing you with her sickness anyway. That's your choice to make."

They heard Matt's voice demand Jesse and Colin to come out of the house.

Colin looked back at the table and noticed Laura's facial muscles grimacing as her arms enveloped her abdomen. "Fine." He turned to Jannie. "You heard the choice Jesse gave me. I'm choosing my life so I can live it the best I can. I'm sorry, Jannie."

Jesse stepped over, grabbed Laura's arm, and roughly

jerked her toward him. He wrapped his arm around her neck and pulled her close. Laura cried out in surprise and bent over slightly with a painful cramp. "Let's get outside before Matt starts shooting."

Jannie quickly wrapped her arms around Colin and sobbed as she kissed him. "We can still be together...I'll wait. I'll follow you. I'll do anything!" She wept and hugged him to weep on his shoulder.

Colin said, "Forgive me, Jannie. I made a promise, and I intend to keep it. No matter what happens, just remember, I truly think I love you."

Jesse scowled. "She'll kill you and my kid with her hacking up a lung. She's dying of consumption. You don't want to marry her, Colin. She's nothing but a town whore. Even Aunt Mattie told you that. Let's go before they start shooting up the house." He kissed Laura roughly on the cheek and dragged her towards the door.

Colin kissed Jannie. "I am going to marry you and take you and your children away from this place and your crazy family. But you got to trust me that this is for the best. And forgive me."

"I will. I swear I will," Jannie said through her tears. "I'll wait for you as long as long as it takes."

He smiled. "Faithfully? I'm the only one from now on?"

"I swear it on my life."

"That'll last until tonight, maybe," Mattie said with a bitter scowl. Her brow lowered, and her mouth dropped in horror when she saw a large red patch of blood on the back of Laura's blue dress as Jesse dragged her outside onto the porch.

CHAPTER TWENTY-SEVEN

MATT AND THE OTHERS HAD RIDDEN HARD AND stopped at two ranches along the way to trade their tired horses for fresh ones so they could keep pushing hard through the miles. Once they entered the town of Natoma and approached the large, ugly black home of the Sperrys, Matt had his small posse spread out and held their rifles at the ready. He made it clear that no shots were to be fired because there were innocent women and children in the house.

Matt shouted, "Jesse Helms, come out with your hands up, and no one will get hurt. If you shoot one time, I can't promise anyone inside will survive. You and Colin Kennedy come out, and you better have Laura, or I'll hang you both here and now!"

A minute later, the door opened and Jesse Helms stepped out onto the porch with an arm around Laura's neck and the other raised. He was not wearing his gun belt nor was he armed in any way. His snide grin was wide and taunting. "Oh, I surrender, Marshal. You might want to congratulate us. This little lady and I were married today. You're interfering with our honeymoon, but we'll delay that for a bit," Jesse said without any concern. He squeezed his arm, pulling her tight against him. He puckered his lips and kissed her on the cheek. "Meet my..."

A gunshot was fired from inside the house that was aimed at the back of Jesse's head. The .45 caliber bullet hit its mark, blowing a hole through Jesse's head, and spraying out blood, bone fragments and brain matter onto the ground. Jesse's lifeless body was propelled forward off the porch and crumpled over the edge with a massive head wound that bled steadily onto the ground. Laura had been dragged to the ground by his arm clenched tightly around her neck. The fall was unexpected, and she hit the ground hard beside Jesse. She landed inches from a growing pool of blood, and the large exit wound between his eyes that gazed lifelessly at her.

A high-pitched squeal escaped Laura's lips as she clawed at the ground in a panic to crawl away from the grotesque remains bleeding profusely. Within seconds, she was four feet away, her eyes unable to leave Jesse's distorted face while she screamed in terror.

"Laura!" Jake shouted and handed his rifle to his brother before dismounting and running to her. He fell to the ground beside her, taking her shaking body in his arms to calm her down, but in shock, she stared at Jesse with wide eyes, not recognizing it was Jake who was holding her.

Chaos erupted as a tall man with long hair stepped out onto the porch with his hands raised. He held his revolver by the barrel high above his head. "I'm surrendering! I had no choice but to kill him. Laura would never be safe with him alive. I promise you. I'm Colin Kennedy. Everything I did, from start to finish, was to protect that young girl from Jesse." Jannie followed him out.

"Jesse!" Mattie screamed and rushed past Jannie and Colin and fell over Jesse's body. She leaned over his back, holding him while wailing deeply.

Colin kept his hands raised as he kneeled to his knees. "I promised Laura I'd get her back home." He nodded with satisfaction. "And I kept my promise. Now she can live free of fearing Jesse taking her again." He peered at Laura. "Marshal, Laura's bleeding!" he shouted over Mattie's wailing and Laura's guttural groans as she wrapped her arms around her stomach. There was blood seeping from under her dress.

Vince stood on the porch in disbelief as he held Jannie's youngest child. Tad stood beside him, staring at Jesse's body in shock. Jannie was on her knees behind Colin, her arms wrapped around his neck affectionately. She stood as Matt approached Colin. "He had to do it, Marshal. Jesse was going to kidnap her again. He said so!"

Matt grabbed Colin's revolver and kicked him down flat for Truet to shackle his wrists. Matt pushed Jannie back and ordered Vince and Tad to step to the far end of the porch to keep them in sight.

Laura cried out and bent over with a severe shooting pain that cramped her abdominal muscles. Her eyes were transfixed on a pool of blood on the ground that was coming from between her legs. Another severe cramp made her cry out as she took hold of the hand that on her. She gazed up to see Jake's concerned face. She whimpered between the excruciating cramping, "Help me."

Jannie coughed and pointed at Laura. "She's miscarrying that baby!"

Morton stood beside his horse, stunned by what was

happening around him. He had spent his life being best friends with his cousin, and despite knowing Jesse could be killed one day by Matt or himself, he was not prepared to see his cousin shot in the back of the head or to hear his mother wailing. He stared bewildered at Jannie, surprised and confused as to why she was not reacting the way he would expect her to. Their cousin, who had been more like a brother for all of their lives, had just been murdered, and she acted more concerned for the man who shot him.

Jannie watched Truet securing Colin's hands behind his back. She grabbed Matt's arm and pleaded, "Please don't take Colin. He killed Jesse to save her life! Jesse was going to take the baby and kill her. He saved her life." She had heard Colin use the excuse of saving the girl's life as his defense and repeated it.

Mattie, overhearing her daughter's words, turned her grieving face toward Jannie. A snarl formed on her lips, and she charged forward like a raging bull and drove her body into Jannie, driving her down onto the porch. The back of Jannie's head hit the wood boards with a hollow sound. Mattie grabbed her daughter's hair in both clenched fists and began slamming the back of Jannie's head into the porch boards. A deep growl escaped from Mattie's clenched snarl as she tried to break Jannie's head open with every slam of her head. Jannie screamed and scratched at her mother's face, arms, and hands as she fought to stop her mother.

"Ma!" Vince shouted and joined Morton to pull Mattie off their sister. "I'll kill you!" Mattie seethed as she was pulled off Jannie with clumps of hair firmly gripped in her clutches. Jannie sobbed between coughs on the porch.

"I'll kill you!" Mattie screamed with a maddening

expression on her face as she reached for Jannie, fighting with her two boys to break free.

"Mother, knock it off!" Morton shouted.

Mattie's rage was transferred to Morton. She began slapping his face with lefts and rights as she screamed, "This is all your fault! You never should have left him. He needed you!"

Morton, blocking the hits, grabbed his mother, and wrapped his arms around her in a tight hug. Mattie, feeling her son's embrace, began to sob as she gave into holding her son tightly. Her deep agony was heard in her voice as she wailed, "You never...should have...left me. I needed you."

Jake, frightened by the blood escaping from Laura, yelled to his brother, "Bode! Laura is bleeding bad! She's hurt."

Jake's voice drew Matt's attention. "Morton," Matt called. He paused when he saw Morton embracing his mother while she sobbed bitterly. "Vince, where can I get her some help!" Matt demanded to know with a pointed finger toward Laura.

Vince, feeling helpless and unsure of what he should do, said, "Tillie."

Morton shouted to his brother, "Vince, take Bode and Jake and get her to the hotel. Then you get Tillie. Hurry up and go. Now!"

Tillie was the closest person Natoma had to a doctor.

Vince shrugged. "Who's Bode and Jake?"

"I'm Bode. We'll get her up. You ride Morton's horse. Take us to the hotel." Bode and Jake helped Laura to stand, though she was bent over, groaning in pain. The pain was overwhelming, and standing up straight felt nearly impossible with every shooting pain that doubled her over in agony. With no other choice, they set her in Jake's saddle, covering the seat with sticky blood. Jake jumped up behind her. Vince climbed onto Morton's horse and led them toward town.

Morton could feel the strength of his mother's arms tightly holding him as she sobbed bitterly on his shoulder. He had never heard her cry like that before. He gasped, "I'm sorry, Ma."

"I...miss...you so much," Mattie bawled, refusing to let Morton go.

Jannie coughed between her sobs. Colin stood with his hands secured behind his back. He wished he could hold Jannie and wipe away the blood from the back of her head. He reassured her, "Jannie, it will be okay. It will."

Jannie climbed to her feet and stepped quickly across the porch to hug him. "I'll wait for you." She pleaded to Matt, "He didn't do anything wrong. Please don't arrest him. Jesse was planning to take that girl far away when he got out of jail. Colin shot him to save her life. We want to get married. Please don't arrest him. Please, Marshal Bannister."

It had all happened so fast and unexpectedly. Matt had too many things to watch and worried about another shooter coming out onto the porch. He kept his eyes on Tad Sperry, but Tad had not moved, helped, or impeded in any way. Knowing everything that had happened was under control, he exhaled and said, "That's for the court to decide, not me. Truet, let's take him and go to the hotel to check on Laura."

"Matt," Morton said, "I'm needed here for a while."

Matt nodded understandably. "We'll be at the hotel. Take your time."

———

TILLIE WAS a petite Chinese lady in her sixties with gray hair and a wrinkled, square-shaped face. She lived in a tiny shack along the creek not far from the tannery where she worked. Tillie had become the one person that most people in Natoma came to when there was anyone injured or sick for medical help. Over the years, her knowledge of Chinese medicine had saved many lives in town and earned her a reputation as the town doctor.

Tillie came out of the hotel room with blood-stained hands and wrists. A folded-over towel held the remains of a tiny human fetus. She put the towel in a cigar box to be buried in the cemetery and carried it into the hotel lobby, where the others waited.

Tillie spoke bluntly and with a Chinese accent. "The girl is resting and will be fine, but the baby is gone. She must name baby girl and bury her." She handed the box to Matt.

"I'll see to it," Matt said.

"She'll be okay?" Jake asked before Matt could.

"Yes. I just say so."

"Is she awake?" Matt asked.

"No. I just say so. You let her rest. She needs rest for two days." She held up two fingers. "Two days, you understand? Then she can leave. She asked for Jake?"

"That's me," Jake said quietly.

"You be there when she wakes up. But do not wake her up. Be quiet and watch her sleep. She'll wake when her body tells her so. Understand?"

"Yes, ma'am," Jake said respectfully.

Matt exhaled with relief. "Thank you, Jesus." He had been praying for Laura to get through the miscarriage without any serious troubles. He stood and spoke to Truet and Morton, who had joined them. "I'm going to send a wire to her parents and let them know that she is safe and will be home in a few days. I'll send Holly a wire, as well. When I come back, we'll take Colin and start back for Branson, throw him in jail and then..." He yawned. "I'm going home. I don't know about you, fellas, but I want to sleep in my own bed tonight. I'll be back."

It took Matt a lot longer than expected to come back to the hotel. When he did, he said, "Colin, didn't you say Tim was your cousin?"

Colin spoke. "Yes, he is. And I'll tell you again, Tim didn't have a choice but to keep his mouth shut. He's a good kid. I'm sure he feels bad enough about what happened, but he didn't do a darn thing to stay in jail. He has never hurt anyone."

"I'm sorry, Colin, but I received a wire after I sent my two stating that a group of sheep shooters broke into the jail and hung Tim and your other two friends. They were all buried in the Hollister Cemetery earlier this morning. I'm sorry. I'll give you a few minutes to say goodbye to Jannie, and then we're leaving."

———

LAURA OPENED her eyes and blinked rapidly to focus on the face that leaned over the bed. "Jake?" A warm smile slowly formed on her lips. "You're here?"

"You better believe it." His eyes grew thick with moisture. "I've been sitting here for three hours watching you. You're more beautiful than ever. I have missed you so much."

Her arms reached up to hug him. She pulled him close to her and began to weep. "I love you! Don't ever disappear from me again." She kissed him, placing her hands on his cheeks and looked into his eyes.

"I didn't plan to."

"I know." Her smile slowly faded. "I lost my baby." She did not feel the joy that she had thought she might when she had prayed to have a miscarriage days before. She sniffled. "Jake, I prayed I would have a miscarriage, but now I wish I didn't. It was my baby."

Jake nodded. "I know."

Laura's brow wrinkled with concern. "Do you still want to marry me? Even after…"

Jake sniffled. "Laura, even if you had the baby, I would have married you and raised it as my own if that was what it took to live my life with you. What happens to you happens to me. That is what love and marriage are about: becoming one. That baby would have been our firstborn, but now, when we get married, we'll have a baby together."

Laura ran her fingers along his scar. "You, Jake Thomas, still make my heart melt. I love you so much."

Jake's grin widened with a warm gaze. "You have no idea how relieved I am to hear that. I love you, Laura. I'll love you more every day until the day I die."

EPILOGUE

As Matt told the story to Alex Wentworth, Christine spoke with a frail voice, "Matt, I'm not feeling well."

"What's the matter, my lady?" he asked with concern.

"I don't know. I suddenly don't feel well. Odd. Like I'm going to faint."

Matt stood slowly as his aging knees ached. "Let's get you in bed, sweetheart. Do you need a doctor?"

"I just need to lie down."

"Excuse me, Alex. That's enough storytelling for today. I need to get my lady to bed. If you'll excuse me." He pushed Christine's wheelchair out of the room. "Rory," he called. "I need your assistance."

The concern in Matt's expression revealed the depth of his love for Christine. Alex had a fiancée named Denise Aggelar, with whom he was very much in love. The photos of Matt and Christine hanging on the walls of their house when they were young were a reminder of the wilder days in Branson. Matt's badge and gun belt were worn in several of the photos. Alex wandered casually from room to room, looking at pictures, paintings, and other things that were placed on shelves and elsewhere. Matt and Christine's life together had accumulated many things, but the one thing that showed their greatest wealth was the love they had for one another.

After a few minutes, Rory Jackson entered the room to find Alex looking at photos on the wall. "I don't believe Matt's going to be in the mood to tell more stories today. He is lying down beside Christine."

Alex nodded with an understanding. "He sure loves her, doesn't he?"

Rory hesitated to answer as she thought back over the years. "Very much so. Their love for each other is truly inspiring. Sometimes, two people get it right. They certainly did."

"You never married, Miss Jackson?"

She shook her head. "No. I was engaged once. I fell for him like a child falling out of a tree." Her warm smile slowly faded into a deep frown. "He was a good man."

"What happened?"

She shook her head. "I'm sure Matt will tell you about my fiancé and me when the time is right. He was telling you about saving Laura Whitehead from that animal, Jesse Helms, today. He'll tell you soon enough, I'm sure. In the meantime, I need to look after Miss Christine."

"Is she going to be all right?"

"Yes. Occasionally, she has these dizzy spells. You have a good day, Mr. Wentworth. You can come back next Sunday after church. I'm sure they will both be feeling better then."

"Can I ask you a question? Matt didn't say, did Jake and Laura get married?"

Rory smiled. "You should take a drive up to Hollister and visit the Long T Ranch and ask them yourself. Yes, they did. And in case you're wondering, they raised a whole passel of children."

"Whatever happened to Holly Fairchild?"

Rory wrinkled her nose. "That's a story Matt will have to tell you himself. Come back next week, and maybe he will. But I never know what story he is going tell next. Good day, Mr. Wentworth."

"What about Colin Kennedy? Did he marry Jannie Sperry, or was he hanged for Sheriff Emmerson's murder?"

Rory smiled. "I can answer that. He was arrested and found not guilty of murder because they couldn't prove he shot anyone, but they could prove that he protected Laura. He still served time for his part in the kidnapping of Laura, but only a few months. And then, yes, he did marry Jannie Sperry. Now, if you will excuse me, I need to attend to Christine. Have a good day, Alex."

A LOOK AT

The Matt Bannister Series

A BREWING STORM RUNS DEEPER THAN PRIDE OR HONOR IN THIS CHRISTIAN WESTERN MYSTERY COLLECTION.

Fifteen years ago, the young Matt Bannister ran away from the town of Willow Falls. Now a famed US Deputy Marshal, he's coming home to reconcile with family.

But all too quickly, he realizes that old feuds unsettled never die— and he must confront his painful past. Good thing Matt is a fighter, a killer, and a tough man who isn't afraid to stand his ground against anyone.

As the tempest of the past collides with the present, Matt encounters religious persecution, murder, kidnapping, and lies— and his unyielding spirit becomes the beacon of redemption in a world haunted by shadows.

Join Matt Bannister on a relentless quest for redemption as he faces a storm of secrets and danger.

AVAILABLE NOW

ACKNOWLEDGMENTS

For all the years that I have been writing, my family has always been the most supportive of me. So, with that, I want to thank my wife, Cathy. Without her support and encouragement, I wouldn't be able to do as much writing as I do. Our children are also very supportive, and I want to thank them for being encouraging as well. Mike, Jessica, Chevelle, Katie, and Keith...thank you. My son Keith deserves more credit, though. He reads everything I write and is not shy about telling me what he thinks and offering suggestions that quite often I follow. His interest in the books and the hours he puts into reading them, marking them up, and sharing his opinions while doing his college work to keep his grades up are admirable. Thank you, Keith.

I also want to thank Micheal Gear and Kathleen O'Neal Gear for their help and suggestions with this book. Their keen wisdom and knowledge of how to tell a story were a feedback that I certainly appreciate.

Finally, I want to thank CKN Christian Publishing, Patience Bramlett, Sharmaine Gobind, Ellie Folden, Mike Bray, Jake Bray, and the rest of the team who make CKN and Wolfpack Publishing the fantastic company that it is.

ABOUT THE AUTHOR

Ken Pratt and his wife, Cathy, have been married for twenty-two years and are blessed with five children and six grandchildren. They live on the Oregon Coast where they are currently raising the youngest of their children.

Ken grew up in the small farming community of Dayton, Oregon, where he worked to make a living. But his true passion always lay with writing.

Having a busy family, the only "free" time Ken has to write is late at night—getting no more than five hours of sleep every day. He has penned several novels that are being published, along with several children's stories.